The near purple color of the moon a few moments ago was gradually replaced by a duller red that hinted of orange. The reflection on the cliffs was amazing. It was as if the red walls were actually glowing in the moonlight. It was a remarkable sight.

Then, as if on cue, the coyotes started their singing again. And yes, Kate admitted, it was beautiful, the sounds bouncing around in the canyons below them. Lee stirred, moving away, and then stood. She held out her hand to Kate.

"Dance with me."

Their eyes met in the moonlight.

"I've always wanted to dance up here," Lee explained.

Kate nodded slowly. It was too perfect for her to refuse. Too . . . *romantic*. She took Lee's hand and let herself be pulled to her feet. And the coyotes obliged, their song fading to the background as Lee's arms pulled Kate closer. Kate's hand trembled as she slipped it over Lee's shoulder and she prayed Lee couldn't hear her thundering heartbeat.

They were too close, really. Yet Kate ached to be closer. Another few inches and she would feel Lee's breasts against her own. Another few inches and their thighs would brush. She squeezed her eyes shut, trying to call up an image of Robin, anything to break the spell that Lee had cast on her.

COYOTE
SKY

GERRI HILL

Bella
BOOKS
2006

Editor: Anna Chinappi
Cover designer: LA Callaghan

ISBN-13: 978-0-7394-7252-1

To Judy "McNews" Underwood.
May you dance by the song of the coyotes very, very soon.

Acknowledgments

Thanks very much to Harriet Holland and Judy Underwood. I appreciate your comments/feedback on my early attempts at *Coyote Sky*.

About the Author

Gerri lives in East Texas, deep in the pines, with her partner, Diane. They share their log cabin and adjoining five acres with two labs, Max and Zach, and four cats. A huge vegetable garden that overflows in the summer is her pride and joy. Besides giving in to her overactive green thumb, Gerri loves to "hike the woods" with the dogs, a pair of binoculars (bird watching), and at least one camera! For more, visit Gerri's Web site at www.gerrihill.com.

CHAPTER ONE

Kate sat in traffic wondering why on earth she'd attempted a trek across Dallas during rush hour. She adjusted the AC, took a deep breath and tried not to think of the pack of cigarettes she kept with her—just in case.

"If it wasn't so damn hot," she murmured, pointing the vent toward her. It was only mid-May, but already the summer heat was showing itself. She glanced affectionately at the cigarettes then forced her eyes back to the road. She didn't know why she tormented herself with them. She'd been in various stages of quitting for the last two years, finally able to count days between cigarettes instead of hours. And this time, it had been four days. Well, three days, nine hours and a handful of minutes. *But who's counting?*

Her cell rang, thankfully distracting her from the nicotine fit she was about to have. She smiled when she saw the number displayed. Brenda had been gone nearly three months and Kate was surprised how much she missed her friend.

"Hi!" she greeted.

"Hey, kiddo."

Kate grinned. "You can't call me kiddo. I'm thirty-seven."

"Yes, and I'm fifty-seven, so that makes you a kiddo, darling."

Kate laughed. Brenda had been calling her kiddo since they'd first met, eight years ago. She pretended to be offended, but honestly, she'd miss the affectionate name if Brenda stopped.

"So, how is the desert? Do you miss the city yet?"

"I told you, this is not the desert. In fact, I'm not even in Santa Fe anymore. I've moved farther up in the mountains and right now I'm staring across a canyon, seeing the beautiful sandstone cliffs that inspired Georgia O'Keefe. Oh, Kate, you should see it in the mornings. It's breathtaking."

Kate nodded. "So, I guess that means you're painting. How's it coming?"

"Oh, darling, I absolutely adore the freedom to express myself this way. It has been so uplifting to be here, I can't even describe it."

Kate shook her head. She had met Brenda Granbury in a writing class eight years ago when the wealthy widow decided she was ready to write her first novel. A bit eccentric—okay, *very* eccentric—but they had hit it off despite their twenty-year age difference. And over the years, Kate had watched as Brenda tried her hand at writing, sculpting, pottery and now painting. "There's an artist inside, just waiting to break free," Brenda said on many an occasion. So, Kate encouraged her in all her pursuits, even though she knew that Brenda didn't have one ounce of artistic talent. It made Brenda happy to try and that's all that really mattered.

"Well, I'm glad you're enjoying yourself." Kate inched along in traffic. "Do you have plans to return soon? I miss our weekly dinners."

"Oh, I miss you, Kate, but I don't miss the city at all. In fact, I've moved from the lodge here in Coyote after only a few days, moved to one of the summer homes up the mountain a ways." She paused. "An interesting group of people live here, Kate. Artists all. And, I seem to have found myself in a lesbian mecca."

2

"Oh, Brenda, please! Your gaydar is nonexistent." Kate turned the AC up again as the traffic came to another stop. "You thought I was straight for the first month you knew me."

"That's not fair. You were pretending to be straight. That should be illegal."

"I wasn't pretending to be straight!"

"Kate, darling, you *still* pretend to be straight!"

"I do not! Just because I've not announced publicly that I'm gay doesn't mean that I'm hiding. For God's sake! Is it necessary that people know *everything* about you?"

"Of course not. Now tell me, how's the book coming?"

Kate closed her eyes and leaned her head back, silently shaking her head. "It's coming."

"I guess that means you still have writer's block."

"I hate that term, Brenda. There is no such thing as writer's block. You either have a story to tell or you don't. It has nothing to do with so-called writer's block."

"And?"

Kate crept along in traffic, her eyes staring ahead. "And I guess I don't have a story to tell."

"Darling, why don't you take a break?"

"A break from what? Not writing?"

"A break from *there*, from the city. Come stay with me for awhile," Brenda suggested. "Coyote is a lovely little town."

"In New Mexico? In the *summer*? Brenda, the Dallas heat is enough, I certainly don't want to go to the desert."

Brenda laughed. "It was forty-one degrees when I got up this morning. It was lovely. What was it there at eight a.m.? Seventy-five and humid already?"

"Oh, Brenda, it's not just that." She looked wearily out at the traffic. "What am I supposed to do with Robin?"

"Good Lord, is she still in the picture?"

"She lives with me, Brenda. Of course she's in the picture."

"Something I *still* fail to comprehend. It's not like you're in love with the woman."

"I'm sorry you don't see it, but I do love her, Brenda."

"You love chocolate too. I said *in* love, darling."

Sadly, Kate knew she was right, but she refused to give Brenda any more ammunition where Robin was concerned. After two years of casual dating, Robin's apartment complex was sold and her rent nearly doubled. Kate did what she felt any friend would do. She offered her place until Robin could find something else. Robin moved into Kate's bedroom, not the spare, and now, six months later, Kate assumed she had stopped looking for a place of her own.

And it wasn't so bad, really. They got along well. And Robin could cook, something Kate *hated* to do. So even though the sex wasn't mind-boggling—or frequent—it was enough to sustain their relationship.

"So? What do you say?" Brenda asked, jarring Kate from her musings.

"New Mexico?"

"It would be good for you, Kate. A change of scenery."

"I don't know, Brenda." She looked at the endless traffic ahead of her and sighed, her glance going to her stash of cigarettes. "Tell me again what the temperature was today."

CHAPTER TWO

"New Mexico? But why?"

Kate looked at their bed, which was cluttered with clothes she'd pulled from her closet and drawers—jeans, shorts and practically every T-shirt Kate owned. Should she really trust Brenda's advice on packing? *Casual clothes, darling. All casual.* Maybe it wouldn't hurt to throw in some slacks and a dressy blouse or two.

"Kate?"

"Hmm?" She looked at Robin, forgetting that she was even in the room. "Sorry. What?"

"I asked why are you going to New Mexico?"

She paused. "To write. I have an October deadline and I'm on page twenty. Brenda seems to think a change of scenery would do wonders."

"Surely you don't plan to be gone until October, Kate."

"No. But you could always come visit, you know." The words were out before Kate could stop them. Brenda seemed to think that it was Robin's presence in her apartment, in her life, that was causing Kate's writer's block. Of course, Kate didn't *have* writer's block.

"Well, I suppose I could take a long weekend here and there. I could even take some extended time in July, perhaps."

Kate shook her head. "We'll see. I may not have time for more than an occasional weekend, Robin. It's really going to be a working trip."

"I've never been to Santa Fe."

"Brenda's not in Santa Fe anymore. Some little town, up in the mountains—Coyote." Kate folded the clothes she'd tossed on the bed, surprised at the excitement she felt. Perhaps Brenda was right. A change of scenery might be just the thing she needed to kick-start her writing.

"Well, I know I'll miss you," Robin said as she moved behind Kate, pulling her close.

Kate resisted the urge to stiffen. Instead, turning into Robin's embrace, she welcomed her gentle kisses. She didn't even protest when Robin pulled her to the bed, their weight crushing the neatly folded T-shirts. As Robin's hand slipped inside her panties, Kate noted absently that she'd have to refold her shirts again, perhaps even wash and dry them to get the wrinkles out.

I wonder if I need to bring a jacket . . .

CHAPTER THREE

Brenda studied her painting, wondering why her sandstone cliffs looked nothing like the view spread out before her. Well, the colors were there, at least.

"It looks lovely, Simone."

Brenda turned, smiling at the petite young woman who was patiently teaching her to paint and who insisted on calling her Simone. Harmony was wearing her usual white. Today it was a long, comfortable sundress, her sandals and painted toes just peeking out beneath the hem.

"Lovely? I wouldn't go that far," she said.

"You must have patience. Your colors are magnificent today." Harmony handed her a small crystal she had been fingering. "Here. Squeeze tight. Feel the energy," she said quietly.

Brenda did as she was told, imagining energy pulses vibrating from the crystal she held in her hand. She knew she would pocket the crystal later, then add it to the growing collection she had. Harmony and Sunshine seemed to have an endless supply of them.

"Ariel tells me you have a friend coming. You must be excited."

"Yes, a young friend from Dallas. She's a writer. She'll fit right in."

"I don't read much, I'm afraid. What's she done?"

"She writes a private investigator series. She's working on number seven. The Masters. Paul and Jennifer. They pretend to be a married couple in the books."

Harmony shook her head. "Sorry. Never heard of them."

Brenda shrugged. The first three books in the series were best sellers. The last three, well, she'd never tell Kate this, but the last three were real stinkers.

"Come to dinner tonight, Simone. Sunshine says Ariel has a new young thing and we want to meet her."

Brenda snorted. "Don't know why. She'll have *another* new young thing next week."

Harmony laughed. "She does stay busy, doesn't she?"

Brenda smiled. Yes, Lee—or Ariel, as Harmony and Sunshine called her—did stay busy with the young women who seemed to flock to her. She'd become friends with the county sheriff, but she'd long ago lost count of the number of women Lee brought around.

Brenda fanned herself as she waited for Kate's plane. Her straw hat and oversized sunglasses did nothing to keep the noontime sun at bay. As much as she'd enjoyed her stay in Santa Fe—spending endless hours visiting the art galleries—she was glad she'd moved up higher into the mountains. Not cold by any means, not this time of year, but the daytime temperatures had yet to reach eighty. Here in Santa Fe under a cloudless sky she figured it was above ninety already, reminding her of the cursed Dallas heat. Perhaps that was why only two others had braved the patio for lunch. The airport grill—famous for its green chili burgers, she was told—was packed inside, the air conditioning humming quietly in the background. But Brenda was anxious to see her friend, so she sat at the edge of the patio, watching as a plane prepared to land.

"Flight four thirty-nine from Albuquerque, now approaching."

"Finally," she muttered. She stood, watching as the plane touched down, its wheels bouncing only once, then taxied smoothly the rest of the short runway. It was a small jet, holding about twenty people, but on this Wednesday she doubted it was even half full.

Moving to the edge of the patio, she squinted into the sun as she watched the hatch open and the stairs descend. Kate was the fourth to deplane, a large backpack slung over one shoulder, and Brenda grinned, not realizing how much she had missed her young friend. She watched as Kate brushed the blond hair off her forehead, then slipped on her own sunglasses.

"Katie!" Brenda waved, watching as Kate shielded her eyes and lifted a hand in greeting.

Brenda walked down the steps of the patio, her sandals clicking on the hot asphalt as she hurried to the plane. She was engulfed in a tight hug, then surprised by a quick punch on the arm.

"You said it wasn't hot here," Kate reminded her, her eyes moving over the shimmering asphalt around them.

Brenda grinned. "I said it wasn't hot where I was staying. Why do you think I moved up the mountain?"

Kate turned in a circle taking in her surroundings, her eyes widening at the beautiful mesas and plateaus in the distance. She turned back to Brenda, slipping her sunglasses on top of her head.

"But it's beautiful, Brenda. I haven't been here in ten years or more."

"We're in an airport, darling. It's not beautiful. Out there," she pointed. "Now that's beautiful." She linked arms with Kate. "How much luggage do you have?"

Kate gave a wry smile. "Two somewhat large suitcases."

Brenda shook her head. "I told you to pack casual, didn't I? Jeans, shorts and the like." She pointed to herself. "I've worn these same capri pants three times this week."

Kate smiled. "I don't believe that's something I would be advertising. You do laundry, right? I mean, I know you have a housekeeper in Dallas, but you know *how* to do laundry, don't you?"

"I'm not that pampered, Kate. Of course I know how to do laundry. I just choose not to do it."

Kate rolled her eyes. "Don't tell me you have someone who does that for you here?"

"Well of course I do. I refuse to stoop to that level. She comes once a week and it's worked out beautifully. In fact, I'm thinking of having her come more often. She's a wonderful cook."

Kate nodded. "Will I get to take advantage of this service?"

"*Mi casa es su casa*, darling," Brenda said with a wave of her hand.

"This might be a good summer after all."

"I'm glad you didn't insist on doing the Santa Fe thing today. It's just too hot to be walking the streets."

Kate grinned. "But as you told me, it's a *dry* heat."

"That was just to get you out here. We'll come down here one evening when it's cooled some, eat Mexican food, stay the night, then hit the galleries the next morning. And I know I'm being ridiculous, Kate, because we've shopped in Dallas before when it was a hundred degrees. Maybe it's my age. I just can't seem to tolerate the heat anymore."

Kate studied her friend as she drove them out of Santa Fe and headed up the interstate highway. Brenda looked different. But maybe it was just the casual clothes, the sleeveless blouse that threw her. Kate drew her eyebrows together. Brenda's trademark bright red lipstick was missing. Kate moved closer. My God, does she even have *any* makeup on?

"What are you doing?"

"Take those ridiculous sunglasses off."

"Whatever for?"

Kate reached over and pulled them off, her eyes widening. "Oh my God."

"What?"

"The Brenda I know would not even leave her *bedroom* without makeup, much less leave her house. What has *happened* to you?"

"Give me those," Brenda said, snatching the sunglasses from Kate and putting them back on her face. "Nothing has happened. This is just a new phase in my life, darling."

"I thought painting was the new phase."

"Yes, it is. And I have met some wonderful people up here, all kind of . . . *earthy* people."

"*Earthy*?"

Brenda waved her hand. "Natural. Peaceful."

"Oh God, you haven't stopped shaving, have you?"

"No, I still shave and bathe, Kate. But you're right. Can you see me in Dallas, looking like this in public?"

"So, you've quit wearing makeup? Whatever for?"

"I have quit decorating myself, yes. It was as if I was trying to hide the true me beneath makeup and clothes and diamonds."

Kate's eyes flew to Brenda's fingers. Missing were the three rings Kate had never seen her without. "Brenda, please tell me you've not joined a cult and been brainwashed."

Brenda laughed, slapping Kate's leg affectionately. "Oh, Kate, darling, nothing that exciting, I'm afraid. I'm fifty-seven years old Kate, and for the first time in more years than I can remember, I am among strangers. They know nothing of my past, of my husband, of the wealth that I have. One day, while I was still in Santa Fe, I was dressing, fixing my face, finding the perfect, elegant dress to wear to dinner, sorting through my jewelry when it hit me. Nobody knew me here. I didn't have to dress the part. If I wanted to wear those cool linen shorts that I'd bought, no one would think me underdressed."

"Brenda, I've been telling you for years that you didn't have to dress the part. It's not like he's around any longer to force you."

"Oh, I know. But it was such a habit after twenty-five years. All of his so-called friends still thought I'd married him only for his money. So I had to be extra careful."

Kate smirked. "Well, he was thirty years older than you."

"I'll tell you now, Kate, I never was in love with him. I cared for him and grew to love him over the years, but I was never in love. And something his friends would be shocked at, for he was such a strong man, but he was *impotent*." She whispered the last word.

Kate smiled. "So, you did marry him for his money."

Brenda shrugged. "I grew up in Beaver's Creek, Oklahoma. It was an accomplishment just to graduate high school."

"You were twenty-five when you met him. Hardly high school."

"Twenty-four and it didn't matter. I was still in Beaver's Creek. Best waitress the Beaver Saloon had ever had, in case I haven't mentioned it before."

"You have, but I still don't know what it has to do with here and now, and why you've suddenly quit making yourself up."

Brenda laughed. "Kate, darling, the simple truth is, I don't *have* to make myself up any longer. Don't you see? In Dallas, around our old friends, around the *wives* of our friends, I had to play a part. And I was good at it, I admit. But here, it no longer applies."

"But Brenda, you can't just let yourself go just because you're away from your normal friends and your normal life."

"Kate, do I look like I've let myself go?"

"Actually, no, you look wonderful," Kate admitted. Brenda's normally pallid skin had a healthy glow. Even her hair style had changed. The dull, hair-sprayed style she normally sported had been trimmed and left natural. Well, as natural as a bottle of blond hair color will get you.

"Thank you. I feel wonderful. And I can't wait for you to meet everyone. But Kate, you have to promise to keep an open mind."

"Brenda, I am the most open-minded person you know."

"In your dreams, darling." Brenda pointed out the window. "That's the Rio Chama. We'll come upon the lake soon, but the canyons around here are magnificent. You won't believe the colors, Kate."

Kate looked out the window, for the first time admiring the scenery as they climbed higher into the mountains. Hard to believe that just that morning, she was fighting traffic around the airport in Dallas and now here she was, far removed from the city and all its noise and hustle.

Brenda slowed as the highway came to an intersection. She pointed quickly to their right. "Taos is that way," she said as she got in the left-hand lane. "Coyote is this way."

"What exactly is Coyote?"

"Oh, it's just a dot on the map, really. They do have a very nice lodge, though. I stayed there three days. But the area is filled with summer homes, most owned or rented by artists. I was lucky enough to find one to rent through the summer." She glanced quickly at Kate. "It's costing a small fortune, but I hardly care. It's well worth it. I can't wait for you to see the view in the mornings. The sunrise just brings everything to life. Now I know why Georgia O'Keefe found such inspiration there."

"In *Coyote*?" Kate asked. "Where you're staying?"

"Oh, yes, darling. The locals say she came often to paint the cliffs. Why, there are even pictures of her at the bakery."

Kate bit her lower lip. "Are there any real trees, Brenda? Other than this," she said, pointing to the small, stunted trees that graced the landscape.

"Trees?"

"I mean, you're not taking me to a desert with cliffs, right?"

Brenda laughed. "I promise, no desert. Well, they call it the high desert, but really, there are trees. It's quite beautiful, Kate. And higher up in the mountains, there are pine and spruce forests."

Kate nodded, enjoying the scenery that sped past as Brenda drove them deeper into the wilderness. It could be fun, she thought. And if it wasn't, she could always head back to Dallas any time.

"So, tell me about these new friends of yours," Kate suggested. "And why do I have to keep an open mind?"

"Well, there's Sunshine and Harmony. I have no idea their ages or real names. They're somewhere between twenty and forty. Very earthy. They're into crystals."

"Sunshine and *Harmony*? Are you joking?"

"Oh, no. Harmony is teaching me to paint. She's very talented. She has her own gallery in Santa Fe."

"*Harmony*? Who names their child Harmony?"

Brenda sighed. "Kate, I told you to keep an open mind. They are very nice. Now their friend Starlight, she's a little strange."

Kate rolled her eyes. "You're just messing with me, right? *Starlight*?"

"Obviously, those are not their real names, Kate. That's just what they go by. Harmony has this habit of naming people. It seems to stick."

"Okay. Who else?"

"Well, I can't wait for you to meet the sheriff."

"The sheriff? You're friends with the sheriff?"

"Yes. She's something else. I swear, Kate, if I was ever curious about playing for your team, she'd be the one I'd pick. She's got this magnetism about her. I can't explain it."

"Good Lord, Brenda!"

"I'm serious. Don't think I haven't thought about giving lesbianism a try, just because of her."

Kate laughed. "You don't give it a try, Brenda. You either are or you aren't."

"Well, that hasn't stopped a parade of young blond things from throwing themselves at her, most of them straight and curious. Apparently she's very talented."

"And she what? *Teaches* them? Sex?"

Brenda grinned. "What would you do, darling, if twenty-year-old blonds were begging to share your bed?"

"Brenda, I'm thirty-seven years old. Twenty-somethings do not beg to share my bed. And if they did, I'd send them home to their mothers, that's what I'd do."

Brenda nodded as she made a turn off the highway. "Yes, I'm afraid you would, kiddo. Lee, however, doesn't seem to have that problem." Brenda glanced at Kate. "Of course, she's not thirty-seven. In fact, I have no idea her age, either. Young, I'm sure."

Kate took a deep breath. "Okay, so far you've mentioned three *earth* fairies and a sex maniac sheriff. Have you met anyone *normal*, Brenda?"

Brenda laughed as they topped a rise. "That's what I have you for, darling."

"Oh my God," Kate murmured. She gripped the dash, her eyes scanning the vastness laid out before her.

Brenda nodded. "Those were my exact words, I believe, when I first saw this."

Kate pointed. "The mountains there, is that Taos?"

"No, no. Taos is to the east." Brenda motioned out her window. "That's actually south, from where we came. Polvadera Peak is over eleven thousand feet. But the main canyons are to our north. You'll learn much more about the area from Lee. She's agreed to be your tour guide. She's quite knowledgeable of the area."

"Wait. *Lee*? As in the sex person?"

"She's really very nice, Kate."

"Uh-huh. And we'll have so much in common. I'm in a monogamous, committed relationship. And she's teaching straight girls how to have sex. You know how I feel about promiscuous women, Brenda. They get you into trouble one way or the other."

"Well, if you leave your sex lives out of it, I believe you'll have something in common. Aside from you, she's probably the most normal person I know here. That's why I know you'll get along."

"Brenda, by now you know how I am. I've never been into the whole casual sex scene," she said with a wave of her arm. "I think it's disgusting, actually. I mean, we're not animals. We're not fucking like bunnies."

"Obviously *you're* not, darling."

"And what is that supposed to mean?"

"You know what that means, you don't need me to spell it out."

Kate grabbed the dash again as Brenda turned off onto a bumpy dirt road. "You know where you're going, right?"

"Of course. If we'd stayed on the main road, it would have taken us into Coyote. We'll go there tomorrow and I'll show you around. This road will take us to our summer home, Kate. You're just going to love it."

15

"I'm sure I will, Brenda. But do you have any neighbors?" she asked as she looked around—trees, rocks and little else.

"Not close neighbors like in the city, of course not. The house we're staying at sits on more than two hundred acres. I've walked most of it."

Kate stared. The Brenda she knew did not walk. In fact, she was known to get in her car and drive to the end of her driveway to check the mail. She closed her eyes. *God, I hope she hasn't been brainwashed by some earthy cult!*

"What?"

Kate shook her head. "Nothing, it's just . . . you're *walking*?"

"I'm telling you, darling, this is the best thing I've ever done for myself. You've known me for years, Kate. You know I've never really been into nature and all that crap," she said with a laugh. "But out here, I'm actually learning the names of plants, if you can believe that."

"Well, I can't," Kate murmured. Then, as she stared, "My God."

"Oh, yes. Beautiful."

The large adobe home came into view, but it was not the house that drew Kate's attention. No, the cliffs that spread out behind the house held her. The red sandstone reflected the afternoon sun, causing her to squint as she admired them.

"Oh, Brenda, now I see why you love it here."

"I told you my view was incredible. The house is built so that the cliffs are visible from nearly every angle."

As soon as Brenda parked, Kate was out, her arms spread wide. The heat that she was expecting was absent. It was pleasant, dry. The air smelled fresh. "Pine trees, Brenda?" she asked.

"Piñon pines and scrub oaks, primarily. There are some ponderosa pines mixed in, mostly in the wetter areas and up higher in the mountains."

Kate grinned. "And you know the names of trees. Oh my."

CHAPTER FOUR

Lee stared at her bed, watching the young woman sleep, wishing she could remember her name. She closed her eyes. *Tiffany? Bethany?*

She rubbed her face, smelling the remnants of their lovemaking. Perhaps she would enjoy it more if she could remember their names. She finally moved away into her bathroom. She closed the door before turning on the light. She stood there naked, the mirror reflecting back at her. She noticed two things. One, a bruise on her right breast. No doubt the blond had bitten down as she climaxed. And two, she needed a haircut. She dismissed the bruise, instead brushing at the dark hair that covered her ears, trying to tuck the errant ends. She deftly avoided meeting her own eyes in the mirror. She already knew what they would reflect—an emptiness that was getting harder and harder to hide.

Occasional sex with a cute young thing was one thing. But damn, she wasn't twenty anymore. She could hardly keep up.

Did I really just think that?

She shook her head as she stepped into the shower. Maybe she was just past all that. Jumping from bed to bed in college was considered an accomplishment, but hell, she was—

"Getting old." She stuck her head under the water. Her birthday was fast approaching and she was dreading it. Thirty was too young for a crisis. Surely she could wait until forty for that. She turned around, letting the warm water bounce off her back. Maybe she needed to talk it out with Brenda. Surprisingly, she had become friends with the older woman. Perhaps because compared to Harmony and the girls, Brenda seemed almost normal. Of course, the Indian chanting she'd taken up was suspect. And Lee didn't know why she'd agreed to show her writer friend around. She wondered if she'd be able to lie and tell her she liked her books when, really, she couldn't even make it through the last one.

Her eyes popped open when she heard the shower door open. Tiffany or Bethany stood there, stark naked, eyes traveling over Lee's wet body.

"You are something else, Sheriff." One manicured hand reached out, nails scratching lightly across Lee's breast. "My boyfriend could learn a thing or two from you."

"Yeah? Maybe you can teach him," Lee murmured before pulling the young woman into the shower with her.

CHAPTER FIVE

"What the hell is that?"

Kate rolled over, eyes still closed. *Chanting?* They had just gone to bed, why in the world was Brenda *chanting?* Kate sat up and leaned on her elbows, listening. She was surprised at the gentle pink color reflecting off the cliffs that greeted her through her opened window.

Dawn? Already?

She lay back down. She couldn't remember the last time she'd slept through the night. Up for water, up to pee, something. Never sleeping like a rock all night. But still, who got up at this ungodly hour? To *chant* no less.

But she couldn't get back to sleep, the monotone chanting was drifting in through the window. She tossed off her covers, enjoying the cool crispness of the morning air. Grabbing her robe from the end of the bed, Kate walked barefoot through the open house, staring. Everywhere she looked, the cliffs reflected the sunrise.

Now she knew why no curtains or blinds were hung. Who would want to close out this sight?

The French doors were left open to the patio, and she walked there, finally seeing Brenda. She was perched on a rock, not far from the expanse of the deck, her head bobbing slowly as she continued to chant. For some reason, the sound was comforting as the sun rose. Kate watched a bit longer, then silently crept back inside, not wanting to disturb Brenda. She would start coffee instead. It was only then that she glanced at her watch.

"*Five thirty!* That's insane," she murmured.

But soon, the smell of coffee had her waiting somewhat patiently, as she drummed her fingers on the marble countertop, watching the last of the drops fall before snatching the pot and filling her cup. After her first sip, she gave an audible approval, turning to find Brenda watching her.

"You like?"

Kate nodded. "Kinda nutty."

"Piñon coffee."

"Piñon? Like the tree?"

Brenda moved past her, filling her own cup. "Yes, from the piñon nuts." She smiled when she took a sip. "So, how did you sleep, darling?"

"Like a rock. You were right. Leaving the windows open was a good idea. I had the covers up to my neck, feeling almost like winter."

"Yes, it's so pleasant sleeping in the cool air, isn't it? And speaking of fresh air, I've noticed that you've not had a single cigarette since you've been here."

Kate stared. "Actually, I haven't even thought of it."

"How long has it been?"

"Well, if I don't count the one I had while waiting at the airport, it's been over two weeks."

"Wonderful, darling. I knew you could do it."

Kate watched her friend as she poured more coffee. She was still puzzled by her appearance. The wealthy widow she knew from

Dallas was considered nothing if not glamorous. Always impeccably dressed, makeup applied to perfection and not a hair out of place. The woman who stood before her now, clad in loose khaki pants, soft leather moccasins and an oversized cotton shirt that appeared to be hand-painted, would never pass for her Brenda.

"So, are you going to tell me what all that noise was?"

Brenda laughed, nearly spilling her coffee. "I think I should be offended."

"And I think you should have warned me. I thought it was the middle of the night. Of course to some, five thirty *is* the middle of the night."

"Well, that *noise* is a form of meditation. Some call it Indian chanting, but it's a little more than that. Starlight has been teaching me."

"Uh-huh, I see. *Starlight*. Figures," Kate murmured.

"Oh, Kate, I told you to keep an open mind. It gets me outside at the very cusp of dawn. I'm able to completely close my mind to everything. It's wonderful. It's very relaxing. Maybe you should try it."

Kate shook her head. "Don't think it's for me, Brenda."

"Oh, well, I was the same way at first. I thought she was loony, but Harmony said it might help with my painting."

"Speaking of that, when are you going to show me what you've done?"

"Oh, I don't know, Kate. Maybe I'll be like you. You won't let me even peek at your books until they're finished."

"And maybe that was a mistake. Maybe the last one wouldn't have sucked if I'd let you read it first."

Brenda raised her eyebrows.

"Okay, the last two, then."

Brenda nodded. "I really hope you'll be able to write here, darling. I think being out here will allow you to clear your mind."

"Why do you think my mind needs clearing?"

Brenda lowered her coffee cup, looking Kate straight in the eyes. "Because you've not been writing, and because your last few were stinkers. I think you need to refocus, get something fresh going."

"Stinkers?"

"No offense, darling, but yes, stinkers."

Kate went to refill her coffee, nodding. "You're right. They stunk. I just feel like I'm muddling along in their lives, not going anywhere. I mean, I hardly know these characters anymore."

"And that's exactly how the last few books have panned out. And as a fan who has read every book you've written, I didn't recognize the characters, either. My only advice, because as you know, I'm not a writer, is to *do* something with them. I mean, move them along in their relationship or have them end this silly cat-and-mouse they've been doing."

"Silly?"

"Yes, silly. At the beginning, you wanted them to get together and it was cute how they pretended to be married. Even your take on their flirting seemed real, even though I know you have no idea how to flirt with a guy."

"What do you mean by that?"

"I mean that in a nice way, darling, but you're gay. And even though you pretend to be straight sometimes, you're still gay. And I have been around you in straight bars before and you have no clue."

"I do *not* pretend to be straight!"

"Darling, your publisher doesn't know you're gay. Hell, some of your so-called friends don't know you're gay."

"Brenda, just because I don't announce it to them doesn't mean they don't know."

Brenda dismissed her comment with a wave of her hand. "As usual, we are talking in circles about this subject. And if you choose to be secretive about it, that's your business. But we were talking about Jennifer and Paul."

Kate nodded. "So you're tired of their flirting?"

"Darling, after six books and they've not even *kissed* . . . yes, it's time to move on."

"That's just it. I don't know where to go. It just doesn't feel right to have them as a real couple. I mean a real couple that has sex. You know, I view them almost as a brother and sister, so to make their relationship sexual is just gross."

Brenda patted her hand. "You'll think of something, but please don't keep it going in the same direction. I'm not sure your readers could suffer through another one."

Kate stared out the windows, the sun now fully over the cliffs, the gentle pinks of the canyons changing to a brighter orange. She couldn't decide which color was more beautiful.

"I think I'll take a few days to relax, Brenda, then open up the book again. You may be right. This could be good for me out here."

"We'll have a grand time, darling. In fact—"

Her sentence was cut short by a quick knock on the patio door only seconds before it opened.

Brenda smiled. "That'll be Harmony."

"Good Lord, it's barely six."

A petite woman with long flowing blond hair walked in, her white sundress reaching below her knees. She paused, taking a deep breath.

"Ahhh, piñon," she murmured, closing her eyes. She then looked up, nodding briefly at Kate. "How are you this morning, Simone?"

Kate's eyes widened and she quickly looked behind them, wondering who the hell Simone was. Her eyes widened further when Brenda answered her.

"So wonderful, Harmony. Good morning to you. This is my friend, Kate. Kate, this is Harmony."

Kate stared, trying to force a smile onto her face. "Hello . . . *Harmony*."

"Oh my." Harmony spread her arms. "Such negative energy, Simone. Do you feel it?"

"Oh, yes."

Harmony held out her hand to Kate. "Here, take this. Squeeze it. Feel the energy."

Kate opened her palm, seeing the stone that Harmony had placed there. She arched one eyebrow. "It's a rock," she said dryly.

The audible gasp from Harmony nearly caused Kate to laugh, but she bit her lip, fingering the stone in her hands.

"That is no *rock*. That is an elestial crystal. It is very powerful." She then snatched the stone from Kate's open palm. "Perhaps you're not quite ready. Your negative energy is very strong."

Kate opened her mouth to speak, then closed it again. She turned to Brenda, eyebrows raised.

Brenda smiled, giving Kate a subtle wink.

"We should go, Simone. The colors will fade soon."

"I'm ready. My bag is already on the deck." Brenda turned to Kate. "Time for my lesson. I'll be back before noon, so make yourself at home. We'll eat lunch in Coyote, and I'll show you around."

Kate nodded silently, her frown more pronounced as the two women walked out onto the deck.

Simone? Who the hell is Simone?

CHAPTER SIX

"That's the only grocery store in town," Brenda pointed as they drove slowly down the main street of Coyote.

"Why does she call you Simone? Furthermore, why do you answer to it?"

"Will you get over the Simone thing already! It's just what she calls me, darling. Can't you leave it at that?"

"But it's not your name," Kate said for the fourth time.

Brenda loosened her grip on the steering wheel and squeezed Kate's leg affectionately. "Perhaps we need to work on your negative energy. Bad karma, Harmony says."

"Bad karma, my ass," Kate muttered.

Brenda laughed. "That's my Kate." Then she pulled over to the curb and pointed. "The best bakery I have ever been in. Their pastries are out of this world, but it's the lunch menu that draws most. Green chilies on practically everything, so be prepared."

"I like spicy food."

"Yes, but this is not Tex-Mex." Brenda opened her door, then stopped. "Oh, my," she whispered. "Look. Have you ever seen a sexier sight?"

Kate followed her gaze, watching long bare legs swing out of a dusty Jeep. Her eyes moved past scuffed hiking boots and up very toned thighs, her mind not quite acknowledging the gun and holster strapped to the woman's waist. A brilliant white sleeveless shirt contrasted nicely with her healthy tan but it was the hazel, laughing eyes that held Kate's attention as the woman pulled her sunglasses off.

"Brenda! Good to see you," the woman said as she walked toward their car.

"Lee," Brenda greeted. She got out, motioning for Kate to do the same. "I want you to meet my friend, Kate."

Lee bent at the waist, peering into the car as Kate fumbled with the door. Lee opened it for her, stepping back as an embarrassed Kate crawled from the car. *This was the sex maniac sheriff?*

"Thank you."

Lee grinned. "All my pleasure."

"Kate, this is Lee, the county sheriff. Lee, Kate Winters."

"I've read your books, Miss Winters. Well, I don't think I've managed to get through the last one yet. Very nice to meet you."

Kate stared at the hand that was held out to her. She was nearly afraid to touch it. But she politely extended her own, surprised at its softness.

"Nice to meet you too. Brenda has told me a little about you." Kate could hear the distaste in her own voice and hoped this woman wouldn't notice. She didn't intend to be rude to the sex maniac.

Again, the laughing eyes captured Kate's. "She has?" Lee turned to Brenda. "Spreading nasty rumors, Simone?"

"Hardly rumors and hardly nasty, darling." Brenda glanced down the sidewalk. "In fact, I believe here comes a member of your fan club now."

"Sheriff Foxx! There you are!"

Kate's eyebrows shot up as she realized the woman was barely out of her teens. Sheriff *Foxx*? Surely to God that couldn't be her real name. *Foxx*?

"What can I do for you?"

"I'm Tiffany's friend. Erin."

"Tiffany?"

"From last night."

Lee nodded. "Oh, yes. That Tiffany."

"Well, I'm having some . . . some car trouble. I thought maybe you could help me. Tiffany said you were very good with your hands."

Lee smiled. "Of course." She turned back to Brenda and Kate. "Duty calls, ladies. Nice to meet you, Miss Winters. Brenda asked me to show you around a bit. I'll come by this evening to collect you. We'll do a quick tour before dark."

Kate stared, shocked that this young girl was so blatantly flirting with the local sheriff. Not only that, but Sheriff *Foxx* seemed to be taking her up on it. Kate shook her head. She had no desire to spend time with this woman whose actions she found to be repugnant and repulsive, not to mention irresponsible and immature. "No, that's okay. I'm fine. Besides, I'm sure you'll be plenty busy."

Lee's eyes twinkled. "Oh, this won't take all day, trust me. Just seems these girls have a lot of car trouble."

"Well, lucky you're available to assist them, then," Kate said, unable to keep the sarcasm out of her voice.

Lee laughed. "Brenda, exactly what have you been telling her?"

Brenda waved her away. "Oh, don't mind Kate. Go help the young girl with her car."

Kate purposefully turned her head as those long legs walked away her. But as she followed Brenda into the bakery, she couldn't help but sneak a peek at the local sheriff. Her hair was dark, nearly black, cut in a short, attractive style. Grudgingly, Kate admitted that a young, twenty-something—gay or straight—

would have a hard time resisting the attractive sheriff. Animal magnetism was something she'd never used to describe a woman before, but this one was oozing with it.

"I swear, I don't know how she does it," Brenda said as she slid into a booth. "They just flock to her. I doubt she has a spare minute alone."

"Car trouble," Kate murmured. "Can't they think of something a little more original?"

Brenda laughed. "I'm sure they've used all the excuses they can think of. One friend tells a friend and so on."

Kate leaned forward. "You don't think she was taking that girl somewhere to have sex, do you?"

Brenda shrugged. "You never know with Lee. Her reputation precedes her, so it's assumed, I suppose."

Kate shook her head. "It's disgusting. Not to mention, they are complete strangers. You could get as much satisfaction from a hooker."

"Well, I see you're doing so well with keeping that open mind, darling."

"But Brenda, don't you find it disturbing that the local sheriff is out *banging* the tourists? My God, that one wasn't even of legal age!"

Brenda laughed. "Banging? Oh Kate, darling, we have got to get you out more."

"I'm serious. Isn't the county afraid of a lawsuit or something?"

"Lawsuit? For what? And it's not like she's going to get one of them pregnant, Katie. And trust me, *they* come on to her, not the other way around." Brenda patted Kate's arm, her voice turning serious. "You need to lighten up, darling. Lee has become a friend. What she does with her private life is none of my business."

Kate frowned. "Do you think I'm being judgmental?"

"You think?"

Kate nodded. "Probably. And after meeting Harmony, the sheriff did seem almost normal."

Brenda laughed. "Harmony will grow on you." She pointed at

the menu Kate had yet to look at. "Ten lunch burritos to choose from. I've tried them all except the portabella mushroom and spinach."

"What? Too healthy for you?"

"Yes. A burrito should be greasy and spicy."

"And despite all that, you look like you've lost weight."

"Oh, I've shed a few pounds," Brenda said. "It's just being outdoors and having activity, I think. And of course, the weekly dinners at Harmony and Sunshine's place. They are total vegetarians, so it is nothing but healthy there."

"Weekly dinners?"

"Oh, yes. Most weeks. And you'll join us, of course. Sometimes it's only six or eight of us. Other times, there will be twenty or more. Just depends who Harmony meets during the week."

"Every week?"

"Tuesdays. And if not every week, then at least two out of the month."

"You don't do like . . . chanting and stuff, do you?"

Brenda laughed. "I swear, Katie, I never knew you were such a stick-in-the-mud!"

Kate closed her menu, her eyes moving among the patrons in the small bakery. It was then that she realized that she was probably the most conservatively dressed one there, something she would never have considered herself in Dallas. But here, among all these *earthy* people in their leather hiking sandals and cotton shorts, all looking tanned and fit, she felt a bit old and out of place. Even Brenda, still clad in her baggy khakis and soft moccasins, looked more suited to the atmosphere of this local eatery.

"What will you have?"

Kate smiled. "I think I'll live dangerously and try the portabella and spinach."

"Figures." Brenda waved to a waitress who came over immediately. "Hi Remmy. Meet my friend Kate. She's from Dallas."

"Hello, Kate. You must be the one with writer's block."

Kate glared at Brenda. "I'm the writer, yes."

29

"Well, I hope you like it here as much as Simone does."

Kate ignored the quiet laugh Brenda gave her and pointed at the menu. "I'll have the portabella mushroom and spinach, please."

"Of course."

"Remmy, make mine the black bean and beef, extra cheese."

"The usual tea?"

"Oh, yes. For both of us." Brenda grasped Kate's hand as soon as Remmy walked away. "The most fabulous herbal tea you'll ever taste."

Kate leaned forward. "Does anyone here call you Brenda?"

"Mostly just Lee. She doesn't quite get Harmony."

"Well, at least we have that in common."

"Is this your car?" Lee asked. They stopped next to a candy apple red sports car. It looked like it was fresh off of a showroom floor. Lee couldn't imagine that it wouldn't start.

"Yes. You like it?"

Lee nodded. "Nice. Looks fast."

"Oh, it's very fast," Erin purred. "Maybe you want to take it for a spin?"

Lee's lips twitched. "I thought it wouldn't start?" She smiled as the young woman had the grace to blush.

"Well, I mean if you can get it to start, then you're welcome to take it out. I mean, maybe we could take a drive this evening or something."

Lee studied her. It would be so easy. A quick drive in the sports car, then take her back to the house. And like her friend Tiffany, she would be eager and willing to try anything. All because their young boyfriends didn't have a clue as how to please them.

But for some reason, Lee wasn't in the mood. No, tonight she craved some normal, adult conversation with a woman who wanted nothing from her. She just didn't have the energy to repeat the night she'd just spent with Tiffany.

"You know, as much fun as that sounds, I've already got plans this evening," she said quietly. The stricken look on the girl's face almost made her change her mind. Almost.

"Oh." The girl shifted her feet. "Well, maybe some other night, you know, when you're free."

Lee nodded. "Sure, Erin. How long will you be in town?"

"Until the end of next week."

"Okay. Well then maybe we'll hook up." Lee pointed at the car. "Let's see about getting her started."

CHAPTER SEVEN

"Promise me you'll be nice to her."

"I just don't know why you set this up. I don't need a babysitter or someone to show me around."

Brenda had just gotten off the phone with Lee who was on her way over. Kate remained adamant that she did not need a tour of the county.

"I told you, she's knowledgeable of the area and you'll enjoy it. It's so beautiful out there, darling. I think you just need to relax a little and open your mind."

Kate pointed a finger at Brenda. "Do not mention my so-called negative energy again. I have no negative energy," she stated loudly.

Brenda only smiled. "Of course not, darling."

"And I'm not entirely convinced that you've not been brain-washed by this cult of earth fairies."

Brenda laughed and dismissed her with a wave of her hand.

"Think what you like, but I've never felt better in my entire life. So if they are brainwashing me with positive energy and meditation, all the better."

Kate sighed. "You're right. In the eight years I've known you, I've never seen you more relaxed. Maybe I do have a little negative energy," Kate admitted.

Brenda nodded. "It'll be good for you here, Katie. Take a few days to relax, then find you a cool spot outside to sit and write. It'll flow for you here, darling. You watch."

Kate stared out the windows to the cliffs. The colors in this early evening light were almost as brilliant as the mornings were. Yes, she could imagine taking her laptop out and sitting in one of the many nooks of their multi-leveled deck. Of course, she wondered how much writing she would get done with the view of the cliffs distracting her. A quick knock on the side patio door brought her out of her musings.

"That'll be Lee. No one ever uses the front door and Harmony and the girls always come around to the deck," Brenda said as she moved to open the door. "For some reason, Lee has taken to using the side patio."

It was with annoyance that Kate acknowledged the sexual magnetism the local sheriff exuded—and this just from walking into the room. A twenty-year-old wouldn't stand a chance. Yes, this woman was nothing but trouble.

"Hi, Brenda. Miss Winters," Lee greeted.

"It's Kate, please. You'll have me looking around for my mother if you continue with Miss Winters."

"Of course."

Twinkling eyes captured Kate's without trouble and she mentally kicked herself for not being able to pull away. This woman was a player, she reminded herself. And as soon as they were alone, she was going to make it perfectly clear to the sex maniac sheriff that she was involved with someone. Robin was no doubt sitting at home, alone. It was only then that Kate realized they had not spoken since Robin had dropped her off at the airport the previous morning. She had not even thought to check her cell phone for messages much less service.

"I brought you some wine, Brenda." Lee held up a jug. "You mentioned the other night that you were running low."

"Oh, darling, how sweet of you." Brenda took the jug, then showed it to Kate. "Sangria wine. Lee makes the best."

"You make your own wine?"

Lee shrugged. "Secret recipe." Then she winked. "But it's got some kick."

"Why don't you have a taste before you go?" Brenda offered.

Kate shook her head. "No, thanks." *Did she just wink at me?*

"Maybe after our tour, she'll feel like a glass," Lee said, her twinkling eyes still able to hold Kate's.

"Where will you take her this evening?" Brenda asked.

"Oh, we'll just do the cliff road. Won't have time for much else before it gets dark. I thought maybe Saturday, we could go out earlier and do a real tour."

Kate watched the two as they planned her week. Brenda had something up her sleeve, Kate was almost certain. And if it had *anything* to do with trying to set her up with this . . . this sheriff person, Kate would kill her.

"Well, you should go before the suns gets too low. The colors are still good," Brenda said as she nearly shoved them out the door.

Kate glared at her. "We need to talk," she hissed just as the door was shut in her face. She found herself alone with Lee Foxx. She smiled, hoping it looked more genuine than it felt. "Lead on, Sheriff."

"The Jeep hasn't seen a top since winter. I hope you won't get cold, but the temperature drops once the sun sets."

Kate paused, glancing at her own bare legs before looking at Lee's.

Lee smiled, a smile that made her eyes twinkle and Kate was again held by them.

"I'm used to it. But we won't be out long, so you should be fine."

Soon, Kate was sitting in the dusty Jeep, bouncing down the

dirt road toward the cliffs. There was no door to hold on to, so she grasped the dash with one hand and the seat with the other. Lee finally slowed.

"Sorry, but I wanted to try to catch it before the sun set, but I guess we're too late."

Kate looked to the west, still seeing the orange sun barely hanging on to the day. "Catch what?"

"There's a spot where it overlooks the river. The cliffs reflect beautifully at sunset." Lee too looked to the sky. "Might have to catch it another day though."

Kate relaxed a little, the rocks outside her opened door not speeding by quite as quickly.

"Have you started writing yet?"

Kate blinked. "Excuse me?"

Lee shrugged. "Brenda says you have writer's block."

"I swear, is there anyone here she *hasn't* told?"

"I liked the first few books. The last few, well, no offense, but they sucked."

Kate's eyes widened. She couldn't believe this woman, this *stranger*, had just said her writing sucked.

"You're a literary critic, I take it?" Kate asked, her voice dripping with sarcasm.

But Lee laughed. "No. I just read them. And I think I've figured out what the problem is."

Kate forced a smile. "Well, please tell me."

"Jennifer. She's the problem."

"What's wrong with Jennifer?"

"Well, there's nothing wrong with her, except she's still pretending to have an interest in Paul. And Paul, he's a nice guy and all, but he just doesn't get Jenn's juices flowing."

Kate's eyes widened. "*Excuse me?*"

Lee grinned. "Jenn is obviously a lesbian. Why are you holding her back?"

"A *lesbian*? Where in the world did you get that idea?"

"Oh, come on. She's strong, she's cute as hell, she can kick butt and she's in her thirties and never married, never had a steady boyfriend. And you try to make us believe that she's got a romantic interest in Paul? Hell, if it wasn't for the forced flirting with these characters, I'd think Paul was gay too."

"Oh my God! I cannot believe you are even saying this. Paul is in *love* with Jennifer."

"In love? You call that love? Have they even kissed? It's gotten to the point where I'm not sure they even like each other. And that's why I haven't been able to finish your last book. I want to scream at them, I want to scream at Jennifer! Get a clue! You're a dyke!"

Kate was too shocked and angry to even notice the laughing eyes of this . . . this maniac. If the Jeep had been going any slower, she would have thrown herself out! Instead, she turned, glaring at Lee.

"You obviously have *no idea* how to weave a story together," she said through gritted teeth. "The little *escapades* you have with your young, straight girls cannot pass as life experiences that you want to share in book form. Jennifer Masters is no *lesbian*."

Lee slowed the Jeep, the grin on her face showing the laugh lines around her eyes. Despite her anger, Kate wondered how old this woman was. She'd assumed, at first meeting, that Lee was barely twenty-five.

"*Escapades*? What in the world has Brenda been telling you?"

"She didn't have to tell me much. Besides, I was there today when your little friend showed up. *Car trouble*?"

Lee laughed. "Oh yeah. Forgot about that."

"I take it you were able to help her."

"Whew, it was fast and sleek."

"I don't need details," Kate said dryly.

"I'm talking about her car. Candy apple red, two-door sports car, ragtop. She let me take it for a spin."

"No doubt. I guess the car trouble wasn't serious."

"Battery cable was loose. Didn't take but a second. Then we had a spin. It was fast."

"Hope you enjoyed it."

"Oh, I did. She could fly."

Kate stared out the window, biting her tongue. It didn't matter in the least what this woman did in her spare time. If she chose to fuck every eighteen-year-old tourist that visited the county, what business was it of Kate's? And if the locals didn't mind their sheriff cavorting around like the sex-crazed woman she must be, why should she?

"There's the river over there, the Rio Pueblo," Lee said, pointing to their right. "We're too late to catch the full effect of the sunset though."

Kate turned her head, looking over her shoulder, her breath leaving her at the beauty of it.

"It's beautiful," she murmured, her anger fading. "What is it we're missing?"

"If we catch the full sunset, the reflection off the water and the cliffs is so magnificent, it'll bring you to your knees."

Kate turned, surprised at the sincerity in Lee's eyes. This woman, who she imagined to be conceited and full of herself, seemed genuinely touched by the beauty of their surroundings.

"You like?" Lee asked.

Kate nodded. "Yes. Very much." She met Lee's eyes. "Do you take your young women here?"

Lee laughed, her eyes sparkling. "No. I don't think they're all too interested in the natural scenery around here. They're more into the nightlife." She drove on. "We can drive down to the river. There's still time. It'll be cooler, though."

Kate nodded. "I'm fine."

They drove in silence for awhile, then Lee turned, watching her. "Brenda says you're seeing someone."

"Yes I am. We live together."

"It's that serious? Brenda acted like it was a passing thing."

"She would. She doesn't like Robin."

"So, your Robin is okay with you being gone?"

Kate smiled. "I didn't really give her a choice."

Lee nodded. "A woman in control of her own life. I like that."

CHAPTER EIGHT

"So where did you go?"

Kate stared at Brenda, wondering at her curiosity. Again, she felt the woman had something up her sleeve.

"On the cliff road until the sun set. Then we drove down to the river. It was nearly dark, though, so the views weren't very good."

"I don't know why she came so late," Brenda said. "Saturday will be better."

"So she says." Kate accepted the glass of sangria wine that Brenda offered her. Sweet, with a definite kick.

"But you were nice to her?"

"No."

"*No?*"

Kate moved to the sofa, curling her bare feet under her as Brenda settled in the giant recliner that faced the deck. It was full dark outside, but with the French doors opened, they were able to see stars twinkling over the canyon.

"She had the audacity to tell me my books sucked. And then she accused Jennifer Masters of being a *lesbian*, of all things."

Brenda laughed, nearly spilling her wine. Kate glared at her.

"Well, she is a bit of a dyke, darling."

"My Jennifer is no *dyke*! What books have you been reading?"

"Let's just say, compared to Paul, she's a bit butch, you have to admit. How many times has Jennifer been the one to save the day, while he sits idly by in his designer suits, hoping not to get dirty."

"That's because I've tried to portray Jennifer as a strong role model for women."

"Exactly. One that doesn't need a man around to save her."

Kate shook her head. "That doesn't make her a lesbian."

"No, of course it doesn't. But if she had sex with a man occasionally, that might make it more convincing. And I don't mean Paul. As you said, they are almost like brother and sister."

Kate sipped her wine and stared out the window, wondering what she was going to do with her characters. She'd painstakingly created them years ago, turning Jennifer into a hero that women of all ages could look up to. Paul was the dashing, charming man in her life, the man who supposedly ran their agency, the man who pretended to be her husband. And a man who Kate had unknowingly turned into a flaming queen!

Brenda stood, sensing that Kate wanted some alone time. "I'm going to take a long bath and read a bit before bed, darling. Help yourself to more of Lee's wine, if you want."

Kate looked up, nodding. "What are you reading?"

"Oh, local history. I have a book on the Native Americans who lived here. The Anasazi and Pueblo Indians. It's so fascinating. I'm learning about medicine wheels now."

Kate smiled. "You've really taken to this area, haven't you?"

"Yes, I have. In fact, I've been thinking more and more of simply selling everything in Dallas, including the company, and moving here permanently."

Kate stared at her. "Are you serious?"

"What is there for me in Dallas, darling? A thirty-room estate that I share with no one? Business associates and old friends of Al's that I have no desire to spend time with but I'm required to? Or perhaps the charity events that I attend because it's expected of me when in reality, I loathe them." At Kate's stricken look, Brenda smiled and tipped her wine glass at her. "Oh, kiddo, I'm just thinking about it. By the time winter comes, I may be dying to get back to Dallas."

Kate watched as Brenda walked from the room, her moccasins silent on the tile floor. Yes, she didn't doubt that Brenda had been thinking of moving here permanently. She was a different person up here. Kate had never seen her more relaxed. She seemed to be at peace with herself, with her life. Which for Brenda, was quite unusual. In Dallas, nearly every day was spent at some event or other representing her late husband. Brenda's life was a total whirlwind and her lone escape was when she and Kate got away for their weekly dinner date.

Kate had never really thought about it before, but it must have been exhausting for Brenda, having to dress the part, *play* the part, day after day. Her husband's oil company and subsequent holdings made him a very prominent Dallas businessman. And even though she had little say in how the company was run today, she still owned it. And with that, came responsibilities and commitments that Brenda had apparently grown weary of. No, Kate couldn't blame her if she wanted to escape from it all. She grinned, imagining the frumpy ladies of Brenda's bridge club finding her on a rock, chanting.

CHAPTER NINE

Friday morning after Harmony and *Simone* left for their art class, Kate took Brenda's advice and decided to explore the area around their house. But as Kate stumbled over a rock in her walking shoes, she decided her first purchase was going to be a nice pair of hiking boots. And maybe a pair or two of those cute hiking shorts that everyone seemed to wear around here.

As she followed the trail Brenda had pointed out, she let her mind clear and simply absorbed the beauty around her. The smell of the piñon pines and junipers was intoxicating, and she took deep breaths, wondering if she'd ever smelled air as fresh before. She stopped when the trail parted the piñons at the edge of one of the small canyons. Her eyes widened, the yellow and red rock cliffs across the canyon seemingly on fire, contrasting beautifully with the nearly cobalt sky that surrounded them, not even one cloud to mar the perfection.

Something Lee said the evening before came back to her. *"It'll bring you to your knees."* Yes. It very nearly did. She almost wished someone was here to share this with her, but then she felt an immediate sense of peace settle over her as she realized how completely alone she was. She spread her arms out, wanting to embrace the beauty before her.

She finally walked on, her eyes sliding again and again to the multi-hued sandstone cliffs. Yes, she could very well imagine Georgia O'Keefe here with palette and paintbrush in hand, painting the very cliffs that Kate now viewed. No wonder Brenda found inspiration here.

"Simone, you're becoming so bold with your colors. I love it."

Brenda stared at her canvas, then looked to the cliffs. She couldn't hide her smile. It was the best work she had produced so far. "It actually kinda looks like the cliffs, doesn't it?"

Harmony spread her arms wide, both hands clutched in fists, no doubt squeezing a crystal.

"Your positive energy is flowing this morning, Simone. And it's reflected here on canvas." She opened one palm, offering the crystal to the sun, and they both watched as the light reflected off the glass-like stone. Then, in a flash, Harmony tossed the stone into the canyon. "For another soul to find one day." She turned to Brenda. "Next week, we'll work on your depth perception. Instead of painting just the cliffs, we'll move it back and include the canyon rim and perhaps a tree or two."

"Trees? Oh, Harmony, I don't think I'm ready for trees."

"You'll do fine," she said, as she helped gather Brenda's things. "I hear that Ariel is going to show your friend around tomorrow."

"Her name is Kate," Brenda said. "And yes, Lee has agreed to be tour guide. In fact, she took her out yesterday evening along the cliff road."

"I'm surprised. Kate is not Ariel's normal choice for company."

Brenda laughed. "No, she's certainly not. But trust me, there's nothing romantic going on between them. Kate has a girlfriend back home, although I hate to use that term to describe Robin. I despise the woman. And anyway, Kate is very old-fashioned. She finds Lee's behavior where the young girls are concerned to be a bit boorish, I'm afraid."

"Sunshine has a theory about Ariel, you know."

"And what's that?" Brenda asked as they made their way back to the house.

"She is a lost soul on a journey, yet she doesn't know for what it is she searches."

Brenda smiled, but said nothing, knowing Harmony would continue.

"Sunshine says her eyes look nearly hollow sometimes, as if her very life is being drained."

Brenda shrugged. "She always seems happy to me."

"Outwardly, yes. I'm talking about her inner life, her soul. But Sunshine says her journey is nearing its end."

Brenda stopped. "*What?* You don't mean—"

"No. Ariel is fine. I mean she will soon find that for which she has been searching."

Brenda knew not to question Sunshine's theories. Harmony called her a *seer*. And on more than one occasion, Sunshine had proved to be somewhat of a prophet.

Kate looked up when she heard footsteps approach. She smiled at Brenda, then watched Harmony round the corner of the house, presumably to leave.

"What are you doing, darling?"

"Working on my book."

Brenda raised her eyebrows. There was no laptop, no notebook, not even pen and paper.

Kate smiled again. "Working on it in my head."

"I see. And how is it coming?"

"I may have a few changes in store. We'll see."

"Good." Brenda joined Kate on the rock, both of them looking out to the cliffs. "Did you enjoy your walk?"

"Very much. There was one part where the sun must have been hitting it just right, but it looked like the cliffs were on fire."

Brenda nodded. "I know the spot. Once I get my colors down better, Harmony is going to let me paint it."

"How's that going, by the way?"

"Excellent, darling! I will actually show you what I did this morning. My cliffs look like cliffs today!"

Kate laughed, remembering the pottery class she suffered through with Brenda. Finally, the woman was able to make a bowl. Everyone else had progressed on to more complex vases and sculptures. "So, I guess this means you are enjoying it?"

"I absolutely adore it. I feel a bit of Georgia O'Keefe in me while I have a paintbrush in my hand."

"I'm happy for you, Brenda. I was thinking last night that I've never seen you more relaxed and at peace with yourself."

"At peace, yes. A perfect word." Brenda paused, looking at Kate. "You know, this spring, when I first told you I was coming out here to paint, you never really asked me why."

Kate shrugged. "I guess I just assumed it was another endeavor you wanted to try."

"Yes, I suppose it was at the time. It was part of the reason, anyway. There is something I never told you, Kate. Never told anyone, in fact. But the last year or so, my doctor was prescribing antidepressants for me."

"Brenda? Really? Why didn't you say something?"

"Oh, darling, I was too embarrassed to tell you."

"That's not something to be embarrassed about. A lot of people—"

"Yes, I know, darling, but I didn't want to be one of them. Besides, the drugs were slowly zapping the part of me that was *me*. I stopped feeling, I stopped caring. I was just in la-la land, where everything was rosy all the time."

"Now that you mention it, I guess I did notice that you had mellowed quite a bit."

"Mellowed! Now there's a word!"

"So, I take it you're off them now?"

"Oh, yes. I flushed them down the toilet in the first hotel I stayed in on my way out here. It was the strangest feeling, Katie, with my car all packed and Dallas in my rearview mirror. It was like this weight being lifted off my shoulders. I can't really describe the euphoria I felt. It must be what it's like to be released from prison after thirty years. I felt truly free."

"And that's the real reason you don't want to go back?" Kate guessed.

"One of many reasons, darling. You do know that my lone happiness in that life was you, don't you?"

Kate was touched by the sincerity of Brenda's words. Touched and saddened. "I'm sorry."

"Sorry? Oh, I'm not sorry. How insignificant it seemed at the time, the day we met. I didn't realize how starved I was for friendship, Kate. And I certainly didn't expect to find it in someone as young as you."

Kate smiled. "Thank you."

"But with that said, the longer I stay here, the harder it will be to leave. Do you understand?"

"I understand. I certainly don't expect you to come back just to keep me company."

"I'm not going to make a rash decision, Katie. I'm not going to sell everything, hoping that this is what I want. I may stay a year and then decide. Or I might wake up next week, call Thomas and tell him to sell. Or I may decide that Dallas really is home."

"I just want you to be happy. And if you do decide to stay here, don't doubt that I won't make myself a nuisance by visiting."

Brenda leaned over and quickly kissed Kate's cheek. "I love you, you know."

Kate was nearly embarrassed by the tears that formed in her eyes. "I love you too," she murmured, aware that it was the first time the two of them had ever uttered those words to each other.

"Now, I'm thinking a very light lunch is in order for I feel a bit like splurging this evening."

"How so?"

"Steaks on the grill? How does that sound?"

"Sounds wonderful. Will we get to enjoy more of that sangria?"

Brenda laughed. "I told you Lee made the best. It's downright addictive."

CHAPTER TEN

Lee sat on the top step of her deck, sipping her second glass of sangria wine. She glanced occasionally into her bedroom, then looked back toward the fading colors of what was a fabulous sunset. Erin, unlike her friend Tiffany, hadn't had the stamina for a prolonged session in bed. In fact, after only her second orgasm, she'd crashed. Lee looked at her watch. Two hours had passed. She sighed, thinking it was just as well. She hadn't really planned on looking up the young woman, anyway, but she'd spied the red sports car speeding outside of Coyote and she just couldn't resist. Knowing that the girl's boyfriend was expecting her for dinner only added to the temptation of a quick conquest of the young college student. And she supposed she should go wake her so she could run back to her friends.

Lee sighed again, wondering at the loneliness that had been creeping up more and more lately. Again, she wanted to blame it on her age, which, in just a few short hours, would officially be thirty. But it was more than that, she knew, she just couldn't put her finger on it. Maybe she was finally growing up. Maybe it was time to settle down.

She snorted. *My God, you're only thirty, not dead!*

No, she wasn't the settling down type. She'd always known that. She couldn't imagine settling down with someone, moving in together, sharing the same bed, night after night. How boring. How *depressing*. No, she liked her current arrangements just fine. No strings, no attachments, just sex. And sometimes, really good sex.

And sometimes really bad sex, she thought as the glanced again into her bedroom. Oh well. There were worse ways to spend a Friday afternoon.

CHAPTER ELEVEN

Kate contemplated opening up her laptop, then decided against it. She had ideas for Jennifer and Paul and she wanted to get started on them. But Lee was due any minute. She'd called first thing that morning, to remind Kate of their tour of the county. Kate had almost asked Brenda to tell Lee she was canceling, to tell her she wanted to start writing, but decided against it. She figured it was a trip she would just get over and done with today, then Brenda would leave her alone about the history of the area. Not that she wasn't interested. But being stuck for several hours in a Jeep with Sheriff Foxx—she could think of other things she'd rather do.

Like write.

"I think Lee's here," Brenda called from out on the deck.

Kate looked around her room, wondering if she needed to take anything. On impulse, she grabbed the small digital camera she'd purchased just for this trip. When she walked out into the living room, Lee was already inside. Brown hiking shorts and a white, sleeveless T-shirt—Kate assumed this was the normal attire for the sheriff. Only today, the gun and holster were missing. And Kate admitted that clothes did make a person. Tan, fit. Outdoorsy. Kate couldn't imagine this woman in a city. Again, without warning, Kate felt the pull of Lee Foxx. She waited, watching as Lee turned, their eyes meeting. Lee smiled, the corners of her eyes crinkling up just slightly. Kate nodded, hating the fact that she was not immune to the charms of this woman. *Charms?* The woman had yet to open her mouth. No, she simply emitted *pheromones* or something and it was extremely annoying to realize she was no different than the young tourists that flocked to the sheriff.

Oh, but she was different. She was a mature woman in a stable relationship, and she had no interest in Lee Foxx. None whatsoever, in fact.

"Hi. I was just about to say hello to Brenda."

"I'm in no hurry," Kate said, motioning to the opened patio door.

"Come on out, Lee," Brenda called.

Kate smiled when she saw her friend. Brenda was sitting in the sun, bare legs showing beneath her oversized shirt. The book she'd been reading lay open on her lap.

"A beautiful morning, isn't it?" Lee commented.

"Oh, darling, so wonderful. I can't imagine people staying inside their houses on mornings like this." She smiled up at Kate. "All ready, dear?"

"I suppose." Kate glanced at Lee. "Do I need anything?"

"Nope. Although you may want to bring shorts along. It'll get warm in about an hour or so."

Kate slipped her hands in the pockets of her loose fitting jeans and shook her head. "I'll be fine."

Lee shrugged. "Suit yourself."

"Will you be back in time for lunch? I could whip something up," Brenda offered.

"Actually, I went by the bakery. I've got a picnic basket."

"Oh, how lovely, darling."

A picnic? Kate sighed. She supposed the quick tour of the canyons she'd envisioned was not to be. And really, it wasn't fair. For the first time in *months*, she itched to write. She actually had ideas for a change. But no, she would spend the better part of the day stuck in a Jeep with the local sheriff.

Lee studied the quiet woman sitting beside her, a woman who didn't look like she wanted a tour of the river canyon.

"Brenda said you were looking forward to today," Lee said. "I get the impression she lied."

"Do you?" Kate turned in her seat. "This was her idea, not mine. She seemed to think I would enjoy it here a little more if I was somewhat familiar with the area."

"She's probably speaking from experience." Lee slowed the Jeep, then turned off the main road, climbing higher into the backcountry. "We'll start up top. I'll try not to bore you," she added with a smile. "This is BLM land around here, so it's public."

"What's that?"

"BLM? It's Bureau of Land Management. The restrictions aren't quite as severe as on national forest land. As a whole though, most of the county is national forest, with just pockets of private land."

Kate held on to the dash as they rounded a sharp curve on the dirt road and climbed higher.

"You came in from the northeast there," Lee said, pointing out her window. "That's the Rio Chama. But all of the canyons around here were cut by the Rio Pueblo. That's what we saw the other night."

"What about the lake? Brenda pointed it out when I first got here."

"They dammed up the Rio Chama, past the deep canyon. Canon De Chama has some great river rafting, but it's gotten to be real touristy in the last few years. There used to be just two outfit-

51

ters there, so the river was still wild," she said. "Now, there are rafts everywhere."

Kate shook her head. "You've lost me. Outfitters?"

"Sorry. They rent out rafts, provide river tours with guides, things like that."

"How do you know so much about this area? Are you from here originally?"

Lee laughed. "No. I grew up in Phoenix. I was in college before I made my first trip out here."

Kate frowned. College? She'd assumed the woman was barely past college age now. She turned in her seat. "How old are you?"

Lee stared. "How old? Why?"

"What do you mean, why?"

"Why do you want to know? What difference does it make?"

"What is it with you people and age?"

"You people? What are you talking about?"

Kate shrugged. "Brenda says Harmony and Sunshine are somewhere between twenty and forty, but they won't say. I don't understand what the big deal is. It's just a number."

"Oh, yeah? Well how old are you?"

Kate smiled. "I'm nearly thirty-eight."

"Nearly?" Lee slowed the Jeep. "That mountain over there, that's Polvadera Peak. You had a great view of it coming up from Santa Fe." She drove on, turning back to Kate. "And you are probably the first woman I've met who rounds up her age, not down."

"Well, when my birthday hits and they call me thirty-eight, I've actually successfully completed thirty-eight years and I'm working on number thirty-nine." She shrugged. "So technically, I guess I could say I'm nearly thirty-nine."

Lee practically slammed on her brakes. "*What?* You're thirty-seven but you're technically thirty-nine?"

Kate smiled. "Well, it's simple math, Lee. When you're born, they don't call you zero, they wait until you've completed your first year, then say you're one."

Lee stared, her mouth opened. "So, you're saying, if someone is twenty-nine, about to be thirty, when their actual birthday comes, and they think they're thirty, they've really already done thirty, they're already starting on freakin' thirty-one!" she said, her voice loud.

It was Kate's turn to stare. "Yeah," she said slowly. "Doesn't take a rocket scientist," she murmured.

"So if someone's having a crisis over turning thirty, they should have had their damn crisis at twenty-eight, not twenty-nine!" She leaned her head back. "Good God."

Kate smiled, then laughed. When Lee rolled her head toward her, Kate laughed harder. "Let me guess. You're about to turn thirty?"

Lee smiled, then started the Jeep again. "I *thought* I was about to turn thirty, yes. Apparently, I'm starting on freakin' thirty-one."

"Well, if it's any consolation, I never would have guessed you to be thirty."

"And why's that? My boyish good looks?" she teased.

"Maybe it's the age of the women you date. The little girl the other day couldn't have even been eighteen."

"Eighteen? No, she was a junior in college. Perfectly legal. And how do you know about who I date? What in the world has Brenda been telling you?"

"Just that you have a penchant for young blonds, mostly tourists, mostly straight."

Lee laughed. "Well, they do tend to have more stamina."

Kate shook her head. "Aren't you afraid of catching something?"

"Catching something?"

"A *disease*," she said pointedly.

"It's not like I don't use protection. I mean, I'm not stupid."

"What do you use? Latex gloves?"

Lee laughed again. "Good one, Miss Winters. Yes, I have a never-ending supply of disposable gloves under my bed." She took her right hand off the wheel and wiggled her fingers. "Protects these from catching something!"

Kate raised her eyebrows. "So what are they called? Dental dams?"

Lee nodded. "Don't you use them?"

"God, no. Robin and I have been together a couple of years. I can't imagine a latex tongue coming at me."

"A couple of years? What? Are you exclusive?"

"Of course. That's what being in a relationship means. But I suppose you don't know anything about that."

Lee pulled off of the dirt road and stopped the Jeep. She got out and stretched, arms reaching high into the blue sky. "God, what a morning," she said. "Come on, I'll show you the view."

Kate got out, doing the same, although not with as much production as Lee had. She simply rolled her shoulders around, then straightened her back.

"So, you trust that she's exclusive too?"

"Robin? Yes. I mean, we live together."

"So, you've signed a pact in blood or something?"

"No. But when you're in a relationship, when you live together, it's just assumed, I suppose."

Lee grinned. "You haven't discussed it? Are you crazy?"

"What are you insinuating? You don't know me and you've not even met Robin."

"I don't know you, but I know women."

"From the children you date? I doubt it."

Lee tilted her head. "Well, at your age, I suppose they do look like children."

Kate stared, only barely resisting the urge to slap the arrogant grin off her face. *Would that be considered assaulting a peace officer?* Instead, she shoved both hands into her pockets and forced a smile to her face. "Good one, Sheriff. You forget, however, that I don't have a problem with age. You, on the other hand, are having a mid-life crisis at thirty!"

Lee scowled. "Look, that stays between us."

"That you're having a crisis?"

"No! That I'm thirty."

"No one knows you're thirty?"

54

"No. And no one knows it's my birthday, either."

"Again, I don't understand the big deal, but fine. I won't spread nasty rumors about your age."

"Thank you."

"When is it, anyway?"

"What?"

Kate rolled her eyes. "Your birthday."

"Oh." Lee looked away, shielding her eyes against the sun. "It's actually now."

"Now?"

Lee nodded. "Today."

Again Kate stared. "Today is your birthday and you're spending it driving me around? Why in the world?"

Lee shrugged. "Well, I told Brenda I would, for one thing. And I like being out here. I don't really take the time to do this much anymore, so this is enjoyable."

"I appreciate that, but shouldn't you be with someone close to you? Like one of your girlfriends?"

Lee grinned and Kate was captivated by the tiny laugh lines around her eyes. Hazel eyes that actually twinkled when she smiled.

"They're not exactly what you'd call girlfriends, Kate. You were right, mostly tourists. Here one day, gone the next."

"And you like living like that? How sad."

Lee leaned closer. "You like sleeping day after day after day with the same woman? How sad."

Kate laughed and clapped Lee on her shoulder. "Well, here's some news for you, Sheriff. There will come a day when the twenty-year-olds won't even notice you. You'll be too *old* for them! Why, you could be their mother!"

"You're cruel, Kate Winters. Very, very cruel."

"I've got the perfect spot for lunch," Lee said. She pulled off the dirt road, driving the Jeep around the scrub oaks. They both bounced in their seats as the Jeep maneuvered the rocks.

"I'm just guessing here, but this isn't really a road, is it," Kate said as she held onto the dash.

"Not really, no. But I want to show you something."

Lee's "I want to show you something" were words Kate had heard all morning. And honestly, she'd loved every minute of it. She slid her glance to the sheriff, allowing herself a quick, unobserved inspection of the woman sitting next to her. Dark, wind-blown hair was in disarray around her face and small, fashionable sunglasses hid her eyes. But the smile on Lee's face indicated she was enjoying herself too, and Kate nodded, finally looking away. Sheriff Foxx had proven to be a knowledgeable tour guide and entertaining as well. Despite her reservations about this trip, she was glad Brenda had insisted she take it. If for nothing else, she realized her negative perception of Lee Foxx might have been a bit unwarranted. Granted, she liked to date younger women—much younger women—but that didn't mean she was the horrible person Kate had envisioned. In fact, Kate admitted that she actually enjoyed her company.

Lee pulled to a stop, moving the Jeep as close as possible to a piñon pine. Kate moved out of the way as the low-lying limbs brushed her arm through the door opening.

"Just trying to get some shade," Lee explained. Then she stood on the seat, leaning over the top of the opened Jeep, binoculars pressed close to her eyes. "Golden eagle over the canyon," she murmured.

"Where?"

Lee lowered the glasses. "Too far now." She glanced down at Kate. "Have you ever seen one? In the wild?"

Kate shook her head.

"Awesome. When they soar overhead, not even a bald eagle can match it for its magnificence."

"Well, I hope I get to see one, then."

Their eyes met for a second, then Lee smiled. "Come on. I want to show you something before we eat. Bring your camera."

Kate climbed out of the Jeep, stretching her back before following Lee. As she skirted a cactus, again she was reminded that she needed to purchase a pair of hiking boots.

"What are you doing?"

"Trying to avoid this cactus thing."

"I told you—"

"I know, I need hiking boots."

Lee stopped, motioning Kate to come closer. "Over here. Stand up there."

Kate attempted to climb on the rock pile, embarrassed when Lee grabbed her waist and gave a push. She steadied herself, then looked where Lee pointed, her eyes widening.

"Oh my God," she whispered. "It's like . . . like an oasis or something."

"Yeah, kinda. It's not quite as arid around here to warrant an oasis, but really, that's what I call it."

"What is it? I mean, there's a waterfall and everything." Kate reached her hand out. "Binoculars?"

Lee handed them over, smiling as Kate scanned the small canyon.

"So come on, tell me about it," Kate said, her eyes never leaving the waterfall.

"It's Lost Creek. It starts way back in the mountains and disappears underground three or four times before it reaches here. About two hundred yards upstream, it goes underground again, only to come out there, causing the waterfall."

"How high is it?"

"Oh, I don't know. Eighty to a hundred feet, maybe."

"There's a pool?"

"Oh, yeah, it's wonderful. Crystal clear water, about ten or fifteen feet deep. Then it flows down the canyon and hits the Rio Pueblo."

"It's so lush looking down there," Kate said.

"That's where the oasis part comes in. Water year round, a lot of the vegetation in that canyon is unique to that area only. It's beautiful down there."

Kate lowered the binoculars, turning. "So when are we going down?"

Lee laughed. "Oh, no. I don't think you can make it down there."

"Why not? How many times have you been?" Kate turned back to the oasis, this time training her camera on the waterfall instead of the binoculars.

"I've been about a dozen times. But it's not easy. Really, the normal access point is climbing up the river canyon but it's very steep in places. It's about a nine-hour hike. Very few make it all the way."

"But you did."

"Well, no. I didn't come up from the canyon."

Kate's eyes widened. "You go down from up here?"

Lee nodded. "It's extremely steep in parts, and you need climbing gear to get back out, but it only takes about an hour to get down. It's just the coming out that's a bitch."

Kate climbed off the rocks, handing Lee the binoculars. "So, when can we go?"

"I don't think so, Kate. No offense, but it's kinda strenuous. I'm not certain you could make it."

Kate put her hands on her hips. "What are you saying?"

"I'm saying you just don't look like you could make it."

Kate waved her hand toward the oasis. "How hard can it be? You go down the hill, play in the water, then climb back up the hill." She shrugged. "It doesn't seem that difficult."

Lee smiled, her eyes twinkling. "Again, no offense, but you'd never make it back up. How embarrassing would it be to have to call search and rescue to get you out?"

Kate looked back again, noting the steepness of the canyon. Lee was probably right.

"Okay. Maybe so. It just looks so inviting."

"We can always go to the river, if you want to enjoy the water."

"I've never rafted," Kate said. "I'm a big chicken when it comes to things like that."

"It's fun. It can be addictive."

Lee lifted the picnic basket from the Jeep and the blanket, then motioned for Kate to grab the cooler. She spread the blanket in the shade of piñon pines, then sat down, crossing her legs easily.

"Wish you'd brought shorts, don't you," Lee stated. She pulled out a jug from the cooler and took two plastic cups from the basket.

"Yes, I wish I had shorts," Kate admitted as she sat down, tugging the jeans up so she could cross her legs. She reached for the cup Lee handed her. "Is this that herbal tea from the bakery?"

"Yes. It's good, isn't it?"

Kate took a big swallow, nodding. "Unique flavor. What is it?"

"There's a little bit of everything in there, she won't say exactly."

At the bottom of the basket was a warmer, and Lee lifted the lid, pleased that the burritos were still warm. "I didn't know what kind you liked, so there are four, all different. Two with chicken, one beef and one vegetarian."

"It doesn't matter. Brenda says they are all good."

"There is a chicken with roasted chipotle peppers. It's pretty spicy."

"And the beef?"

"It's got avocado and onions on it."

"Hand it over," Kate said. She loved avocadoes.

"Good. The chipotle one is my favorite," Lee said.

Kate took a bite, unable to hold back her moan. "Oh, my," she murmured with her mouth full. "This is wonderful."

Lee nodded and bit into her own, a satisfied grin as she tasted the hot peppers. She watched Kate as she ate, the other woman looking up and studying her as well from time to time. It was warm, the sun high, but in the shade with a light breeze blowing, it was pleasant. Still, she didn't doubt Kate was hot in her jeans. She raised an amused eyebrow when Kate wadded up the foil that wrapped the burrito. She'd finished it in maybe four bites.

"How did you end up here, Lee?" Kate asked unexpectedly when she leaned over to refill her tea.

Lee grinned, her white teeth shining against her smooth, tan face. Kate answered the smile with one of her own. "Wrong question?"

"No, no. It's just funny how life turns out, is all." She handed Kate another burrito.

"Oh, I'm not sure I can eat a whole one." But Kate took it anyway, unwrapping the foil to reveal the warm tortilla inside.

"It's chicken. Or would you rather have the veggie one?"

Kate shook her head, taking a bite of the chicken. "Mmm. This is good too. I had the veggie one the other day," she explained, then pointed at Lee. "So tell me."

Lee shrugged. "It was the cure for a broken heart."

"*You* had a broken heart? Doesn't that mean you have to actually be in some sort of a relationship for that?"

"Well, I was young once, thought I'd give it a try." Lee took a swallow of tea, thinking back. It had been a long time since she'd reminisced about her first trip out here. "Sophomore in college, Arizona State," she started. "My first real girlfriend," she said with a smile. "Angela Bernard. She was quite the catch around campus and I thought I was hot shit. But, it goes back to that trust thing you were talking about. I *assumed* we were committed to each other, even though we didn't talk about it. I mean, we were together. I never thought for a minute that she was seeing someone else. Hell, I gave up dating. I thought she had too."

"Oops."

"Yeah, oops. She and my good friend, Sarah, were going at it in her dorm room. That wasn't real pretty to walk in on."

"What happened?"

"Oh, the usual. I'm nearly hysterical that she's in bed with my best friend and she's claiming that it's no big deal, we were only dating, after all."

"Sucks."

"Yeah. So, spring break, I get invited to go river rafting in New Mexico. I didn't care where, I just wanted to get away. Came up here to the Rio Chama and I fell in love with the area and with rafting. I came back that same summer and worked on the river as a guide. It held more appeal than college but I went back to school for another year. The summer between my junior and senior years, I came back here to work again—and never left."

"You had one year left of college and you quit? What were you majoring in?"

Lee laughed. "Nothing. I didn't have a clue as to what I wanted to do."

"I would have thought you were a jock," Kate said.

"Oh, I played a little basketball. I wasn't tall enough, or good enough to be a starter," she said. "But we still had our share of groupies."

"And the sheriff part of it all?"

Lee shrugged. "I lost the lottery."

Kate waited for her to explain.

"There's this little river bar—a dive, really—where the locals hang out. One night, Old Man Carpenter came in." Lee grinned. "That's what everyone called him, Old Man Carpenter, like that was his proper name. He'd been sheriff for nearly fifty years. Well, he walks up to the bar, put his badge and his gun up there, and just said 'I quit'."

"And you have a lottery instead of an election?"

"You have to have somebody to run before you can have an election," Lee said. "And I didn't really know what was going on, anyway. I was twenty-two and just happy to be working on the river."

Kate leaned back on her elbows, enjoying the story. She motioned for Lee to continue.

"Everybody in the bar puts their name in a pot, and it gets passed back down the bar. Old Man Carpenter shuffles through the papers, then pulls out a name." Lee laughed. "You should have seen his face. He moves his hat back and scratches his head, then silently hands the paper to Opal." At Kate's raised eyebrows, Lee explained. "Opal owns the bar. He was bartending that night," she said. "Anyway, Opal reads the name, shakes his head, then passed the paper on. And so it went, everyone reading the name and passing it on."

"So, what? Nobody wanted a woman as the sheriff?"

Lee shook her head. "It wasn't my name. The paper finally reaches Gus Hormel. Gus reads his name, picks up his beer bottle and asks, 'Do I get to carry a gun?'" Lee grinned. "Everyone yells 'no'!" Lee took a swallow of tea before continuing. "Gus is the town drunk."

"I see."

"So, Old Man Carpenter reaches in the pot and pulls out a second name." Lee pointed at herself. "That's how I ended up on the ballot."

"And no one opposed you?"

"Hell, no. Nobody wants this job."

"Can't be that bad. I mean, do you even have any crime?"

"That's just it. No *man* wanted this job." Lee shrugged. "No crime, no action. Just the occasional traffic accident."

"But you could have turned it down if you didn't really want it, right?"

"Sure. In fact, I tried to. I mean, I was living down at the river in a little shack. I wasn't sheriff material. I played on the river and played with the tourists," she admitted. "I was young. I didn't want the responsibility."

"But?" Kate prompted.

"But, Neil Shriker made me an offer," she said. "The Shrikers have the largest ranch in the county. He donated a piece of his property and all the other ranchers chipped in and they built this cute little cabin for me. They also tossed in a Jeep as the official sheriff's vehicle and upped the salary a little to make it more appealing."

"Sweetened the pot a bit?"

"Just a bit. So, the county has a sheriff and I'm off the river," she said. "And it's worked out. I mean, I went down to Albuquerque and had some training so I'm not completely over my head."

"And now you love it?"

"Sure. I've grown to love it. And the locals, well they treat me as if I've been here my whole life. And it saves them having to do another lottery." Lee picked up a rock and tossed it between her hands a few times. "But the last couple of years, with more tourists in town, things aren't always slow. We had a nasty accident down on River Road last year. An SUV with six college students inside went around a curve too fast. They ended up in the river."

"How bad?"

Lee shook her head. "All dead. It was very, very sad. They were out here having a good time, enjoying the summer."

"Alcohol?"

"Oh, sure, college kids out for a good time. But it was early in the evening, it was raining and they didn't know the road. That was the real cause."

"And you had six sets of parents to deal with," Kate guessed.

"Yeah. That's something I hope I don't ever have to do again." Lee straightened her shoulders, then tossed the small rock she'd been fingering to the side. "So, that's the story." She grinned. "And then here we are."

Kate tipped her cup of tea toward Lee. "And here we are, Sheriff."

CHAPTER TWELVE

"It's after three," Brenda said when Kate walked in through the opened patio doors.

"You keeping tabs?"

"Well, no. I just didn't think you could stand each other's company that long, darling." Brenda closed the book she'd been reading and patted the leather sofa beside her. "Sit. Tell me all about it."

Kate laughed. "Tell you what? I understand Lee's given you the same tour."

"Our tour was barely two hours long. I dare say you got the extended version."

Kate nodded and joined Brenda on the sofa, sliding down until her legs stretched out in front of her. "Extended yes, but I enjoyed it, even though I'm exhausted." She rolled her head toward Brenda. "Thank you for making me go."

"And Lee? Were you nice to her?"

"Yes, I was nice to her."

"I told you you'd like her."

"Well, she's entertaining, at least. Although I still find her taste in women to be deplorable."

"Oh, to each his own, I say."

Kate smiled, knowing Brenda's fondness for Lee. So, she changed the subject. "Did you paint today?"

"No. Harmony only comes during the week. I find if I attempt to paint on my own, it just sets me back. Besides, I felt in the mood to be lazy, darling." She held up her book. "And not a history novel. Trashy sex," she said with a laugh. "You know, it's been awhile for me."

"Well, now that you're away from Dallas, away from that crowd, you could always date."

"Date? Here?" Brenda laughed. "Besides the handful of old married ranchers that live in the county, my choices are lesbians or college boys coming to the river for the summer."

"Well that goes to show the company you keep," Kate teased.

"Oh, darling, I'm not interested in dating anyway. I'm enjoying my time, enjoying getting to know myself again. Perhaps when I decide what I'm going to do with my life, I may decide to date." She squeezed Kate's arm. "Date is a scary word for a woman my age, you know."

"Brenda, you're hardly old. And being out here, you look younger than ever."

"Yes, I feel wonderful, but I don't want to complicate things with dating. I'm perfectly happy as things are." She squeezed Kate's arm again. "I think I'm enjoying my solitude. Back home, there were always appointments to keep and dinners to attend. The only time I had alone was when I was sleeping. I never realized I missed the quiet time to just sit and think."

"Brenda, if I'm in your way—"

"Oh, no, no, darling. I didn't mean it that way. I love having you around. Besides, it's not like we're attached at the hip. I have my painting, and hopefully, you'll be immersed in your writing."

"Yes. Actually, this morning, I was a little annoyed about this tour. I had ideas I wanted to get down." She smiled. "I think I'm ready to start, Brenda. I think I know where I'm going to go with Jennifer."

"Fabulous, darling. Are you going to share?"

Kate laughed. "Of course not. You know I don't let anyone read while I'm writing, not even Robin."

Brenda's eyes widened. "Oh, my. I completely forgot, darling. Robin called while you were out."

Kate sat up. "She called? My cell?"

"She said she'd been calling your cell for the last few days. But no, she called the main line. And I don't know why you have an aversion to keeping your phone with you. I do believe that was the purpose of the cell phone, darling."

Kate stood up, pacing. "I hate phones. They're nothing but an interruption. And no, I haven't called her. I haven't even *thought* to call her." She stopped. "What did she say?"

"Well, really, she just wanted to know if you made it safely. I told her your cell service was temperamental, so she was welcome to call on the main line anytime."

"Thanks. But is it temperamental? I haven't even checked."

"No. Service is rather good up here, actually. You'll have to make up your own lie to tell her."

"I better call her. Did she sound mad?"

"Oh my word! So what if she's mad? What's she going to do? She's six hundred miles away."

Kate rubbed her forehead as she walked into her room. She couldn't *believe* she'd forgotten to call Robin. God, she would be so pissed. When she looked at her phone, she was thankful there were only six messages, three of which were from Robin. She debated listening to them first, but decided against it. She paced in her bedroom, listening to the ringing, wondering where Robin could be on a Saturday afternoon. She hung up, then tried Robin's cell. She answered on the second ring.

"It's me," she said. "I'm sorry I missed your call."

"Kate! I was getting worried. I thought you'd at least call and let me know you made it."

"I'm sorry. I just . . . well, Brenda's had me busy and the service is hit-and-miss," she lied.

"That's okay. I'm glad you left the number for the main house line. So, how's the writing going?"

Kate closed her eyes. "It's going good. I'm moving along," she lied again. "Is everything okay there?"

"Oh, sure. Hot as hell, but what's new."

Kate frowned. "Where are you anyway? I hear music."

"Oh, I'm with a couple of friends. We're at a tiny little bar downtown. Early dinner."

Kate's eyes widened. "Okay." *What friends? Robin never went out with friends.* "Well, I'll let you get back to them. I'll check in next week."

"Okay, honey. I miss you already."

Kate nodded. "Miss you too."

Kate tossed the phone on her bed, then opened the window, swinging it out so that she could lean on the ledge. She was thankful there were no screens as she lifted her head into the late afternoon sun. She wasn't sure what she was feeling. She supposed she should feel jealous that Robin was out at a bar on a Saturday afternoon without her, but she wasn't. She was, however, a bit puzzled as to who she could be out with. They didn't really have many mutual friends and on the few occasions that Robin went out alone, it was with a friend from work. Perhaps that was the case now.

But still, Kate was a bit ashamed at the relief she felt. She'd feared that Robin would call daily, making it a ritual while she was gone. And not that she would feel bothered if Robin called, she just didn't want to have to be available. She wanted—needed—to write. She didn't want interruptions.

"Like touring the canyons wasn't," she murmured sarcastically.

But that was over with and now she could concentrate on her writing. And apparently, she wouldn't have to worry quite so much about Robin.

In fact, if she really stopped to think about it, their whole separation was a little strange. Kate's last few days in Dallas, they'd barely seen each other as Kate tried to tie up loose ends before leaving. And Robin had merely dropped her off at the airport, not bothering to wait with her, saying she had an appointment. An appointment for what, Kate hadn't asked. Because truthfully, she didn't really care. She just wanted to catch her flight and be on her way.

It occurred to her then that perhaps she was using this trip as a way to end things with Robin. Unconsciously, of course. And after four or five months of separation, when she returned to Dallas, perhaps they would reevaluate their relationship.

CHAPTER THIRTEEN

"Excellent, Simone. Don't be afraid to be bold."

"You don't think it's too much?"

"It's only too much if you think it's too much," Harmony said.

Brenda studied the canvas, then shook her head. "It's too much. Too bright."

"Look at the cliffs, Simone. What do you see?"

Brenda studied the view in front of her, the sandstone reflecting the afternoon sun. A multitude of reds shone before her, the rusty colors fading to orange as the canyon deepened. She looked back at her canvas.

"I have too much red," she said.

Harmony clapped her hands, then spread her arms just as quickly, palms outstretched as if praying. "Wonderful, Simone. Excellent. I'm so proud."

"Excellent?"

Harmony nodded. "You have too much red. But you saw it

yourself. You didn't need me to point it out." Harmony produced one of her many crystals, pressing it into the palm of Brenda's hand. "Squeeze tight. Keep this one with you, Simone," she said quietly. "It's special."

Brenda didn't ask why. She would do as she was told.

"Perhaps tomorrow, if you feel up to it, we'll hike down a bit. The colors are very different. You need contrast."

"Are you sure? You don't think we're going too fast?"

"It's only a matter of showing you the difference in colors. It's much easier to paint the duller colors of the lower canyon than the magnificence of this," Harmony said, pointing to the still blood-red upper reaches of the canyon.

"Then that's what we'll do."

As they made the walk back, Harmony brought up the weekly Tuesday night dinner.

"Will you bring Kate with you?"

"Of course. Unless there's a problem, darling."

"No, no. I have noticed that her energy is not quite as negative as when I first met her. Perhaps she is releasing it," Harmony suggested.

"More likely she's just relaxing a little bit. She's been writing, so that's a good sign."

"How did her trip with Ariel go?"

"Oh, Lee took her all over the county, I think. It was late afternoon before they got back."

"Again, I'm surprised. Ariel is so fidgety. I can't picture her driving your Kate around all day." Harmony physically shook herself. "I would feel so . . . depleted."

Brenda laughed. "Perhaps Ariel is not as attuned to the negative energy as you are."

Harmony looked skyward. "Perhaps." Then she stopped. "I have a certain fondness for Ariel."

Brenda smiled. "We all do."

"She seems so strong sometimes, yet there is a childlike presence about her that makes you want to protect her."

"And you think she needs protection from Kate?"

"No. As you say, Kate is not fond of her antics with the young women. I doubt they'll even be friends. No, there's something else. I can't quite put my finger on it."

"What about Sunshine?"

"She still thinks Ariel is on a journey. She's going to spend time with her tonight."

Brenda nodded. "I'm looking forward to introducing everyone to Kate."

"Let's hope they all keep an open mind, Simone."

Brenda laughed. "Funny, that's what I told Kate she needed to do."

Lee pulled her Jeep to a stop, wondering why she felt laden by having a date tonight. She *always* brought a date. She glanced at the young blond sitting in her open Jeep, her long hair windblown and tangled. *Britney? Barbara?*

"I warned you it'd be windy," she said. *Beverly?*

"That you did."

Lee got out, then walked around to the passenger's side, holding the door open and helping her down. *Beth?*

"Thank you, Sheriff Foxx," she said, running her hand along Lee's bare arm.

Lee flashed a smile. "My pleasure." She placed her hand lightly on her back, guiding her up the steps. "Remember, keep an open mind. They're kinda . . . well, different," she said.

"But I like different."

"I'm sure you do," Lee murmured as she opened the door.

"Now, Kate, remember, darling . . . keep an open mind."

"Will you stop already? I've met Harmony, I've had a crystal shoved in my hand and I've been told I have bad karma. I'm sure nothing will faze me tonight."

Brenda smiled and linked arms with her. "Yes, but you've not yet met Starlight."

"Nor Sunshine."

"Oh, she's sweet. I'm sure you'll like her."

"And she's Harmony's partner?"

"Yes. They've been together since they were teens, I'm told."

"Amazing." Then Kate stopped. "There won't be any chanting, right?"

"Of course not. It's just a dinner party." They passed the dusty Jeep. "I see Lee's here already. She's usually the last to show up."

"Tell me again how you got involved with these women?"

"They're artists, darling."

"Oh, yeah," Kate murmured, standing back as Brenda opened the front door. "Artists."

She tried to prepare herself, but *nothing* could have prepared her for what she walked into. As soon as they stepped inside, she was engulfed in 1969, right down to beads covering the entryway into a hall. Soft lights, mostly colored, were aimed at the ceiling, some shining on psychedelic prints. *Black lights?* Incense burned and candles flickered, and the soft strands of folk music drifted throughout the house. Kate's eyes widened as she looked at a giant poster of a peace sign, complete with marijuana leaves. Next to that was a black-and-white poster of Janis Joplin, head tossed back with a microphone pressed to her lips. She felt like she was in another place . . . another time.

"Simone! So good to see you again!"

Kate turned, watching a thin, blond-haired woman greet Brenda. She looked like she could be Harmony's sister.

"Sunshine, good evening. Come, meet my friend Kate."

Kate smiled, remembering her first encounter with Harmony. She offered her hand, wondering if a crystal would be placed there.

"Welcome to our home, Kate. So glad you could join us."

"Thank you. Nice to meet you."

Sunshine leaned closer. "Do not be afraid," she whispered. "Your destiny lies here. You can't fight it."

72

Kate stepped back, her eyes wide, but Sunshine was smiling, her eyes friendly.

"Ariel's been asking for you. I'll tell her you're both here."

When she moved away, Kate elbowed Brenda.

"Psst."

"What, darling?"

"Who the hell is Ariel?"

Brenda laughed, again linking arms with Kate. "Ariel is what they call Lee." She pulled Kate closer. "What did she say to you? You looked frightened."

"She said some nonsense about my destiny." Kate leaned closer. "I can't believe I'm saying this, but this place is awesome. I feel like I'm in another era."

"And I feel like a senior in high school, darling." Brenda pointed at another poster. "I had that very print hanging on my bedroom wall. Jefferson Airplane was one of my favorites."

"You think these are originals?" Kate pointed to another. "Look at that Jim Morrison print. That's amazing."

"I'm surprised you even know who Jim Morrison was."

"I'm not that young," Kate said, laughing as Brenda broke into an off-tune version of *Light My Fire*.

"Oh, Kate, those were the days. That's one reason I love coming here. It takes me back, you know. The sixties can be documented and recorded, but you still won't know the true feeling unless you actually lived it, darling. And even in our small corner of Oklahoma, we felt it. Our parents didn't know how to deal with us." Brenda laughed. "They blamed it all on the Beatles, believe it or not!"

"And when you think back, the Beatles were rather tame compared to some."

"Like your Jim Morrison there." Brenda squeezed her arm. "Speaking of bad boys," she said quietly, motioning with her head.

They both laughed as Lee walked up.

"What? Am I dressed funny?" Lee asked.

"Of course not, darling. It was actually a private joke, one I might share with you at a later date." Brenda released Kate's arm. "I'm going to find some of Lee's wine. I'll bring you a glass, Katie."

Lee smiled when Brenda walked off. "I swear, I think she's addicted to the stuff. What about you? Have you developed a taste for it?"

"Actually, yes, we have it nearly every evening."

"Good thing I stashed a jug in the Jeep for you then."

"Thank you, Sheriff." Kate peeked over her shoulder and noticed a young blond woman watching Lee. "Just guessing here, but is that your date?" she asked, motioning to the blond.

Lee turned around, waving as Brandy smiled sweetly at her. Lee smiled at her, then turned back to Kate. "Yeah. Brandy," she said.

"Brandy? What a cute name. Where did you find her?"

Lee blushed slightly. She didn't know why, but she felt nearly embarrassed by Kate's question. So, instead of telling her the truth, that she'd met the girl at the river a couple of weeks ago—in a very skimpy bikini, no less—she lied. "I've known her for awhile. She's going to be here for most of the summer."

"Lucky you. You'll have a fallback if the local tourists dry up."

"Very funny."

"How old is she?"

"I never asked."

"Are you sure she's legal?"

Lee ignored her question, instead motioning toward Sunshine. "What did you think?"

"After meeting Harmony, Sunshine seemed perfectly normal . . . until she whispered something about not fighting my destiny."

"Some say she's a prophet. I've learned not to take what she says lightly."

"Oh, come on. I think maybe she's inhaled too much incense over the years."

Lee laughed. "You get used to them. But I hope I'm around when you meet Starlight."

Kate scanned the crowd. "Is she not here?"

Lee glanced at her watch. "Too early yet."

"Why, Lee, are you still here? I would have brought you a refill."

They both turned as Brenda came over, handing Kate a glass of sangria. Kate smiled her thanks, taking a sip of the sweet wine.

"Just enjoying Kate admonishing me about my date." Lee looked over her shoulder. "And I should get back. She doesn't know a soul here."

"Yes, run along and play," Kate teased. "I'm sure she has a curfew."

"You should be nicer to me if you want to go down to the oasis," Lee tossed over her shoulder as she walked away.

"The oasis? What's that, darling?"

Kate watched Lee walk away, hating the fact that her eyes lingered on her. She finally looked at Brenda, smiling as she touched wineglasses with the older woman.

"Lee didn't take you there on your tour?" Kate asked.

"Like I said, I got the short version."

"Well, I couldn't even begin to tell you where it is, much less find it on my own, but it's a waterfall in this deep canyon. And I call it a canyon, but it's really something that was cut out by this creek. It starts right there at the waterfall." Kate took a sip of wine, flicking her eyes quickly toward Lee. "It's really pretty. I wanted Lee to take me down there, but she doesn't seem to think I could make it back up. She said something about climbing gear."

"Oh, no, darling. That sounds too much like work." She leaned closer, lowering her voice. "Who's the young girl she's with?"

Kate shrugged. "Brandy."

"She looks younger than most, but she's certainly pretty. Lee can find them, can't she?"

"Apparently." Then Kate elbowed Brenda, her eyes wide. "Who in the world is that? Or should I say *what* is that?"

Brenda followed her gaze across the room, then laughed. "That would be Starlight, darling."

"She's like . . . colorless." Kate looked at Brenda. "I've never before seen anyone that white. At least, not anyone alive."

"Starlight is a bit of a night person. She's not fond of the sun."

"She's not a vampire, is she?" Kate whispered teasingly.

"Oh, darling, no. She just functions better at night. Harmony says she's completely reversed from most people."

"She sleeps during the day?"

"Yes. She's up all night, until dawn. And her paintings reflect that. They are all night scenes. You should see her display in Harmony's gallery. Not eerie at all, darling. Very peaceful, calm, serene. She does a lot of water scenes with moon reflections. She can even bring the canyons alive with only moonlight. It's amazing."

Kate held her breath as the porcelain woman walked toward them. Her hair was nearly as white as her skin, and the black dress did nothing to add color back to her features.

"Be nice," Brenda whispered.

"She's the one that chants," Kate stated quietly.

Brenda laughed, patting her arm as Starlight walked up. "How are you tonight, Starlight? I haven't seen you in a couple of weeks."

"So good to see you again, Simone. I'm doing well, thanks."

She took both of Brenda's hands, closing her eyes as she held them. Kate stared, her eyes wide, expecting the woman to break out into a chant. Instead, a soft hum was heard. To her surprise, Brenda joined in. She took a step back, wondering if this woman was perhaps a witch.

"Your energy is good, Simone. You've done well."

"Thank you. I've done all the lessons."

"I think you're ready for the next level. You want to meet this week?"

"Of course. I've been looking forward to it, darling. Will you come over?"

Only then did Starlight open her eyes and they bored into Kate. "You have company now. I don't think it's wise, do you?"

Brenda looked at Kate. "Meet my good friend Kate. She's going to stay with me through summer." To Kate, she said, "This is Starlight."

Kate nodded, watching as this woman looked her over. She finally met her eyes, surprised at the gentleness there.

"Sunshine says you have a purpose here. Harmony says you are full of negative energy."

Kate shrugged. "So they say."

"Perhaps you'd like to join us in our lessons," she offered.

Kate smiled politely, but shook her head. "It's not really my thing," she said.

Starlight studied her for a moment longer, then quickly took her hand and held it. Kate was too startled to pull away.

Starlight glanced at Brenda before releasing her hand. "I suppose we could meet at your place. I don't think her energy is all that bad. Maybe Harmony misread her."

"Wonderful, darling. Perhaps Thursday?"

"I will be over at moonrise."

She left without another word. Kate let out her breath, her eyes still wide as she looked at Brenda. "You have got to be kidding me. Is she *real*?"

"Oh, very real, darling. And she's completely harmless. She is very much a loner, very introverted. Besides coming here for the weekly dinners, I don't think she socializes at all."

Kate held up her empty glass. "I'm going to need a refill after that."

"Of course, darling. Come with me. I'll introduce you to the others." She pointed to the sofa, where four women sat talking quietly among themselves. "I've never met them before. Like I said, you never know who will be here."

Kate was more interested in touring the house than meeting new people, but she followed Brenda into the kitchen. Unlike the living room, the kitchen was well lit and decorated in a more modern style. Perhaps it was only the living area that had been transformed into the sixties. She smiled politely as Harmony stared at her. For some reason, Harmony didn't like her. She would ask Brenda about it later. But now she nodded when Harmony offered more wine.

"Have you met everyone?"

Kate shook her head. "Brenda was about to introduce me around."

Harmony frowned. "Who?"

"Brenda." Then Kate sighed, barely resisting the urge to roll her eyes. "*Simone* is going to introduce me."

"Oh, of course. And I have some colleagues from Santa Fe who made the trip up. I'll introduce you personally. One of them is a fan of yours, I hope you don't mind."

Kate smiled. "Of course not."

When Brenda turned to speak with someone else, Harmony leaned closer, pressing something hard into her palm. A stone, no doubt.

"Sunshine says you are here for a reason, that it's your destiny. She also says you will fight it," Harmony whispered. "It will do no good."

Kate pulled away, angry. "Look, I don't care what Sunshine says. This has nothing to do with destiny. I'm simply spending the summer here to write. And come fall, I'll be heading back to Dallas." She shrugged. "So you see, there's nothing really to fight." She opened her hand then, finding not the expected crystal, but a beautiful jade stone.

"Green is the color for healing and hope," Harmony said quietly. "It also is a symbol of calm and serenity."

Kate sighed. "Look, I can't—"

"Jade brings serenity to the mind by releasing negative thoughts. It also opens the heart to love," she whispered, looking quickly over her shoulder. "You will tell no one I gave this to you."

"But—"

Harmony quickly closed Kate's hand, pressing the stone more firmly into her palm. "Do not fear Ariel," she whispered before leaving.

Oh good Lord, these people are crazy.

"What was that about?" Brenda asked as Harmony hurried away.

Kate discreetly slipped the stone into the pocket of her jeans.

"I'll have to tell you later," she said quietly. "Apparently I'm sworn to secrecy."

Brenda simply raised her eyebrows.

"And I'm telling you, they're all borderline nuts."

"Oh, darling, they're just unique."

"No, they're weird." Kate led Brenda from the kitchen back into the living room. She glanced once at Lee, watching as Brandy hung on her every word. "She's practically in her lap," she muttered.

"Who?"

Kate shook her head. "Nothing." She turned her back to Lee. "Why do they call her Ariel?"

"Lee?" Brenda smiled. "Harmony says it's a Hebrew word. It means lion, or God's lion, I can't remember. You'll have to ask Harmony."

Kate smirked. "Right. Next time we're having lunch together, I'll ask her."

By the time dinner was served, Kate had switched from Lee's wine to water. For some reason, the wine made her irritable as she watched Lee with the young blond. So she suffered through the informal meal, sitting at the bar in the kitchen with Brenda. The others were scattered across the living room as the dining room table only sat four.

"What is this?" she whispered as she shoved the food around with her fork. She thought she recognized spinach in it.

"I call most of Harmony's dinners tofu surprise," Brenda said with a laugh. "But they're actually very good." Then she lowered her voice. "We'll have a steak on the grill tomorrow night."

Lee watched Kate and Brenda leave, thinking she should go out and give Brenda the wine she'd brought for her. But she could always drop it off at the house. When the door closed, she turned back around, finding the expectant eyes of her date. *Brandy*. Lee sighed.

"You ready to go somewhere a little quieter?" Brandy purred, her hand snaking up Lee's arm.

Lee nodded. "Sure. Let's get out of here."

On the way out, Sunshine intercepted them. She pulled Lee aside, moving away from Brandy.

"Ariel, how do you feel?"

Lee frowned. "I feel great. Should I not?"

Sunshine squeezed both of her hands, then closed her eyes. "Do not fight the Fates, Ariel. You will try, but it will do no good."

Lee gave an amused smile as she looked to the ceiling, wondering what in the world Sunshine was talking about now.

"Sunny, it depends on what the Fates have planned. Besides, I like fighting them."

Sunshine's smile was coy. "Not this time, Ariel," she whispered. "Not this time." She walked away quickly, leaving Lee staring after her.

"So what about your destiny, darling?" Brenda asked on their drive home.

"I don't know what they meant. But both Sunshine and Harmony mentioned it. And Harmony was downright spooky about it." She reached in her pocket and pulled out the jade. "She gave me this." She held it out to Brenda. "She said it would calm me and release my negative energy."

"My God, darling." Brenda turned on the interior lights, holding the stone up. "It's a jade the size of a walnut." She looked closer. "Is it real?"

"I don't know."

"Why would she give you this?" Brenda asked, handing the stone back to Kate.

"Because they're weird, Brenda. She said it's going to heal me and open my heart to love. What the hell does that mean?"

"It has to be from something Sunshine said. I told you she was a seer, darling. She *knows* things."

"Well, before Harmony left, she said I shouldn't fear Ariel. What to you think she meant by that?"

"Fear Ariel? But why would you fear Lee?"

"Exactly."

"Your friends are a little odd, don't you think?"

Lee laughed, turning the Jeep back toward the river instead of her cabin. "That's one way of putting it," she said. "I guess I've gotten used to them over the years."

She tensed up only slightly when Brandy's hand slid over her thigh, threatening to slip between her legs. Lee stilled the hand before it could do just that.

"You're heading back to the lodge," Brandy observed. "I thought we were going to your place." Then she moved closer. "Of course, I'm fairly certain Trudy would love to do a three-way."

There was a time Lee would have jumped at the chance. In fact, early spring, she'd done just that. But something wasn't right and she couldn't put her finger on it. Just the thought of having sex with Brandy—and her friend Trudy—nearly repulsed her. So, she lightly squeezed Brandy's hand before removing it from her thigh.

"I don't think so. Not tonight."

"No? Did you not enjoy yourself the last time?"

Did I? She couldn't recall, actually. It was but a blur, so much like all the others, just stolen minutes with complete strangers.

"You know, it's not that, Brandy, it's just . . . I don't think dinner agreed with me," she lied. "I'm not feeling all that super right now. Maybe we'll hook up later in the week."

"That might be kinda tough, Sheriff. My girlfriend comes in on Thursday."

Lee sighed with relief. "Oh yeah? Is she going to stay with you for awhile?"

"Unfortunately."

"Unfortunately? I would think if you've got a girlfriend, you'd want her around."

"I just turned twenty-two," she said. "I'm too young to be attached and serious, you know what I mean. Like you, you don't have a girlfriend. Now's the time to play. Maybe when I'm older, twenty-seven or so, I might be ready." She turned in the seat, watching Lee. "What about you?"

Lee laughed, debating telling her how old she really was. And old was what she suddenly felt. Instead, she tried to find a graceful way out of the conversation. "I've not really put an age on it, Brandy. I guess, when you meet the right woman, you don't worry about how old you are. And maybe that's what's wrong with you, your girlfriend's not the one."

"Oh, I know she's not. But my mom hates her, so it's fun to irritate her by bringing Jules around."

"Great reason to have a girlfriend," Lee murmured.

CHAPTER FOURTEEN

Kate sat in the shade, her legs stretched out on the chaise lounge, her laptop open as she reread what she'd written while still in Dallas—it was garbage. Just a bunch of ramblings going nowhere. She sighed, leaning her head back, wondering what in the world she was going to do with Jennifer and Paul. Dare she follow Lee's advice? Would her readers totally flip out if Jennifer discovered she was gay?

They investigate a cheating wife, only to find that the wife is cheating with another woman. Jennifer follows them, taking pictures. At first, she's appalled. Then, she feels a kinship. The light bulb goes off. She likes what she sees.

"Oh, good Lord, that sucks," Kate murmured. She looked to the sky, her mind reeling.

The local police request Jennifer's help with locating a former client. A client now accused of murder. The detective she's assigned to is another woman. A beautiful woman. A beautiful gay woman.

"Wonder why they're always beautiful?" Kate said out loud, her thoughts going to Lee. She shook her head, again focusing on Jennifer.

They bicker. The detective thinks private investigating is for losers who couldn't cut it as a cop. Jennifer thinks the detective is arrogant . . . beautiful, but arrogant. Her name is . . . Shane.

Kate rolled her eyes.

Okay, her name is . . . Jordan. Yes, Jordan. They travel together day and night, looking for the client. They run into trouble. Jennifer holds her own, impressing Jordan. Jordan begins to see Jennifer in a different light. And Jennifer, after spending so much time with Jordan, begins to feel an attraction. A physical attraction that she can't explain. She feels drawn to the detective, so much so that she can't concentrate on the case any longer. One night, at a dingy motel, where they're forced to share a bed—

"What are you doing?"

Kate jumped, nearly spilling her laptop. Lee grinned down at her, laughing before pulling over another chair.

"Did I scare you?"

"And what gives you that idea, Sheriff Foxx?" Kate found herself staring at Lee's gun. Somehow, that seemed safer than staring at her legs.

"Maybe it was the tiny scream I heard." She pointed to the laptop. "You working on our Jenn?"

"Maybe."

Lee moved closer. "Can I see?"

Kate slammed the laptop closed. "You most certainly may not!"

"You're not going to make them have sex, are you? Because that would just be disgusting."

"I haven't decided *what* I'm going to do with them," Kate said honestly. "And what are you doing here? Lunch break?"

"Sort of. I was coming by to see if you wanted to go to the oasis," Lee said, wondering at the nervousness she felt.

Kate's eyes widened. "The oasis? But you said I couldn't make it."

"Well, I went out there the other day. I put a few pitons in and left a rope anchored. There's only one really steep area and I think, with some help, you could make it."

Kate smiled. "With some help? I'm assuming you're not referring to search and rescue?"

"No. Just me." Their eyes met, and Lee smiled. "So, what do you say?"

"What are pitons?"

"They're these pointed metal things, you hammer them into crevasses. Climbers use them to hook their ropes onto. Well, they're not so popular anymore, but I thought they'd be good footholds for you."

Kate nodded. "And you want to go . . . like *now*?"

Lee shrugged. "If it's good for you. But I guess you are working, huh?"

Kate hesitated. She really needed to work. But she really wanted a close-up of the oasis. Playtime won out.

"Now's good. What do I need?"

Lee stood, pleased that Kate had agreed. "Hiking boots and a camera, that's it."

"Problem then," Kate said.

"You never bought hiking boots? If you didn't want to pay an arm and a leg at Potters, why haven't you asked Brenda to take you down to Santa Fe?"

"Actually, we're going tomorrow. Shopping is not really my thing, but Brenda says she knows of a place to get boots. Then we're doing a tour of Harmony's gallery, then she's promised to treat me to dinner."

Lee followed Kate inside, looking around for Brenda. "Where's Brenda?"

Kate shook her head. "She and Harmony drove to the river this morning."

"Painting?"

"Yes. And I never would have guessed it in a million years, but Brenda's paintings are actually starting to look good."

"Harmony is really talented. They all are, for that matter. But I prefer Starlight's work best. She's got one where the sun has just set, but there is still color in the sky and the full moon is hanging over the canyon. The moon is orange, the canyons are orange, yet it's a night scene. It's awesome. You'll see it at the gallery. If there was one painting I wished I owned, that would be it."

"Why don't you buy it?"

"Oh, no. Starlight gets big bucks for her paintings. I couldn't even begin to afford it."

Lee followed Kate to the edge of her bedroom, leaning casually on the doorframe as Kate slipped off her sandals and changed into her athletic shoes. The bedroom was neat and tidy, nothing personal of Kate's to see. She watched Kate, a little amused at herself that she actually found her attractive. Not that Kate wasn't cute, she was. Blond hair, blue eyes—Lee's favorite combination. It was just . . . well, Kate wasn't exactly her type. Kate wasn't anywhere *near* her type.

"You're staring."

Lee blinked several times, finally meeting Kate's eyes. "Sorry. I was lost in thought, actually."

Kate walked closer, playfully patting Lee's flat stomach. "You were picturing having to haul me out of the canyon, weren't you," she teased.

Lee smiled, turning to follow Kate back down the hallway. "Yeah. Good thing you're a lightweight."

Kate enjoyed the trip up the mountain, dusty as it was. The sun felt good on her skin, the wind refreshing as it blew through the open Jeep. She thought she'd miss the greenness of the Dallas area, but she found she loved the red rocks, the striking colors of the cliff walls, the starkness of it all. It was all so wild here and she felt a connection to it that she couldn't quite comprehend. Like Brenda, she was falling in love with the area. She looked off in the distance, enjoying the views around her. The road was somewhat familiar and Lee occasionally pointed out the landmarks.

"I didn't even think to take you down to the pueblos," Lee said. She pointed to a rugged looking peak to their left. "There's a pueblo at the base of Cerro Pedernal. They say it was built in twelve seventy-five and could house about a thousand people," she explained.

"Forgive my ignorance, but what are pueblos?"

"You've heard of Mesa Verde in Colorado? The cliff dwellings?"

Kate nodded. "Yes, but I've never been there."

"Those are pueblos. It was like a city. It's awesome how they built all that with only primitive tools. The pueblos around here aren't nearly as extensive as Mesa Verde nor do they get the tourists."

"They're probably more preserved without a bunch of tourists traipsing about," Kate said.

"There's a lot of prehistoric art and native dwellings in this area that few tourists know about. They've uncovered pithouses that the Anasazi people built in about the year five hundred and what they call cave art—pictographs and such. I know of a few places, if you're interested," Lee offered.

Kate smiled. "You're not native to this area, but you love it like you were."

Lee nodded. "Yeah. I can't imagine living anywhere else. This has definitely become home."

Kate watched the scenery as they bounced over the dirt road, the scrub oaks giving way to piñon pines the higher they climbed. Finally Lee pulled off the road, again bouncing them down the makeshift path she'd created. She parked beside the same piñon pine as before.

Lee turned in her seat, watching as Kate surveyed the area. The roar of the falls filled the air and Lee hopped out of the Jeep, scanning the sky out of habit, hoping to catch an eagle soaring overhead. Nothing moved except two lone vultures in the distance.

"You got your camera, right?" Lee asked. She pulled her backpack from the Jeep and slung it over her shoulder. She then took a small waist pack and held it out to Kate. "Here. Use this. You can put your camera inside." She handed her a water bottle she pulled from a cooler. "This goes in the clip there." Lee then removed her holster and gun, tucking it under the front seat of the Jeep.

"I've been meaning to ask you. Is it required you carry a gun? I mean, you said yourself, there's no crime," Kate said as she slipped the small pack around her waist.

"Funny story about that," Lee said. "You may have noticed, I don't wear your normal sheriff's uniform. They are hideous." Lee grinned. "Kinda hard to pick up chicks."

"Oh, I'm sure."

"So, I ordered all these T-shirts with the sheriff's logo on them. And no, I didn't carry a gun. Like you said, what's the point. But Old Man Carpenter said either I wear the uniform or I carry the gun, one or the other." Lee shrugged. "The gun won. Besides, girls seem to love it."

"Yes, I'm sure they do," she murmured. She watched as Lee slipped the backpack on and adjusted the straps. "What's in your pack?"

"First aid kit, extra rope, water. Things like that."

Lee led the way to the canyon but before they took a handful of steps, Lee's cell phone rang.

"Damn," she murmured. She unclipped her phone and flipped it open. "Lee here."

"Lee, it's Opal. Had a break-in last night."

Lee sighed, nodding. "What'd they get? The usual?"

"Yep. Two kegs. Looks like they got a handful of cigarettes too."

"Okay. Well, look, I'm kinda out of commission right now." She winked at Kate. "I'm over by Cerro Pedernal. Let me give Skip a call, see if he's closer."

"Sure thing. But when you crash it this time, I'd like to be there to bust their little asses."

"Now, Opal, you know I can't let you do that. But if they're locals, I'll let you take them to their parents, how's that?"

"Ain't no locals fool enough to break in here and you know it."

"I'll be by later this afternoon, Opal. Give Skip a rundown of what's missing."

She shook her head as she closed her phone. "Every year, never fails," she said, motioning for Kate to follow her.

"What's that?"

"Oh, the bar gets broken into. They steal beer, then try to have a party where we can't find them." She dialed another number while they walked. "Skip? It's me. Need you to run over to Opal's." She nodded. "Last night or could've been this morning, early. I'm out of pocket. I'll check in with you this afternoon."

"Who's Skip?" Kate asked when Lee ended the call.

"Part-time deputy."

"Why part time?"

"Because his father owns the largest ranch in the county so he doesn't need a full-time paying job. Besides, we don't really *need* a deputy, but it's nice to have someone you can count on."

"For times like this when you feel like playing hooky?"

"Exactly. What are the chances that the one time I want to take the afternoon off to play, we have a crime spree?"

Kate raised her eyebrows. "The *one* time? Wasn't it just a few weeks ago that you played with a red sports car?"

Lee shook her head. "No. All I did was get her car started. We may have played the next day, I don't recall," she said with a grin.

Kate followed behind Lee, keeping her eyes on the rocks as they walked—and occasionally sneaking a peek at Lee's legs. She actually *hated* the fact that she found Lee attractive. Telling herself that anyone with a pulse would find Lee attractive didn't seem to help. Because, truthfully, anyone with a pulse was apparently Lee's only requirement for a date. And despite the fact that they were becoming friends, that Kate genuinely liked Lee, she still abhorred her dating practices.

"How's Barbie?" Kate asked.

Lee stopped. "Who?"

"Your date from the other night."

Lee grinned. "Brandy."

Kate shrugged.

Lee continued on, Kate following. "I haven't seen her."

"I thought she was here all summer."

"Yeah. But we didn't really hit it off."

"No? You didn't get lucky?"

"Lucky?" Lee laughed. "So now you want details on my sex life?"

"Of course not. I'm not that desperate."

"Oh, yeah. Forgot you had a girlfriend. You guys been working on your phone sex since you've been gone?"

"Phone sex? You know, Lee, it *is* humanly possible to go weeks, and even months, without having sex."

Lee laughed. "But why would you want to do that?"

"To avoid having phone sex, for one thing."

"Don't like it, huh?"

"It's disgusting. It's masturbating with an audience."

Lee laughed again, then stopped. "Why are you winded?"

"I'm old and out of shape," Kate said without hesitation as she tried to catch her breath. She nearly mentioned the cigarettes she had recently given up, but decided there was no need to bring up that nasty habit.

"You don't look out of shape. It's probably the elevation."

Kate smacked her on the arm. "But you're saying I do look old?"

"I meant no such thing. You look gorgeous, not old," Lee said as she walked on.

Kate stared. *Gorgeous?*

Lee walked on, shaking her head. *Gorgeous?* Geez. Kate probably thinks she was hitting on her or something. She looked back over her shoulder to where Kate still stood. "Well, come on," she said.

Lee led them around the rim of the canyon to the trail she'd made years ago. As far as she knew, no one else had found her trail. She knew the main trail up the canyon from the river was on all the maps, but she rarely heard of someone making the trek to the waterfalls. It was a strenuous hike and to most, not worth the time or the trouble when you could just play in the river canyon.

"Here we are."

Kate looked over the edge, her eyes wide. They were to the left of the waterfall, the creek emerging right out of the cliff wall some forty or fifty feet from the rim. The roar of the falls was loud now as the water crashed on the rocks of the canyon floor. "Maybe you were right. Maybe I can't make it."

"It looks worse than it really is," Lee said. "You'll be fine. Like I said, there's really only one steep area."

"Well, if you don't consider *this* steep, I think I'm in trouble."

"We'll take it slow. The biggest problem is your shoes. They're going to be slippery."

"I promise I'll get hiking boots when we're in Santa Fe."

"Okay. Now remember, bend your knees, try to keep your balance. If you feel like you're stumbling, sit down. It's better to bounce down the trail on your ass than it is to go head over heels."

"Gotcha."

Lee grinned. "Okay, here we go."

She grabbed the same limb of the piñon pine she always did as she slipped over the edge of the rim. She got herself stable, then reached out to help Kate.

"Just hold on to me."

Kate grabbed the tree with one hand, then took Lee's hand with the other. As expected, her shoes slid on the loose rocks, nearly causing her to fall.

"Bend your knees," Lee instructed.

She did, finally getting herself under control.

"Follow me. Be careful of the rocks."

For the first few minutes, Kate actually kept her balance without too much difficulty. She relaxed, taking time to enjoy the waterfall as they went deeper into the canyon. Then, without warning, her feet went out from under her. She landed hard on her backside, scraping her hands in the process as she tried to break her fall.

"Whoa there," Lee said, squatting down beside her. "Hurt?"

"Just my ass," Kate murmured.

Lee smiled, then inspected Kate's hands, rubbing her fingers over the reddening scrapes.

It was just an innocent gesture, but one that caused Kate's heart to skip a beat nonetheless. Embarrassed, she pulled her hand away.

Lee stood and offered a hand to Kate. Their eyes locked together, then Lee smiled. "Come on."

As they continued down, Kate was careful to watch where she stepped, avoiding loose rocks. She mimicked Lee's position, turning sideways as they walked, putting her weight on one leg. Lee was being patient, she knew. She looked to be in incredible shape, and Kate found herself staring at Lee's legs, watching the muscle definition as she walked.

"Up ahead is the ledge," Lee said.

Kate brought her eyes up, looking past Lee. Their trail disappeared over the edge. She looked at Lee. "Let me guess. This is your steep part?"

Lee nodded. "This is it."

They stopped, both peering over the side.

"You have *got* to be kidding," Kate said, shaking her head. "No way in *hell* are you getting me over this ledge."

Lee moved to the side, pulling out a rope from behind a rock. She held it up and smiled.

Kate shook her head. "No. Absolutely not."

"Keep your hands above the knots. That'll be enough support."

"No."

"Then you'll use the pitons for your feet."

"No."

"Look, it's not like you're going to be dangling from the rope. It's more like using stairs. It's only about twelve feet, then we're back on the trail."

Kate stared at Lee, then looked back over the ledge. She shook her head, then brought her eyes back to Lee. "I'm really a wimp when it comes to things like this. I also have no upper body strength. I'm pretty certain that would come in handy right about now."

Lee grinned, then laughed outright at the serious expression on Kate's face. "You'll be fine. I'm going to go down first. I promise, if you fall, I'll catch you."

"Oh, now that's comforting, Lee."

"It'll be over with before you know it."

"Yeah. Falling makes everything go by quicker."

"You're not going to fall." Lee took off her backpack and handed it to Kate. "When I'm down, pull the rope back up and tie it to the backpack. Then just lower it down to me."

Kate nodded. Sure, she could do that. She was fairly certain that would be the only thing she lowered down. She had no intention of going any farther. Then her eyes widened as Lee simply swung off the ledge, lowering herself quickly to the trail below. Their eyes met as Lee looked up at her with a grin.

"Lower the backpack first."

Well, it certainly looked easy enough, Kate thought as she tied the rope to the pack. In fact, Lee made it look so easy that Kate was now too embarrassed to not at least try. She lowered the backpack, trying to talk herself into going over the ledge. Unfortunately, it appeared to be working.

Please Lord, don't let me fall.

"You see the pitons?"

Kate nodded, wondering how in the world those little things would support her weight. She sat down on the ledge, rope held tightly in her hands. The twelve feet Lee mentioned looked twice that, the distance between herself and Lee seemed enormous. She looked at Lee once more, then took a deep breath.

"Turn around and face the ledge," Lee instructed. "It'll be easier. I'll help you with the pitons."

"Are you sure those things will support me?"

"They should. But you'll have the rope, so you shouldn't need to put all of your weight on them."

"She obviously forgot about my lack of upper body strength," Kate murmured.

"What?"

"Nothing," Kate called. "Talking to myself."

She turned, sliding over the edge, wishing she had jeans on as the rocks scraped her thighs. She held tight to the rope, using the knots Lee had made for support.

"About six inches to your right is the first piton," Lee called up to her.

Kate moved her foot, finding the piton. She relaxed a little as she put more weight on it.

"Okay, now just pretend you're walking down a ladder. There's another piton below your left foot, about another ten inches."

Kate lowered herself with the rope, finding the piton. *Okay, so this isn't so bad.*

"You're doing great, Kate. Perfect. The pitons are all about fifteen inches apart."

Lee tilted her head, watching as Kate maneuvered down the wall. She had a perfect view of a very nice ass and she wasn't ashamed to be staring. In fact, Kate had nice legs too.

"Lee?"

"Hmm?" Lee raised her head, blushing crimson as Kate stared back at her.

"I swear, you're such a guy."

"Am not. I was just watching your progress, making sure you didn't fall."

"Uh-huh, sure you were."

"Really."

Kate cleared her throat. "I seem to be stuck."

"Stuck?"

"There aren't any more pitons."

"That's because you're three feet from the ground." Lee walked closer, grabbing both of Kate's legs. "Just lower down the rope. I've got you."

Kate did as she was told, feeling Lee's arms slide up her legs to her waist. Finally, Kate's feet touched solid ground. She let out a contented sigh, untangling herself from Lee's arms.

"Piece of cake, right?"

"I wouldn't go that far," Kate said, rubbing her palms together. "But it was easier than I thought. Your piton idea was wonderful. Thank you."

"I'll take your thank you now. I'm pretty sure you won't be thanking me when we're going up instead of down."

"Oh, yeah. I keep forgetting that this isn't a one-way trip." Kate lifted her shirt slightly, letting the breeze cool her skin.

Lee caught a glimpse of flesh, then turned away, making a show of gathering her backpack. She didn't know why, but she found the gesture to be extremely sexy. *Did you ever think you'd find a thirty-seven-year-old sexy?*

"It's hot," Kate stated.

"Yeah. We're going to be in full sun until the next switchback. Then it levels out a little more as we get closer to the falls." She pointed down the hill. "The trees also get thick." To Lee's surprise, Kate pulled out her camera.

"Stay right there. It's awesome with the falls behind you."

Lee froze, her eyes glued to the camera as Kate framed her.

"Just a tiny smile would be nice," Kate said as she shifted closer.

Lee obliged, standing still until Kate lowered the camera. She raised her eyebrows.

"Perfect." Kate zipped up her waist pack again, then used Lee's shoulder to steady herself. "Lead on."

The next fifteen minutes were nearly straight downhill, then it leveled out, bringing them into a lush, damp forest, as the spray from the waterfall blew about.

"It's beautiful down here."

"Yeah. Nice and cool."

"Oh my God!"

Lee grinned, watching as Kate's eyes found the pool.

"It's . . . it's too beautiful for words."

"I tend to agree with you."

Kate met her eyes. "We shall never tell another soul that this place exists!"

Lee laughed. "What? You want it all to yourself?"

Kate shook her head. "No. I was thinking more of preservation. Can you imagine the damage?"

"Absolutely. That's why I've never shared my trail with anyone."

Kate turned slowly, her eyes meeting Lee's. "No one?"

Lee shook her head. "You're the first."

"Wow. I'm honored," she said quietly.

Lee just shrugged, continuing on down the trail, leaving Kate to follow. It was the truth, but still, there was no need for Kate to know. Lee just had never been compelled to take anyone down here before. It didn't mean anything, for God's sake.

When they reached the edge of the pool, Kate tilted her head back, watching the water cascade over the rock wall on its way down. She'd never been this close to a waterfall before, and truthfully, she'd never been quite so awed by nature. The rock formations, the lush trees . . . and the beautiful, clear water overloaded her senses.

"I take it you like," Lee said.

"I love."

Lee dropped her backpack, smiling at Kate's genuine admiration of the falls. Somehow, she knew Kate would love it down here. That was why she'd made the effort to leave the rope, to place the pitons. It didn't mean anything. Then she grinned, pulling the shirt from her shorts. A dip in the pool was in order. And—God willing—Kate didn't have a swimsuit on under her shorts.

"Feel like a swim?" she asked innocently.

"Oh, God, that sounds good, doesn't it." Kate turned. "I wish you'd told me to bring my suit."

"You don't need a suit. There's no one around."

Kate's jaw dropped open as Lee pulled the shirt over her head. She shouldn't have been surprised that Lee wore no bra, but she was. Before she could take a breath, Lee was naked and diving into the crystal clear water, leaving Kate to stare after her.

Lee surfaced with a scream, shaking her hair from side to side. "Damn! That first dip will get you." She saw Kate's puzzled look. "Cold."

Kate nodded, finally able to avert her eyes. *Like you've never seen a naked woman before.*

"Come on in. It's fabulous."

She was certain she'd never seen a woman as toned as Lee before. Oh, God . . . what the hell? She closed her eyes briefly, then pulled her own shirt over her head. When Lee dipped her head under the water again, Kate ripped her bra off, then her shorts. Standing there—stark naked—she felt empowered, if only for a moment. Lee splashed to the surface and Kate plunged head-first into the pool. *Good God, it's cold!*

She let out her own scream as she surfaced, treading water some ten feet from Lee. "It's freezing!"

"Yeah, ain't it great."

Kate splashed Lee with water, then disappeared again, swimming farther away. On the far end, she was able to stand. She walked into the sunlight, tilting her head back, trying to warm her face.

Damn, she's a goddess. Lee stared, watching the water drip slowly down Kate's neck to her breasts. *Did I just think that? A goddess? What the hell is wrong with you?* She made herself turn away, submerging into the cold water, trying to chase the vision of a naked Kate Winters from her mind.

"Come on, Lee," she murmured. "Get a grip."

"Oh, Lee, this is so fabulous," Kate called from across the pool. "It's heavenly."

"That it is," Lee whispered slowly as her eyes traveled over Kate's wet body. *Yes, a goddess.*

For some reason, Kate didn't feel even slightly self-conscious as she let the sun dry her. Lee was on her own rock, stretched out on her back. Far enough away as to not be threatening—but close enough for Kate to make out every fabulous detail of her body. A part of her knew she should be ashamed for what she was doing. After all, if the tables were reversed and Robin was the one lying naked with a beautiful woman, Kate would be incensed. And she did feel a twinge of guilt, but rationalized with a "doesn't hurt to look." Of course, the guilt wouldn't be quite so strong if she actually *thought* of Robin occasionally.

"We should probably head back up," Lee called.

Kate rolled her head to the side, smiling as she watched Lee sit up. Their eyes held for a moment, then Kate looked away as Lee stood. She gathered her own clothes, dressing with her back to Lee. It was foolish. It wasn't like they hadn't spent the better part of two hours frolicking in the water naked.

"Oh, *now* you're shy," Lee teased.

Kate laughed. "Silly, I know."

"It's okay. It was fun as hell though, wasn't it?"

"Absolutely. I'm so glad you brought me."

"Now, we just have to get you out of here."

Lee shouldered her backpack, then led the way back along the trail. Kate only made the first switchback before she had to stop, panting.

"Okay, so maybe you are a little out of shape."

Kate shook her head. "Smoker," she gasped.

"You *smoke*?" Lee shook her head. "Never would have pegged you for a smoker."

"I officially quit two years ago," Kate said as her breathing returned somewhat to normal. "Actually, I've been on and off for two years. More off than on, I'm proud to say. But technically, I quit at the airport the day I left Dallas."

"Snuck one in, did you?"

Kate grinned. "I hate flying."

"Well, I'm glad you quit. Congratulations. They tell me it's tough."

"Pure hell," Kate admitted as she followed Lee up the trail. "But I feel great."

"We can stop as much as you need."

"Don't worry," Kate huffed. She paused, looking nearly straight up the cliff wall. "Good God," she murmured.

"What?"

"It looks steeper from this angle."

Lee laughed. "Yeah, I'm thinking the rope part is going to be real fun."

"I tried to warn you," Kate said. "No upper body strength."

"We'll manage."

It was all a blur but after four more rest stops, they finally made it to the rock wall. Kate collapsed where they stood, her lungs burning. *Damn cigarettes.*

"You okay?"

Kate could only nod. She rested her arms on her drawn-up knees, hanging her head between her legs as she tried to catch her breath.

Lee slid down beside her, then offered her a drink of water. Kate's bottle was long gone. She took the bottle, taking a long swallow before handing it back.

"I swear, it's like you're jogging up this trail. I think you're trying to kill me."

Lee laughed outright. And she realized she did that a lot around Kate. Laughed. It felt good. Maybe that was why she enjoyed Kate's company so much.

"Jogging? We're practically crawling up the trail."

"You could at least pretend to be winded."

"I'm sure after I have to haul your ass up this rock wall, I will be."

Kate lifted her head, meeting the hazel eyes that danced with amusement. Laughing eyes. She liked them.

Kate smiled at her. "In case you *do* have to haul me up this wall, there's really no need to tell anyone about it, right?"

Lee raised her eyebrows mischievously. "We can probably work something out."

"That sounds dangerous. Maybe I need to give the wall a try first."

"Oh, you'll do fine." Lee stood, offering a hand to Kate. "I'll go first, like before."

"First? But what if I fall?"

"You won't fall. You'll do just the opposite of when you came down. This time, you'll pretend you're climbing *up* a ladder." Lee grabbed hold of a couple of the pitons and gave a jerk. "They're still in tight. Don't be afraid to put your weight on them, just remember to hold tight to the rope."

Kate watched in amazement as Lee walked up the wall, hand over fist on the rope, pulling herself up with ease. *Wow.*

"Tie my backpack like before," Lee called from above.

Kate did as she was told, then waited while Lee pulled the rope up. Kate shielded her eyes from the sun, her eyes locked on the fluid motions of Lee's body.

"Okay, coming down," Lee called, releasing the rope.

Kate stepped back, letting the rope fall where she could reach it. She took hold of the rope, then stared at where the first piton was—her foothold. *Crap.* She glanced up at Lee. "Wonder how I'm going to reach that?"

"It's just three feet. Use the rope to pull yourself up."

"I'll try. But no laughing from the bleachers if I bust my ass!"

Lee grinned. "I promise."

It only took two tries, but Kate did manage to reach the lowest piton. Unfortunately, she put all her weight on it and she felt it slip.

"Don't let go of the rope!" Lee yelled.

Kate didn't. She steadied herself, then like Lee, pulled herself up the wall, hand over fist. Unlike Lee, she did not skip over the very useful pitons. At the top, Lee was squatting, holding out her hand.

"Are you kidding? That means I've got to let go of the rope with one hand," Kate said.

"How else are you going to get up here?" Lee asked reasonably.

"Good point," she murmured. "You won't let me fall, right?"

"Of course not." Then Lee winked. "And then you'll owe me."

Kate rolled her eyes. "Maybe I'd be better off falling!"

But she didn't. Lee grabbed hold of her hand, steadying them both until Kate was ready to push off. Then Lee grabbed both her upper arms, hoisting her onto the ledge. It was a perfect plan. That is . . . until Kate lost her balance, causing Lee to tip backward, pulling Kate with her.

They landed with a thud, Kate lying completely on top of Lee. They both froze, their eyes locking together. Then Lee laughed.

"This could be fun," she murmured. "If only you hadn't knocked the wind out of me."

Kate came to her senses, rolling off Lee immediately.

"I'm so sorry," she said, helping Lee to sit up. "Are you hurt?"

"I'm fine," Lee said as she rubbed the back of her head. "I'm sure this huge knot is nothing."

Kate's eyes widened. She reached around Lee, moving Lee's hands out of the way, gently feeling for the knot. It was the size of a pea. A small pea at that.

"I think you might live."

"Could be a concussion."

"If you're lucky, it'll bruise. Then you'll have something to complain about."

Lee laughed, then stood. "You're not much for sympathy, are you?"

Kate smiled sweetly, then handed Lee her backpack. "Lead on."

But an hour later, still a good fifty feet from the rim, Kate collapsed, waving Lee on.

"No, you go on. I can't make it. I give up," she gasped between breaths.

Lee walked back down the trail where Kate sat, trying to wipe the smile from her face. "So, what now? You going to spend the night here? Just you and the coyotes?"

Kate glared at her. Lee laughed harder.

"We can see the top. We're almost there," Lee said reasonably.

Kate took a swing at her. "You said that thirty minutes ago."

Lee tried another approach. "You're doing great, Kate. It's always harder—much harder—going back up. In fact, I didn't think you'd be able to go as fast as you've been."

Kate stared at her, then started laughing herself. "Oh, God, Lee, you are so full of shit!"

Lee spread her arms wide, her smile contagious. "You doubt me?"

"Oh, yeah. I doubt you, sweetheart."

Lee's smile faltered only slightly. And thankfully, Kate had turned away as she stood. Lee watched as Kate tilted her head back, looking up to the rim where they had to go. *Sweetheart?* Lee took a breath, wondering at the funny feeling that word caused.

"Wonder how many more times I'll have to stop before we get there?"

Lee shook off the feeling, finally walking ahead of Kate. "As many as you need. We're not in that big of a hurry."

"I thought you had a crime scene to investigate," Kate reminded her.

"Oh, just so I'm there before the evening crowd, it'll be fine."

"Well, let's just say if it takes that long for us to reach the rim, you'll have to call search and rescue."

"Kate, the hard part is over. You climbed nearly fifteen feet on a rock wall. This is easy, it's just uphill."

Kate stopped. "Fifteen feet? You said it was barely twelve."

"I may have fibbed a little." Then she stopped too. "Are we resting already?"

Kate shook her head. "No, I'm just slowing down." She stopped again. "And it'll be a miracle if I can even get out of bed tomorrow, much less walk."

"Does that mean you don't want to make this a weekly activity?"

"You ask me that *now*? Before we've even made it out of here?"

"Look," Lee pointed. "Thirty more feet."

Kate sighed. "Yeah, the promised land," she murmured. She walked on, urging Lee to go in front of her with a quick tug on her shorts. She had long ago lost the energy to watch Lee's legs as they walked. She only wanted her in front in case she slipped and fell.

Lee stopped, turned around and reached for Kate. "Okay." She looked up. "I'm going up first. Watch me. Use the tree limbs. I'll pull you over the rim like I did the ledge."

Kate nodded. "Okay."

Like a cat, Lee scampered up the trail, pulling herself up with the help of the piñon pines. At the rim, she swung one leg up, then pulled herself over the top, leaving Kate staring after her. *I'm going to fall.*

"Come on, Kate."

"Why did it seem so easy going down?"

Lee laughed, then sat on the rim, legs swinging casually over the side, waiting.

After a silent count of three, Kate grabbed the lower limb of the pine, pulling herself along, stumbling several times on the rocks. She wondered how much easier it would have been had she owned hiking boots. But she kept going, moving from limb to limb as Lee had done.

"Grab my hand," Lee instructed.

Kate didn't hesitate. The next thing she knew, she was sitting in the bright sunshine, the deep canyon of the waterfall far below them.

"Piece of cake," Lee said.

Kate nodded, then laid flat on her back, relieved she made it. "The next time I ask you to take me somewhere like this, remind me I'm old and out of shape."

CHAPTER FIFTEEN

"Oh, my, darling. Are you okay?"

Kate walked gingerly into the living room, flicking her eyes once at Brenda, then back to the floor as she watched every step she took.

"I'm . . . I'm not sure," she said. "Everything is numb."

Brenda took her arm, steadying her. "I was worried when we got back and you weren't here. Whatever have you done?"

"Lee. Lee took me hiking. To the oasis."

"The waterfall, darling? Down in that bowl?"

Kate nodded. "Yes. Bowl. That's an excellent word for it."

"Oh my."

"I want a shower. I'm starving and I'm exhausted, but I want a shower."

"Okay, go on, darling. Sophia put a nice roast on for us before she left. I'll bring you a glass of wine."

Kate paused. "Sophia? Ahh, your maid service. I'd forgotten." She paused. "She didn't come last week," she stated.

"No, her sister was ill. But she's better than anyone I've ever had in Dallas, darling. Of course, she costs more than anyone I've had in Dallas. But, she's an excellent cook."

"Wonderful," Kate murmured as she walked into her room. She stripped on her way to the bathroom, then eyed the tub instead of the shower. A soak in hot water—extremely hot water—seemed in order. She let the tub fill as she rummaged through the cabinets, looking for bath salts or gel or even bubbles. Something soothing. She grinned when she found the jar of scented bath salts. Then she spied a blue bottle—Soothing Aromatherapy Foaming Bath Oil. *Is that heaven or what?*

"Oh, my, darling."

Kate turned quickly, but she was too tired to feel embarrassed as she stood there naked. She simply reached for the cool glass of sangria that Brenda offered. "Thanks."

Brenda raised her eyebrows as she looked pointedly at Kate's breasts. "You have a sunburn. What in the world did you do?"

"We went swimming."

"Naked? With *Lee*?"

"Yes, with Lee. Brenda, I'm not one of her blond bimbos. We're becoming friends. And I'm surprised that I can even say that about her, but yeah, we're friends. I enjoy her company."

"Well, I'd hoped you would hit it off, darling."

Kate waved her away. "We can't stand here and have a conversation with me naked. It's just weird. Give me an hour to soak and I'll be out."

"Of course. The roast should be ready by then. Yell if you want more wine."

As soon as Brenda closed the door, Kate sank into the hot water, an audible sigh left her body as she submerged to her neck.

"Oh, God, that's good."

She leaned her head back, resting it against the cool tile as she relaxed. She had used muscles today that she wasn't aware she had. And she only knew that because she hurt in places she'd never hurt before. *But it was so damn much fun.*

Yeah. And the more time she spent in Lee's company, the more she liked her. She had fun with Lee. She laughed with Lee. And, surprisingly, she felt comfortable with Lee.

"And she's sexy as hell," she whispered, remembering the way Lee's body looked—stark naked—water dripping off every tanned curve. Then she sighed and shook her head, again hating the fact that she was . . . she was attracted to Lee. And it was so out of character for her. For one thing, Lee was the epitome of what she despised in lesbian relationships. There was nothing healthy about jumping from bed to bed, either physically or emotionally. Yet Lee had turned it into an art. Well, regardless that she found Lee attractive, she could take solace in the fact that she would not end up as one of her bed partners.

She sipped her wine, trying to turn her thoughts to Jennifer and Paul instead of Lee. *Jennifer as a lesbian? What are you thinking?* Despite thinking that Lee had lost her mind when she suggested Jennifer was a lesbian, it was really the only thing that made sense. Especially since she had unknowingly turned her into one in the last few books. And poor Paul, what in the world would she do with him? Would he be heartbroken? Would he be surprised? Or would he, as everyone else apparently, have already suspected?

A knock on the door brought her back to the present. Brenda stuck her head around inside.

"Sorry, but I answered your cell," she said, holding up the phone. "Robin."

"Thank you." Then, as Brenda made a face, Kate stuck her tongue out, still grinning when she answered.

"Hi, honey. I'm not interrupting anything, am I?"

Kate lazily splashed the warm water around her. "I'm in the tub, actually," she said.

"At this hour? Are you okay?"

"Yes. I was out hiking today," she said. "I'm beyond sore."

"Hiking? Doesn't that cut into your writing?"

Kate leaned her head back and closed her eyes as the guilt settled over her. This was Robin, her *girlfriend*. Why did she feel the need to lie? Why couldn't she just tell her the truth? It wasn't like she'd done anything wrong. Was swimming naked with another woman wrong?

"Actually, it did cut into my writing," she admitted. "But Lee offered to take me to the oasis." She waited for the question.

"Who's Lee?"

"She's the local sheriff. Didn't I tell you she is a friend of Brenda's?"

"No, you didn't. But what's the oasis?"

Kate raised her eyebrows, expecting more questions about Lee. For some reason, she thought Robin would be jealous. But why should she? She's not met Lee. She has no idea that Kate finds her attractive.

"The oasis is a waterfall in a canyon. Steep hike down. Killer of a hike going back up."

"I didn't know you liked to hike. Well, I'm glad you're getting out and doing something. I had visions of you locked in your room with your laptop, coming out only to eat."

"No. And actually I spend more time on the deck with my laptop than I do my room. It's so pretty here."

"Well, that's one reason I called. I can get a Friday off in two weeks. I thought maybe I'd come visit. Fly out on that Thursday night. What do you think?"

Kate was aware that she was hesitating and she had no idea why. Of course she should want Robin to visit. She missed her. Right?

"I think that would be wonderful, Robin."

"Great. I'll check on flights. Can you meet me in Santa Fe or shall I just rent a car?"

"It might be better to rent a car. That way, if Brenda is out and about, we won't be without a vehicle," Kate explained.

"Okay, great. I'll call you later with the details." She paused. "I can't wait to see you."

Another stab of guilt as Kate realized she had not really missed Robin. Perhaps this visit would be good for them. They needed to probably spend some time together, get reacquainted. Maybe her earlier thoughts that separation from Robin would make them both realize the emptiness of their relationship was wrong. Maybe the separation would bring them closer together.

She tossed the phone on the mat, dismissing thoughts of Robin. She drained the now cool water, her bath over. Hopefully, dinner would be ready soon. She was starving. And if she didn't pass out from exhaustion, she would write for a couple of hours. She laughed. Jennifer as a lesbian. Wouldn't she have fun trying to write that!

Lee pulled her Jeep in front of Opal's, noting only a handful of locals there. It was still several hours before the summer crowd would leave the river for the day and venture over to the bar. But most nights, the place would be packed. And some nights, the summer crowd would get rowdy. It was on those nights she was thankful to have Skip as her backup. The locals knew he was as easygoing as they came. But at six-foot-five, two-hundred-fifty pounds, he could stop most fights with just a glare.

He waved her inside when he saw her, politely holding the door open for her. "About time you showed up, Foxx. Where the hell were you?"

Lee grinned. "It was official police business, trust me."

"Sure it was. What was her name?"

"For your information, I was actually giving someone a tour. She's a writer. She might use us in her next book."

"What's her name?"

"Kate Winters. You've probably not read—"

"Cool! The Masters. I love those books. But they're based in Los Angeles. Why would she have them out here?"

Great, Lee, he's read her books. Now what? So Lee smiled. "Don't know what she's got planned. I didn't ask." Before Skip could ask more questions, Lee stopped him with a hand on his chest. "What did you find out here?"

"Two kegs, a couple of cases of sodas, about ten cartons of cigarettes and two bottles of cheap bourbon."

"Ten *cartons*? What the hell are they going to do with ten cartons?"

Skip shrugged. "Kids. Hell, they just grabbed shit and ran."

Lee looked up at the tall man behind the bar. "Opal, you got any ideas?"

"No, but I tell you what. The next time this happens, I'll be ready. I'm getting me one of those surveillance cameras," he said as he wiped the bar.

Lee laughed. "You say that every year. And if you'd finally do it once, we wouldn't have to have this conversation every year." She pulled out a barstool and her notepad. "Okay. Let's go over it."

"Closed up at two. I left about two-thirty, like always. Got here about eleven this morning on account I had to meet the beer truck."

"They got in where?"

"Back window in the storage room was busted out," Skip said.

"Any blood or anything? No one got cut on their way in?"

"No. I didn't see anything."

Lee sighed. Same as always. "Well, I guess we need to find ourselves a party. Skip, why don't you call Crumpton's. See if anyone bought a lot of ice. I'll swing by the lodge. They would need a truck to haul off two kegs. Maybe somebody saw something." She stood. "Opal, I'll let you know."

She went back outside, the river canyon already dark even though the sun had not yet set. She looked down the canyon, the water still shimmering with sunlight, reminding her she had not taken Kate to see the sunset.

"Damn," she whispered, shaking her head. For some reason, she couldn't get the writer out of her head. She'd had more fun today than she could remember having in a long while. And it was nice being with a woman who wasn't interested in going to bed with her. And when was the last time she'd thought that. *Not that I wouldn't be interested in going to bed with her.*

"Oh, Lee, she's not your type," she murmured to herself. "Even if she was interested."

"Who the hell are you talking to?"

Lee spun around, finding Skip watching her. "What?"

"What?"

Lee put her hands on her hips, shifting her holster a bit. "What did you find out?"

"Ice is scarce," he said. "They raided the gas station. Even stopped off at the bakery."

"Good. And?"

"Four guys, early twenties. River rats, by the description."

"Probably staying at the lodge, then. You want to hang out there and look for a party tonight?"

"Yeah. I haven't had a stakeout in awhile."

"Skip, you've *never* had a stakeout."

"Do I get to have a gun?"

"No, you don't get a gun. If you find something, you call me. Then we'll deal with it."

"You know, even Barney got to carry a gun."

"Yeah, but he didn't have any bullets."

"Hell, I don't want bullets, Lee. I just want a gun. Apparently, it's good with the women."

She flashed him a smile as she walked off. "How the hell would you know?"

CHAPTER SIXTEEN

"Oh my God," Kate whispered as they walked quietly through the gallery. "They're beautiful."

"Yes, darling. It's almost too much for me to comprehend. I mean, she's taking the time to work with me," Brenda said, spreading her arms. "And she's this talented. I can't imagine what she sees in me."

Kate tugged her arm. "Will you look at the prices! I had no idea!"

Brenda pulled her into another room. "Come, you must see Starlight's work. It's so impressive."

The room was dark, lit only by ceiling lights directed at the paintings, but Kate's breath caught as soon as her eyes fixed on the first display. The river flowed nearly purple, the dark canyon walls glowed a deep red and overhead, the full moon was burgundy.

"Wow," she breathed.

"She brings the night alive, doesn't she?"

Kate nodded, slowly moving along the display. "Oh, my," she whispered. "This is the one Lee was telling me about." And Lee had described it perfectly. The orange moon, the orange canyon walls, yet the sun was no longer in the sky. "I love it."

"Come, darling. This is my favorite."

Brenda led her to a huge painting, nearly floor to ceiling and Kate's mouth dropped open. They were standing practically in the canyon, looking upstream, the red cliff walls curving around to the sky, which still held a bit of color from the sun. But again, it wasn't the sun's light that brought the painting alive. It was the moon, the reflection on the river shimmering on the current, making the water ripple before her eyes.

"I feel like it's moving," Kate whispered.

"Yes. I always feel like I'm on a raft when I stand here."

"What would something like this sell for?"

"Oh, darling, I don't think they could put a price on it. There have been offers, I'm told. Outrageous offers. But Starlight prefers it to stay here."

"Which no doubt drives the price."

Brenda pointed to a vacant wall. "There was one there. I only got to see it one time. It was nearly as moving as this one. She painted it nearly ten years ago. Someone finally made her an offer she couldn't turn down." Brenda looked quickly over her shoulder, then turned back to Kate. "Nearly a hundred thousand dollars," she whispered.

"Oh my God!"

"Shhh," Brenda hissed. "They don't like to talk about money."

"But a hundred grand? For a *painting*?" Kate nudged her arm. "And she's not even dead."

Brenda laughed quietly. "Maybe we should buy a few as an investment."

Kate turned serious. "Do you think? Really?"

"Oh, darling, I'm teasing. Thomas would have a coronary if I were to buy a piece for that price. He seems to think that real estate is the only safe investment."

Kate nodded. "And I guess it's hard to give that kind of money to someone you know."

"Exactly. Because I've no doubt that if I asked them to paint one for me as a gift, they would do it gladly. They are very generous, darling. I know you think them a bit strange, but I've grown to love them."

"Yes, I know. And maybe they are just strange to me because I've never been around people like that. Lee says you get used to them."

"Exactly. And it's not as if I've been around people like them either, Katie. I mean, come on, darling. Dallas? Maybe Austin, but hardly Dallas."

"Yes, but it's been proven that you are *far* more open-minded than I am."

Brenda linked arms with her, pulling her along. "I'm doing my best to loosen you up. And I have the perfect spot for dinner. Their sangria is not anywhere near as good as Lee's but their enchiladas are out of this world."

CHAPTER SEVENTEEN

Kate ran both hands through her hair in frustration, then stared at the sky, barely noticing the approaching evening. She had written nearly four chapters today. In fact, she'd worked nonstop for the last five days. Jennifer had finally met Jordan, the detective.

"But now what?" She sighed. *Hell, I can't write romance.* "Why does it have to be romance?" *Because she's about to meet the love of her life. You can't just skim over it!*

"Are you talking to yourself, darling?"

Kate looked across the deck, watching Brenda as she climbed from her rock perch and stretched.

"How long have you been out there?"

"Oh, an hour, tops. I was practicing my meditation. Starlight comes again tonight."

"I didn't even know you were out here." Kate saved what she'd been working on, then did her own stretching. "I can't believe it's so late."

"But that's wonderful, darling. That means you've been writing."

"Yeah. It's coming. And yes, I do talk to myself when I write."

Brenda walked closer. "When can I see?"

Kate shook her head. "Not yet. It's still, you know, raw. I mean, I'm not even sure that where I'm going is where I need to go. I'm just kinda feeling it out right now."

"If it feels right, darling, then do it. Just let Jennifer grow. I think that's been the problem in the last few books. She's been stagnant. Set her free, darling. Let her *live*."

"It's scary, Brenda. I mean, pretend you're a middle-aged housewife in the Midwest."

"Why on earth would I do that, darling?"

"Because demographics say they are a large majority of my audience. So, you're this woman living in Nebraska, and you get the latest installment of The Masters, and about a quarter of the way through, you realize that Jennifer is acting strange. You realize that Jennifer is looking at women instead of Paul. What do you do?"

Brenda laughed, then clapped loudly. "Wonderful, darling. You're going to take the plunge?"

"Brenda, I'm serious. Your average middle-aged woman in the Midwest is going to be shocked. In fact, she may very well toss the book in the trash without finishing it. Then what? I've lost my base."

"Oh, nonsense, darling. For every narrow-minded Nebraska woman who shuns your book, there will be countless others who will pick it up. You underestimate your lesbian audience. They have stuck with you, thinking Jennifer will see the light, as Lee says. Imagine their reaction when Jennifer finally ditches Paul. It will be so empowering."

Kate sighed. "I'm being realistic here. And most likely, this will be the last book in the series. Jennifer comes out. And suddenly, half of my audience can't relate to her anymore. End of story."

"People have watched Jennifer grow through the years, Katie.

Don't be so surprised if those middle-aged women stick with her. She's like a daughter to them. You've made her so damn lovable already, I doubt her falling in love with another woman will change that. My only advice, darling, is to make it so romantic that they can't possibly turn away from it."

Kate leaned her head back. "And there's the problem. I don't write romance. I don't have a clue as to how to write romance."

Brenda took her hand between both of hers and rubbed it lightly. "Perhaps because you've never lived it, darling."

Kate cocked her head. "Why do you assume that Robin and I have never had a romance?"

"Darling, you forget, I was with you when you met her. And I've seen you together. You never touch."

"That means nothing. In fact—"

She stopped in mid-sentence as Lee bounded up the steps of the deck, flashing the smile that Kate couldn't help but return.

"Ladies, good evening," she greeted.

"Why, Lee, we weren't expecting you."

"Spur of the moment." Lee pointed at Kate. "Come on. Close that thing up. I want to show you something."

Kate stared. "Show me something? Now? It's nearly dark."

"Exactly. It's a coyote sky tonight."

Kate raised her eyebrows. "Coyote sky?"

"Yeah. And come on. We're going to be late if we don't hurry."

Their eyes met. "Are you going to tell me what a coyote sky is?"

Lee smiled. "I can't tell you. I have to show you."

"Of course."

"Oh, Kate, go. It's a beautiful evening," Brenda said.

"Okay, okay." Kate closed her laptop and swung her legs off the lounge. "What do I need?"

"Jeans. It gets cold up there."

Kate stopped. "Up there where?"

Lee pointed to the cliffs. "Up there."

"We're not going to do any climbing or anything, right?"

Lee laughed. "Promise. We'll drive right to it."

Ten minutes later, they were speeding past the canyon road in Lee's opened Jeep, climbing higher toward the cliffs. The sun had set, the sky barely showing color as dusk settled over the canyons. The Jeep's headlights bounced off the rocks and Kate wondered again what it was that Lee wanted to show her. As they topped the last switchback, the expanse of the high desert was evident. Then Lee pointed to their right.

"Oh, wow," Kate said. "That's gorgeous. Absolutely gorgeous."

The full moon had just risen over the cliffs and Kate marveled at its color. Starlight's paintings weren't really exaggerated. The moon was nearly blood red.

"It'll turn orange as it gets higher. But the colors only last for a little while."

Lee pulled off the dirt road, driving them closer to the canyon edge, then stopped. She cocked her head, as if listening. Kate did the same, wondering what they were listening for. Then she jumped from her seat as a high-pitched howl was heard, followed by ten—maybe twenty—others.

"What the hell?"

"Coyotes." Lee opened her door. "Like I said, it's a coyote sky tonight."

Kate hesitated. "Is it safe? I mean, it sounded like it was right over there," she said.

"It's perfectly safe. They sound closer than they are. We'll get echoes from the canyon."

Lee pulled a blanket from the back, and motioned for Kate to follow her. She spread it on a table-like rock, then sat down, crossing her legs under her. Kate joined her, another howl bringing her shoulder-to-shoulder with Lee.

Lee grinned. "I guess I should thank Mr. Coyote for being so close this evening," she teased.

"Very funny. It's just spooky. I've never been this close to them before."

"Surely you hear them from Brenda's."

"Yes. But it's more like little yelps we hear. This was more like a howl. Are you sure it wasn't a wolf?"

"I'm sure. And they are more like yelps. To me, it sounds like they're singing. One starts, then others follow. Listen."

They were both quiet, then it started again. One, high-pitched bark, then from all around them others joined in. Kate again scooted closer to Lee.

"It's like a symphony," Lee whispered. She looked up. "The moon is starting to change."

And it was. The near purple color of the moon a few moments ago was gradually replaced by a duller red that hinted of orange. The reflection on the cliffs was amazing. It was as if the red walls were actually glowing in the moonlight. It was a remarkable sight.

Then, as if on cue, the coyotes started their singing again. And yes, Kate admitted, it was beautiful, the sounds bouncing around in the canyons below them. Lee stirred, moving away, and then stood. She held out her hand to Kate.

"Dance with me."

Their eyes met in the moonlight.

"I've always wanted to dance up here," Lee explained.

Kate nodded slowly. It was too perfect for her to refuse. Too . . . *romantic.* She took Lee's hand and let herself be pulled to her feet. And the coyotes obliged, their song fading to the background as Lee's arms pulled Kate closer. Kate's hand trembled as she slipped it over Lee's shoulder and she prayed Lee couldn't hear her thundering heartbeat.

They were too close, really. Yet Kate ached to be closer. Another few inches and she would feel Lee's breasts against her own. Another few inches and their thighs would brush. She squeezed her eyes shut, trying to call up an image of Robin, anything to break the spell that Lee had cast on her.

Lee was too afraid to do more than slowly shuffle her feet. Her heart was pounding in her chest and she was terrified Kate would hear it. *What is it about this woman that I can't shake?* And why did thoughts of Kate sneak into her mind at all hours of the day and night? And why on earth was she up here dancing with the woman?

Lee finally stopped, letting Kate slip from her arms. It was then that she noticed the pulse beating rapidly in Kate's throat. Their eyes held as they stood there in the moonlight, the coyotes still singing their song. Lee took some comfort in the fact that she affected Kate in some way. She seemed to be as startled by their physical touch as Lee.

Lee shoved her hands in her pockets and took a step back. "Thanks," she murmured.

Kate just nodded, but she too moved away. "It's beautiful up here. Thank you for showing it to me."

Lee took a deep breath, then moved back to the blanket, the spell—thankfully—was broken.

"They seem to go crazy when the moon is full. A few days before and a few days after. The Anasazi people call it a coyote sky when the moon turns red like that."

"Does it happen often?"

"Usually just during the summer months, when the days are longer."

Kate nodded, sitting down again too. Only this time, she left several feet between them.

"You didn't make dinner the other night," Lee said unexpectedly.

"No. I was writing. I didn't want to stop."

"I thought maybe the girls were a bit too strange for you. Sunshine was asking about you."

"Was she talking about my destiny again?"

Lee laughed. "How did you know? She said you were trying to fight the inevitable, whatever that means."

"I wasn't fighting anything. I was just in the middle of a chapter and I didn't want to stop."

"So how's our Jenn coming along?"

Kate smiled. "Actually, Jennifer has met someone."

119

"Oh, yeah?"

Kate met her eyes. "A woman."

Lee leaned closer. "Our Jennifer met a woman?"

Kate nodded. "A detective."

"A detective who is lesbian?"

"Yes."

Their eyes held. "And is Jennifer finally going to fall in love?" Lee whispered.

"I believe she is going to fall head over heels, actually." Kate laughed. "Provided I can learn how to write a little romance."

"Is it hard?"

Kate shrugged. "I've never tried it. Obviously I didn't do so well with Jennifer and Paul."

"That's because they were all wrong for each other. They didn't fit together." Lee picked up a rock and tossed it between her hands. "You could always just rely on real life to guide you."

"What do you mean?"

"Robin. Just think back to when you guys met, how it was." Lee shrugged. "Use that as your guide."

Kate stared, wondering what Lee would say if she knew that Kate could not conjure up even a single event with Robin that she would consider romantic. Why, sitting up here now, with the full moon, *dancing*, was probably the most romantic thing Kate had ever experienced in her life. And it was with someone she wasn't even involved with. Someone she wasn't even *interested* in. Okay, so maybe she was attracted to Lee. That didn't mean she was interested in her, for God's sake. This was Lee, after all.

She forced a smile to her face and glanced up at the moon. "Robin is coming to visit," she said, more as a reminder to herself as anything.

Lee stiffened. "Oh, yeah? Great. You must be excited."

"Of course." Excited? Kate supposed she should be but she wasn't. Not at all. But Lee didn't need to know this.

"I'm sure you miss her."

Kate nodded. "It's been a month."

"Yeah. A long time to sleep alone, huh?"

Kate turned, their eyes meeting. Then she smiled. "Something you wouldn't know about, I'm sure."

Lee stared, wondering what Kate's reaction would be if she knew that no one had shared Lee's bed since . . . since the day before her birthday. Since the day she took Kate on the tour. Since she'd met Kate. Lee swallowed nervously, then stood. *It doesn't mean anything. It wasn't like it was because of Kate that she hadn't been with anyone.*

"You about ready to head back?" Lee asked suddenly, feeling the need to put some distance between them.

Kate watched Lee, wondering what was wrong. She looked agitated. Upset. Kate reached out, wrapping her fingers around Lee's arm.

"What's wrong?" she asked quietly.

Lee stared at Kate's hand, wondering why her skin burned where Kate touched. "Nothing's wrong. It's just . . . I thought you'd had enough. The moon, the stars, coyotes." Lee shrugged.

"I love it, Lee." Kate squeezed her arm before letting her fingers slip away. "Thank you for taking the time to bring me up here."

"Sure."

"Do you do it often?"

"What? Come up here?"

"Bring company. Dance?" she asked quietly.

Lee turned away, wondering again what it was about Kate that pulled her. She cleared her throat.

"I come up here a lot by myself." She shook her head. "I've never brought anyone." She turned back to Kate. "So, no, I've never danced before."

CHAPTER EIGHTEEN

"Are you sure you don't want to meet her at the airport? She's bound to get lost on her way up here."

Kate laughed. "I thought that might please you if she got lost."

"Darling, perhaps if she drove her car into the Rio Chama. But if she only gets lost, that just means we'll have to find her."

"Remember, you promised me you'd be nice to her while she was here."

"And I will. I don't throw a dinner party for just anyone, you know."

"I think you're only doing that so she can meet Sunshine and Harmony."

"It's just a good excuse. Harmony has been so gracious, I think it's time I returned the favor, is all."

"They're vegetarians. What will you cook?"

"Well, *I'm* not going to cook, darling. Sophia will whip something up. She's got a spicy dish she makes with those portabella mushrooms you like so much. And she'll do a chicken dish for those of us who aren't vegetarian."

"Sounds interesting."

"Oh, and I've asked Lee to bring her wine. What's a party up here without Lee's sangria?"

Kate stared. "You invited Lee?"

"Of course, darling. Why wouldn't I?"

"I don't know," she shrugged. "I just didn't think of Lee being here."

"But, darling, the two of you have become friends. Don't you want her to meet Robin?"

Did she? "Of course. And we'll no doubt get to meet her latest," she said dryly.

Brenda raised her eyebrows. "Kate, is there something wrong? Have you and Lee quarreled?"

"No," Kate said, waving her hand dismissively. "I haven't seen Lee since the other night." And as much as she hated it, Lee had never been far from her mind. She didn't know what was wrong with her, but she saw herself dancing with Lee in the desert almost all the time. And for some reason, she was hesitant for Lee to meet Robin. Maybe a part of her was afraid Lee would see through this pretense, this facade, that Kate tried to maintain with Robin. Robin wasn't the love of her life, Kate wasn't in love with her. She thought at one time that she could be. But now that Robin had moved in with her, now that they were *together*, there was little Kate could do. Maybe in the fall, when she went back to Dallas, they would talk. And they could decide if their relationship was satisfying to them both.

But for now, she would pretend she'd missed Robin, pretend she was looking forward to her visit. Pretend that she enjoyed her lovemaking.

"Is that your cell I hear?"

Kate nodded, walking into her bedroom to retrieve her phone. She saw Robin's number. She forced a smile to her face before answering.

"Hey. I guess you made it."

123

"We just landed. I forgot about the time change."

"Yes. And I forgot how hard it'll be for you to try to find us in the dark. Maybe I should meet you somewhere," Kate suggested.

"Well, I've actually had an extremely long day. I was thinking I'd just grab dinner and a hotel room for the night. You wouldn't mind terribly, would you?"

It was with relief that Kate said no, she wouldn't mind in the least.

"Great! Then I'll see you in the morning."

Strange. Very strange, Kate thought. Something wasn't right, but she couldn't put her finger on it. They were acting—talking—like friends, not lovers. She stared at the ceiling. Maybe it wouldn't be so bad, after all. Maybe Robin felt the same way. Maybe Robin came to visit so they could talk.

"Could I get so lucky?" she murmured. But she was being unfair. She had been perfectly satisfied with Robin. Robin was safe. What had changed? *Lee?* She shook her head. No, she refused to believe it had anything to do with Lee Foxx and that damn dancing.

"Was that Robin?" Brenda called.

"Yeah." Kate went back into the kitchen. "Instead of trying to find her way tonight, she's going to stay in Santa Fe and drive up in the morning."

"It's probably for the best. We would no doubt have to call Lee to help look for her."

"And wouldn't *that* be fun," Kate said with a smile.

"Oh, wow, Kate, you were right. It *is* beautiful here." Robin turned a circle on the deck. "And look at you. You look all woodsy," she said.

Kate stood with her hands shoved in the pockets of her hiking shorts, her feet crossed as she leaned on the railing. She glanced at the leather hiking sandals Brenda had talked her into buying. Yes, she supposed she did look woodsy.

"And tan. Do you spend all your time outside?"

Kate nodded. "Pretty much." She pointed to the chaise lounge that had become her writing table. "There's my office."

"Well, that's a tough job."

Robin moved closer, wrapping her arms around Kate's waist. Kate only barely resisted the urge to stiffen.

"It's so good to see you. I'd almost forgotten what you looked like."

"It's only been, what? Five, six weeks? Surely it would take longer than that for you to forget me," Kate said lightly.

"Oh, you know what I mean."

Robin moved away again after only a light kiss on Kate's lips. Kate relaxed.

"So Brenda says we're having a party tomorrow night. Some of your friends."

"Well, they're more Brenda's friends than mine. Although very interesting. Sunshine and Harmony are artists. In fact, Harmony has a gallery in Santa Fe."

"Odd names."

"Oh, yes. And then there's Starlight. Although I don't believe Brenda invited her. I can't even begin to describe Starlight. She has to be experienced. She's a night person."

"Is she an artist too?"

"Yes. She does beautiful work. But she's . . . well, she's odd. She comes over occasionally, late at night, to work with Brenda. She's teaching her some sort of meditation."

"Brenda's always been pretty odd herself. I never quite under-stood your friendship with her."

Kate laughed. "Brenda is just a bit eccentric. And after being here with her, I think eccentric is too strong a word. And when you meet the others, you'll know what I mean."

Robin nodded. "Well, what shall we do today? Are you going to show me around town?"

"Sure. Town consists of a handful of shops. And the bakery. We'll have lunch there." Kate walked back into the house. "We can go now, if you like."

Robin continued to stare at the cliffs. "It's so pleasant. No wonder you stay outside to write." Then she looked at Kate. "You have been writing, haven't you? I didn't even think to ask."

Kate nodded. "Yes. It's coming along nicely." It occurred to her then that Robin rarely inquired about her writing. In fact, had Robin even read her last book? Was she even aware of Kate's dilemma regarding Jennifer and Paul?

"Great. But I hope you'll be able to take a break from it this weekend. I was hoping you could take me to Santa Fe early on Sunday and we could shop. Or tour some galleries."

"Shop? Robin, you shop every weekend in Dallas. I thought you wanted to come up here to get away from the city?"

"Santa Fe is not really a big city, Kate. And I was told there are some lovely jewelry stores there. I've always wanted some silver."

Kate sighed. She hated to shop. And Robin knew it. Robin looked at her expectantly, waiting. But Kate shook her head. She wouldn't spend the better part of a day shopping when she could be writing.

"I don't think so. If you want to shop before your flight, you can head down early. But Robin, that's more than two hours out of my time, just driving. I've got a deadline," she reminded her.

"But honey, we haven't seen each other in over a month. Don't you want to spend some time together?"

"Of course. But I explained that I'm not exactly on vacation. I'm working. And I just can't spare three whole days. Especially when one of them involves shopping."

Robin put her hands on her hips. "Maybe you should have told me that when I suggested coming to visit."

Before Kate could respond, she saw Brenda out of the corner of her eye, her footsteps quiet in her soft moccasins.

"Girls, what are you doing inside?" She looked at Kate. "I thought you'd be out showing her the cliffs."

Kate pointed at Robin's feet—perfectly manicured toenails clad only in dainty, white sandals. Brenda's eyes widened.

"Surely you brought something more suitable?"

Robin shrugged. "It's summer. I just brought sandals. They're perfectly suitable for normal wear."

Brenda and Kate exchanged glances.

"I would offer some of mine, but you look like you're a couple of sizes smaller than me," Brenda said.

Kate nodded. "And me."

"When you said you'd been hiking, I was picturing a nice, smooth hike and bike trail," Robin said with a laugh. "Besides, this outdoor stuff is not really my thing." She turned to Brenda. "I'm trying to talk Kate into taking me shopping on Sunday. Down in Santa Fe. Now that's my idea of fun."

Brenda frowned. "But Katie hates to shop."

"And I never understood that. What woman hates to shop?"

Again, Brenda glanced quickly at Kate before smiling at Robin. "Well, darling, if you want to shop, I'll be happy to take you. Shopping is my specialty, after all."

"You wouldn't mind?"

"Of course not. When is your flight?"

"Not until three."

"Well, we can head down that morning then. Katie, you don't mind, do you?"

Kate smiled her thanks. "Not at all. I can spend the day writing."

"Now, aren't you going to take Robin into Coyote for lunch?"

"Why don't you join us?" Kate asked. She smiled, hoping Brenda would agree. The conversation between herself and Robin was quickly going nowhere.

"Well, if you don't mind," Brenda said with a subtle wink. "I never turn down the bakery, darling."

CHAPTER NINETEEN

Lee stopped the Jeep, pausing with both hands on the steering wheel. She should have made an excuse. She should have just declined the invitation. But no, her curiosity was too much. She just *had* to meet the woman who shared Kate's life.

"Are you okay?"

Lee turned, smiling at her date. Not Brandy, no. But Brandy's friend Trudy. And this would probably send Kate over the edge. Although twenty-two, Trudy looked all of eighteen. An eighteen-year-old model, that is. But for once, she was up front. Trudy knew that when the evening was over, Lee would take her back to the lodge. Tonight, she just needed a date. And Trudy was willing.

"I'm fine. I've just never faked a date before."

"She must be special."

Lee frowned. "She who?"

"Whoever you're trying to make jealous. Because, honestly, I've never had to fake a date before, either," she said as she tossed the blond hair off her shoulder.

Lee got out. "I'm not trying to make anyone jealous. I just didn't want to come alone."

"So why not have a real date?" she asked as Lee held the door open for her. "I don't have anywhere to be tonight."

"Yeah, well, because."

"Because?"

Lee stopped. "Because. Just because."

Trudy patted her arm. "I'll play along. We'll have her so jealous by the end of the evening, she'll be begging for you."

"That smells delicious, Simone. What is it?"

"Oh, I can't take credit for it, Sunshine. Sophia made it for me. Portabella mushrooms and spinach." Brenda pulled a dish from the fridge. "Rice. It just needs to be heated."

Sunshine leaned closer. "This Robin person. She doesn't fit with Kate at all."

Brenda laughed. "I know. I've been telling Kate that for two years."

"She'll know soon. It's only a matter of time."

"What do you mean?"

"Can't you see it? Ariel," Sunshine whispered.

Brenda shook her head. "Oh, no. Not Lee. They've become friends, but Lee is not Kate's type at all. And darling, in case you've not noticed, Kate is about fifteen years older than Lee's normal dates."

"Nonetheless, Simone, it will happen. Watch them tonight."

Brenda smiled. "Okay, I'll watch. But I can assure you, there is nothing there." Brenda took Sunshine's arm, leading her from the kitchen. "Now, let's leave this to finish baking. It's time for sangria."

"Oh, Ariel has us all hooked, doesn't she? Do you suppose she has some secret ingredient in there?"

"I say she should sell the stuff. Or at least share the recipe. It must cost her a fortune to supply it for all our parties."

"She says an old Pueblo chief gave her the recipe with the promise she'd not pass it on."

"What are you two whispering about?" Kate asked from the doorway.

"Ariel's wine," Sunshine said.

Kate held up her glass. "If she doesn't get here soon, we'll be fighting over this. That's it."

The words no sooner left her mouth and Lee walked in, a jug of wine in each hand. But it wasn't the wine Kate was looking at. It was the woman following close behind. Girl, she corrected. *Child.* But a gorgeous child nonetheless.

"Why, Lee, we were just talking about you," Brenda said, taking one of the bottles of wine from her hand. "How are you, darling?"

Lee bent quickly and kissed Brenda's cheek. "Wonderful. How are you?"

"I'm fine. And who is this beautiful woman?"

"Meet Trudy. She's staying at the lodge for the summer."

Kate rolled her eyes. Of course she was. No doubt Lee had her pick of girls from the lodge. Then she looked around for Robin, finding Robin's eyes glued to Lee. And really, she couldn't blame her. Lee's normal jeans had been replaced with soft khakis. Her dark blue shirt was crisp, tucked neatly inside her trim waist. She looked as appealing as ever. When she looked up, she found her eyes captured by Lee's. She answered her smile with one of her own.

"Kate, meet a friend of mine. Trudy. Trudy, this is Kate Winters."

"Miss Winters, nice to meet you. You're the author, right? The Masters?"

"Kate, please."

"Lee, you didn't tell me you knew a famous author," Trudy said.

Kate cleared her throat. "Hardly famous. But welcome to our home, Trudy."

"Kate, aren't you going to introduce me to your friends?"

They all turned as Robin approached, linking arms with Kate as she smiled at Lee.

"Of course. Robin, this is Lee Foxx, local sheriff. And this is her friend, Trudy."

"So you're the sheriff," Robin said, dismissing Trudy.

Lee shrugged. "That's me."

"I understand you've taken my Kate hiking."

"Brenda's had me being tour guide," Lee said, flicking her glance to Kate. "But I've heard a lot about you, Robin." Lee offered her hand and Robin took it, squeezing gently. "Welcome to Coyote."

"Thanks. It's a charming little town."

Lee nodded, looking again at Kate. "Wonder where Brenda ran off to with my wine?"

"Right here, darling," Brenda said, handing Lee a glass. "It's delicious, as always."

"You make wine?" Robin asked.

"Yes. Sangria. It's not like I stomp grapes or anything."

"It's all on the bar, Robin. Why don't you get you a glass? And one for Lee's friend too. Show her where the bar is." Brenda leaned closer to Lee. "I'm assuming she's of age, darling," she whispered as Robin and Trudy walked away.

Lee laughed. "I expected that question from Kate, not you." Then Lee locked glances with Kate. "So that's your Robin."

Kate nodded.

Lee shook her head. "Not what I expected."

"What do you mean by that?"

"Nothing. She just doesn't seem your type."

"My type? And just what is my type?"

Lee shook her head. "She's way too feminine for you."

"*What?*"

"Well, she is."

"I tend to agree with Lee," Brenda said.

Kate glared. "Well, you would." Then Kate faced Lee. "And I suppose you're going to say that Trudy is of legal age?"

"Twenty-two. But she's cute, isn't she?"

Kate patted Lee's stomach as she walked by. "Children are always adorable," she murmured.

Lee stared after her, her hand absently going to her midsection where Kate had touched. She wondered if Kate knew how often she did that. Touched her. Then she smiled at Brenda. "She's very funny."

"Oh, yes, darling. An absolute comedian," Brenda said with a laugh. "And you two do enjoy sparring, don't you."

"Simone, this mushroom dish is so wonderful. You must get the recipe," Harmony said over dinner.

Robin nudged Kate. "Who's Simone?"

Kate smiled. "Brenda."

"I don't understand."

Kate shook her head. "Neither do I."

"I'll have Sophia write it down for you, Harmony. I'm glad you enjoy it." Brenda glanced at the others. "Can I get anyone else a second helping?"

"I'll have a scoop of that chicken, please," Trudy said as she held out her plate to Brenda.

Lee looked across the table at Kate, waiting only a moment before Kate looked up, locking glances with her. Then Lee slid her eyes to Robin, who was staring blankly at her plate, as if lost in thought. She shook her head. No, they didn't go together at all.

"I hope everyone has saved room for dessert," Brenda said. "Sophia makes the best apple pie you will ever eat. And, for those who wish to indulge, there is vanilla ice cream."

"Oh, Simone, I will never turn down apple pie."

Kate stood. "I'll get it, Brenda. Sit."

"Are you sure?"

"Of course."

Lee stood too. "I'll help." Then she grinned. "I've got dibs on the ice cream."

As soon as the kitchen door swung closed, Kate turned. "I could have managed, you know."

"Probably." Lee moved to the freezer, finding the ice cream. "But we haven't had a second alone." She placed the ice cream on the bar, then faced Kate. "Is everything okay?"

"Of course. What do you mean?"

"I just haven't seen you in awhile. I guess you're happy Robin is here."

"Why shouldn't I be?" Kate asked defensively.

"Just asking." Lee glanced over her shoulder at the door, then back to Kate. "Why exactly are you dating?"

"Dating? We're not dating. We live together. Perhaps I should ask you the same question."

Lee grinned. "At least there's hope for Trudy. But you and Robin. Geez, Kate, you don't go together at all."

"Oh, and I'm supposed to take dating advice from *you*? Trudy's like the tenth woman I've seen you with."

"You know you're exaggerating. And we're talking about you. Robin's like a lipstick lesbian."

"And? So?"

"So? Who's going to fix stuff?"

"Fix stuff? What the hell are you talking about?"

"If the toilet leaks or if the door hangs or any number of things. Who's going to fix them?"

Kate stared. "We live in an apartment. We have a maintenance man."

Lee shook her head. "She's just not for you. Like I said earlier, she's too femme."

"Oh, so now you're playing the butch-femme card. And your little Trudy girl fits perfectly into your vision of the ideal lesbian couple," Kate said, her voice rising. "Well, for your information, I think that's a load of crap!" She pointed her finger at Lee. "There's no way in hell that you can possibly have any sort of a relationship with someone who is young enough to be your daughter!"

"She's twenty-two!"

"She looks sixteen!"

"And what business is it of yours?"

"Exactly my point! Stay out of my business, I'll stay out of yours."

"Like I care who you sleep with."

"You must," Kate muttered. "You're critiquing her."

Kate walked away, only to be pulled back around by a hand on her arm. Kate's breath caught as their eyes held. It was only then she realized they were both breathing hard. She swallowed, watching Lee, watching her hazel eyes turn dark.

When Lee moved closer, Kate was powerless. She stood there, her eyes still locked with Lee's as Lee's arms pulled her. The few feet that separated them disappeared quickly. Kate didn't resist—couldn't resist—when Lee moved closer. Her mouth opened, meeting Lee's seeking lips without hesitation. She felt herself melting, heard herself moaning as Lee deepened the kiss. It was only when she felt her hand slide up Lee's arm, when she felt her body try to mold itself to Lee as Lee cupped her hips, did she come to her senses.

She finally pulled away, her eyes wide.

"I can't *believe* you did that," she hissed, her fingers touching her lips where only seconds before Lee's mouth had been. "Robin is just in the next room!"

Lee shook her head, but she didn't know what to say. She had no idea what had possessed her to kiss Kate.

Kate shoved the ice cream at Lee, pointing to the door. "Out!"

"I thought you quit smoking, darling."

Kate turned in the darkness, watching as Brenda walked quietly along the deck. The cigarette burned and Kate watched the smoke as it drifted above them.

"I have. I did," she said quietly.

"Where's Robin?"

"Sleeping."

"Are you okay?"

Was she okay? No, not really. Robin had wanted to make love. Kate couldn't think of a reason not to. And as Robin touched her, as Robin's mouth suckled her breast, all Kate could think of was Lee. All she could think of was Lee's kiss. And as Kate climaxed, it was Lee she felt, not Robin. And no doubt, at this very moment, Lee was in bed with a young woman named Trudy.

"No, not really," she said as she took a drag on her cigarette.

"Want to talk?"

"I just feel out of sorts is all," she said.

"Tell me if it's none of my business, darling, but is it Lee?"

Kate turned quickly. "Why would you think that?"

"Your voices were raised in the kitchen." At Kate's horrified look, Brenda shook her head. "We couldn't hear what you were saying. But when you came out, you both looked so . . . well, very strange." She took the cigarette from Kate, stomping it out with her foot. "You had an argument, obviously. Is there anything I can do?"

Kate smiled. "Lee and I seem to have a volatile relationship. That's not anything to worry about."

Brenda studied her, noting that her eyes wouldn't quite meet her own. Perhaps Sunshine was right. Perhaps there was something between the two of them after all.

Lee sat alone on her deck, watching the moon as it hovered overhead. She'd dropped Trudy off with barely a good-bye. She was still in shock.

You kissed her.

"She kissed me back," she said out loud to the big sky spread out over her.

In fact, Lee would swear she'd heard Kate moan. But hell, who would know? Lee's heart had been pounding so hard, she could hardly hear a thing. *You've lost your mind, that's all there is to it. You actually kissed her.*

She shook her head. "And Robin, God, they are *so* wrong for each other." *They're probably in bed right now, touching, making love.*

She held her head in her hands. "No. No, no, no. Do not go there."

But the fact remained. She kissed her.

And now there would likely be hell to pay.

CHAPTER TWENTY

"Darling, are you going to miss dinner again this week?"

Kate looked up from her laptop. "What time is it?"

"After six. There's still time, if you want to go."

Kate hesitated. Lee would be there, no doubt. And Lee would be there with a date. But she'd avoided her all last week. She couldn't very well hide out indefinitely.

"Okay. Let me grab a shower." She closed up her laptop, swinging her legs off the chaise lounge.

"If you don't mind my asking, how far along are you?"

Kate grinned. "Chapter twenty-one. And no, they've not had sex."

"Good God, woman, what are you waiting for?"

"I'm waiting for the right moment. They haven't really talked about it, you know. I mean, Jordan knows that Jennifer is *looking* at her. And Jennifer knows that she's about to explode any time Jordan comes close. But, they've not talked."

"Sometimes action is better than talking anyway."

"Well, it would all be wonderful if I knew how to write a romance. So, I'm kinda making this up as I go."

"Maybe you should let me read it, darling. I mean, surely you need *someone* to read it first."

"You can only read it if you pretend to be a housewife from the Midwest."

"Oh, pooh. I'll pretend to be a housewife. But I refuse to be from the Midwest."

"Fine. Maybe tomorrow I'll let you read it."

"You look troubled, Ariel." Sunshine placed a crystal into Lee's palm. "Squeeze tight. Feel the energy."

Lee did as she was told. What could it hurt?

"You wish to talk?"

Lee shook her head. "I'm fine."

"No, you're not. You are fighting the Fates, Ariel. I warned you not to."

"What are you talking about?"

Sunshine looked past her to the young woman sitting on the sofa alone. "Who have you brought this time, Ariel?"

Lee followed her gaze. "That's Missy."

"And you found her where?"

Lee grinned. "She's staying at the lodge. You remember Trudy? She's a friend of hers."

"It's futile."

"Oh, I don't know. She seems willing."

Sunshine reached out, placing her palm on Lee's chest, above her left breast. "Your heart already knows, Ariel. Yet you fight it still."

Lee stared. "What are you talking about?"

Sunshine lowered her voice. "You know who I speak of, Ariel. She fights it as well."

❧

Kate's eyes widened as Brenda slipped a white envelope into Lee's Jeep.

"What are you doing?"

"Payment."

Kate raised her eyebrows. "For?"

"Wine, darling. She's refused to accept money from me. I'm hoping she'll take this. It's a gift certificate."

"Why won't she take money?"

"I'm not sure. I think she feels almost burdened by this recipe she has."

"Why won't she just share it so everyone can make their own?"

"It's secret, darling. She's bound by a promise. Sunshine says a Pueblo chief gave her the recipe."

"Well, as much as you all drink of it, I think everyone should pay her."

"I agree, although Lee can be stubborn."

Brenda knocked once on the door, then entered. Kate was again drawn to the atmosphere that Sunshine and Harmony had created. Tonight, music from the Beatles drifted through the speakers.

"Oh, wonderful," Brenda said. "Harmony says they have the entire collection of Beatles records."

Kate nodded, but her eyes had already found Lee. She was sitting on the sofa, smiling at a young girl whose arms were wrapped around her shoulders.

"My God, must it always be someone new?" Kate murmured.

Brenda laughed. "I don't have to ask who you're talking about. Lee's Lee, darling."

"That she is."

Lee looked up, feeling her presence and hating the fact that she did. But Kate had already slid her eyes away. Lee turned to Missy, the girl's arms still wrapped around her. She slowly untangled them.

"You want something to drink?"

139

"Just a Coke. Or water. I'm not really a drinker."

Lee nodded. "I'll bring you a Coke. Be right back."

Lee felt the urge to talk to Kate, to apologize, if nothing else. Whatever had transpired, Lee had initiated it. She'd hoped to talk to Kate last week, but Kate hadn't joined Brenda for their weekly dinner, and Lee couldn't work up the nerve to go to their house. But Kate was here now.

As soon as she walked into the kitchen, she found herself face to face with her. They both stopped, staring.

Then Kate moved out of the way, intending to sidestep Lee.

"We should talk," Lee murmured.

Kate stared. "Why?"

Lee lowered her head. "I should apologize."

Kate smiled, patting Lee's stomach as she walked past. "Accepted."

Lee whipped around. "What? That's it?"

Kate shrugged. "Is there more?"

Lee grabbed her arm, pulling her into the hallway. "Of course there's more. You kissed me too."

"I most certainly did not."

Lee's eyes widened. "What? You deny it?"

"Why on earth would I kiss you?"

"Well, I don't know. Why on earth would *I* kiss *you*?"

"Look, it doesn't matter. And obviously you've moved past it. Who is it tonight? Barbie?"

Lee blushed. "Missy," she said quietly.

"Missy. How cute." Kate turned to move away but Lee grabbed her arm again, stopping her.

"I take it Robin enjoyed her stay here?"

Kate shrugged. "I suppose. Brenda took her shopping down in Santa Fe. I assume that was the highlight of her trip."

Lee shook her head. "She's not right for you. What do you have in common?"

"Don't start that again, please. Before you start criticizing my love life, perhaps you should look at your own."

Their eyes met, both searching.

"You can't possibly be in love with her. I watched you. You don't look at her like you're in love with her. I never once saw you touch."

Kate bristled. "If touching is a requirement, then you must be in love with half of the children staying at the lodge."

"No. And just because I may bring a date to these functions, doesn't mean that I'm sleeping with them."

"Oh, please, you really don't expect me to believe that?"

Lee smiled slightly. "What? Are you jealous of them?"

"Right. I'm as jealous of them as you are of Robin."

Their eyes met and held. Kate swallowed nervously at the look in Lee's eyes. The hazel eyes darkened, just like they had before. *I swear, if she tries to kiss me* . . .

"Are you two arguing again?" Brenda walked between them, smiling. "I've never known two friends to go at it as much as you. Lovers, yes, but not friends." She linked arms with them both. "Now, Lee, how about you introduce us to that pretty young girl you have."

Lee and Kate exchanged glances, both wondering what Brenda might have interrupted.

CHAPTER TWENTY-ONE

Kate paced, watching as Brenda's eyes were glued to the laptop. She didn't like anyone reading her work until it was finished, but she knew this time she'd have to make an exception. And who better than Brenda. But still, for the past two hours, she'd been pacing as Brenda read.

"Well?"

Brenda sighed. "Darling, I'm not going to comment every time I turn a page." She waved her away. "Now, go do something. I can't even enjoy it with you breathing down my neck."

But Kate didn't want to do anything. Whenever she wasn't working on Jennifer's love life, she was worried about her own. And whenever she was alone, Lee inevitably crept into her mind. She wanted to get past the kiss. She wanted to be able to see Lee as her friend—they were friends—without having to explain and justify what happened that night. Because, truthfully, it was all a blur.

What wasn't a blur was Robin. That night was probably the

best sex they'd ever had. The only problem was, it wasn't Robin who brought her to orgasm.

And she had to do something about it. She felt a need to confess to Robin, to tell her that she had a nearly uncontrollable attraction to Lee. She knew what kind of person Lee was, she knew how many lovers she had. But it didn't matter. Her body still reacted to Lee like it hadn't to any other woman before. And yes, she found that she was jealous of all the young women Lee paraded around.

And she also knew, if they were alone, if Lee should try to kiss her, Kate would not protest.

That's what scared her the most. She was powerless.

"I just think you need more sex."

"It's not a sex book. It's not even a romance. It's a murder mystery."

"Readers have been waiting through six books for Jennifer to fall in love. Finally, she does. And I, as a reader, want to know about it."

Kate blushed. "I can't write sex."

"Oh, darling, I don't mean details. We straight women aren't going to want details. But you've hardly given us *anything*! They kiss, then wake up in bed together? Please! Give us a little *something*!"

Kate shook her head. "I don't know *how*. I told you, I'm just not good at writing this romance stuff. I think the whole thing is silly, anyway."

"Silly?"

"Yes, silly. It's all just made-up crap. Things like that don't happen in real life. Romance is so . . . so artificial."

Brenda frowned. "Artificial?"

Kate paced. "Fake. Made-up. A pretense."

"Kate, darling, what are you talking about?"

Kate met her eyes. "You were right. There was no romance with Robin. In fact, I have a hard time recalling the first time we kissed, the first time we slept together. It just happened. It was just another step." She turned and leaned on the railing of the deck, staring out toward the cliffs. "There were no fireworks. There was never an *ache* to be with her."

"Yet, what? You're together, you live together, you have a life together."

"Exactly. Like Jennifer was with Paul. There were no fireworks. She was just there. That I could write. But now, now she's met Jordan. She's *attracted* to Jordan. She *feels* things when she's around Jordan. Things she doesn't quite know what to do with." Kate turned. "Things *I* don't know what to do with. How am I supposed to write this, Brenda?"

"Are you asking for Jennifer? Or are you asking for yourself?" she asked gently.

Kate held her eyes for a second longer, then looked away. "I curse myself, Brenda. I told myself she didn't affect me. I told myself I didn't really even like her." She shook her head. "But I'm no different than any other living, breathing woman. If she asked, I couldn't say no."

Brenda stood and moved closer, wrapping one arm around Kate.

"Lee has a way about her that is hard to resist."

Kate shook her head. "It shouldn't even be an issue. I mean, technically, I'm involved with someone. And you know my rules, Brenda."

"I won't get into your relationship with Robin. You know my feelings on that. But, has Lee done something, darling? I mean, has she . . . *tried* something?"

"No." She smiled. "Actually, we were becoming friends. But something changed." Kate moved away, pacing again. "You remember the night she took me to the cliffs, the coyote sky?"

"Yes."

Kate met her eyes. "It was . . . it was *romantic*. We danced."

"Danced where?"

144

"Up there," Kate said, looking toward the cliffs. "She said the coyotes were singing."

Brenda smiled. "And then?"

"Then nothing. It was like we both realized what we were doing at the same time. We pulled apart. Started talking. I told her that Robin was coming. Then, after that, everything changed. She wanted to come back down. And then she just disappeared. When I saw her again, it was at the party here. And all we did was argue."

"In the kitchen. Yes, I remember."

"She kissed me."

"*What?* Oh, my, darling."

Kate met her eyes. "I kissed her back."

"I see."

"But I freaked. I mean, Robin was there. Robin is my *girl-friend.*"

"And so the next time you saw each other, at Harmony's, you did nothing but bicker."

"Right."

Brenda smiled, then laughed. "I finally see it, darling."

"See what?"

"The correlation between you and Jennifer. This Jordan woman you've created. She's a little bit on the naughty side, she has a little bit of a past. She could be dangerous. Yet Jennifer is *attracted* to that. Just as you are attracted to Lee."

Kate grabbed the bridge of her nose, rubbing lightly. "I don't *want* to be attracted to Lee. I'm in a relationship."

Brenda smiled. "No, you're in a pickle, darling."

"You're not being much help."

"Well, I thought I was trying to help with Jennifer's relation-ship. I had no idea we had to deal with you as well."

CHAPTER TWENTY-TWO

Kate sat quietly on Brenda's rock, watching as the sun faded behind the cliffs. Her laptop lay unopened on her chaise lounge. She'd tried four times to write the love scene between Jennifer and Jordan. And four times she'd deleted it without daring to let Brenda see it. Each time, it either turned out cold, calculated, clinical. There was no flow, no emotion.

And there must be emotion.

After the fourth try, it dawned on her that she was writing her own story.

How depressing is that? "Very," she said out loud.

But she refused to think about Lee. She refused to think about their dance and how her heart pounded. And she certainly refused to think about the stolen kiss in the kitchen.

Lee had been conspicuously absent. Or perhaps it was Kate who was absent. She'd not attended the last two dinners. She'd stayed home. She was writing. And she dutifully called Robin three times a week. And none of that changed the fact that she couldn't get Lee out of her mind.

"Am I interrupting?"

Kate jumped, nearly falling from the rock. Lee stood at the edge of the deck, watching her.

"You scared the crap out of me," she said.

Lee shrugged. "Sorry." Then she nervously shoved her hands in her pockets. She cleared her throat, then looked at Kate, the evening shadows making it hard to read her eyes. "It's a coyote sky tonight. Come with me to the cliffs."

As their eyes held, Kate slowly shook her head. "I don't . . . I don't think so."

"Please?"

"Lee, no."

Lee walked closer. "Why not?" she asked quietly.

"You know why."

Lee shook her head. "No." She held out her hand. "Come on, Kate. We'll talk."

Kate knew she shouldn't go. She *knew* it. But the truth was, she *wanted* to go. She'd missed Lee. She'd missed being around her.

"Please come with me."

She held Lee's eyes in the shadows, conscious of her heart that pounded just a little too fast.

They were both quiet as Lee drove them higher. The blood-red moon was just beginning to turn, the colors fading as it drifted higher in the sky. But it wasn't the moon that Lee came to see.

She'd skipped Harmony's dinner two weeks ago because she was afraid to be around Kate. She was afraid she'd do something stupid again. But when she found out that Kate hadn't gone either, she felt foolish. So, last week, she showed up, alone, hoping to get a chance to talk to Kate. But again Kate didn't show. Brenda said she'd been working.

Now, three weeks since they'd seen each other, Lee thought

they could talk. She would apologize again. Hopefully, they could go back to the way they were—friends.

But damn, all it took was one look and she forgot all about apologizing, she forgot all about being friends. She didn't know what it was, she couldn't even begin to explain it, but she was *insanely* attracted to Kate. The fact that she thought about her constantly should have been a clue. The only thing that made her feel slightly better was that she knew Kate was fighting her own attraction. That one, brief kiss they'd shared was intense enough to tell her that. Kate denied it, but Lee distinctly remembered Kate's mouth opening, remembered the tiny moan Kate had tried to hide. And she remembered the way Kate's hips had pressed hard against her own.

"I'd forgotten how red it got," Kate said when they parked. It was the first words spoken between them.

"Yeah. But we're a little later than last time. The colors are starting to fade."

Kate jumped as the howl of a coyote startled her. "And I'd forgotten how close they sound up here."

Lee hadn't thought to bring the blanket, so they leaned against the Jeep, watching the colorful glow of the cliffs as the moonlight bounced off them.

Again, a chorus of howls surrounded them. Kate inched closer, her eyes darting back and forth, trying to see into the darkness.

"It's okay. They're not that close. And even if they were, they would never attack or anything. They're more scared of us than we are of them."

Kate smiled. "Speak for yourself." She sighed as she stared at the moon. "It's so beautiful. I wish you'd reminded me to bring my camera."

"Sorry. I wasn't thinking of that. I was too shocked that you'd agreed to come up here with me."

Kate turned. "We both know I shouldn't have, Lee."

"Do we?"

Kate met her eyes. "Don't we?"

"I . . . I kinda missed you," Lee said quietly. Then she smiled. "No one to argue with."

Kate closed her eyes. "I missed you being around too," she admitted.

"So, you're not still mad at me?"

Kate leaned back against the Jeep. "Was I mad? I don't remember." Mad wasn't really the right word. She'd been upset, sure. But she no longer knew if she was upset because Lee kissed her or upset because she'd responded to her.

"And Robin, everything's okay with you guys?"

Kate shook her head. "I don't want to talk about Robin tonight," she said quietly.

Lee nodded. "Okay."

They were quiet, watching the moon reflecting off the cliff, listening to the occasional howl of the coyotes. It was nice. It was . . . companionable.

Then a sharp, high-pitched scream right behind them brought Kate nearly into Lee's arms.

"Holy shit! What the hell was that?"

"Mountain lion," Lee said calmly.

"Mountain lion?"

"He was pretty close. He's probably in the trees over there across the road."

"Should we leave?"

"No. He'll take off when he gets our scent."

Kate looked nervously over her shoulder, too afraid to move away from Lee. But standing there next to her, feeling her warmth on this cool summer evening, she was too afraid to stay where she was.

"Listen," Lee whispered near her ear.

Kate stilled, her shoulder still pressed against Lee. Then the chorus began, first down below in the canyons, then all around them. The coyotes were singing.

"I swear, it's as pretty as any symphony," Lee murmured.

Kate nodded silently, her heart drumming to life at Lee's nearness. She should move, she knew. She was too close, Lee was too close. And if she didn't move soon, she would do something stupid.

"Kate," Lee whispered.

Kate was aware of the rise and fall of her chest as she tried to catch her breath, tried to breathe normally.

"Kate . . ."

She knew it was a mistake the second she turned toward the voice. Their eyes met in the moonlight. Lee's normal hazel eyes were dark, hinting at desire . . . and Kate was afraid of what Lee saw in her own. Lee moved, standing in front of her, blocking her view of the cliffs. She had no choice but to look at Lee. Involuntarily, her hands came out, resting on Lee's forearms. *Just to keep her away, nothing more.*

"Don't," Kate whispered.

Lee stood there, her glance dropping to Kate's mouth, then back again to meet her eyes.

Kate shook her head, aware that she was pulling Lee closer to her. "Don't you dare kiss me," she murmured.

"How can I not?"

Kate let her arms slide around Lee's shoulders, her eyes closing. "Don't," she whispered again as her mouth opened to Lee.

Lee's kiss was soft, light upon her lips. Kate couldn't contain the quiet moan that escaped. She pulled Lee closer, her mouth opening, her tongue slowly, deliberately battling with Lee's. She knew she should stop, she knew she should pull away . . . but she couldn't. Her heart had never pounded like this from a woman's kiss. Her body had never melted before, just from the closeness of a woman. And she was certain her mouth had never been so thoroughly kissed before.

But still, the kisses she could have controlled. She could stop and walk away at any moment, she was certain. Her mistake was moving closer, her mistake was parting her thighs, letting Lee's strong leg move between them. A flood of wetness soaked her jeans and she realized she'd lost the battle. *Had she even been fighting?* She moaned, feeling Lee's hand shyly stroke her breast. She leaned her head back, loving the feel of Lee's lips as they moved across her neck to the hollow of her throat.

Without thinking, without even knowing what she was doing, she took Lee's hand from her breast, sliding it between their bodies. She groaned as she pressed Lee's fingers against her aching clit. She heard Lee's answering moan as Lee felt her wetness through her jeans.

Lee pulled back, her eyes searching Kate's. She shook her head, intending to pull away, but Kate held her hand tight against her.

"Yes," she whispered.

Lee closed her eyes, fighting with herself, knowing she should stop, knowing she should pull away. Tomorrow, Kate would be angry. Tomorrow, Kate most likely wouldn't even speak to her. But tonight, right now, Kate wanted her. And as Lee's fingers felt the wetness that soaked Kate's jeans, all she could think about was being inside her.

Without another thought, expert hands unbuttoned jeans and slid the zipper down in one motion. Her mouth captured Kate's again as her hand slipped inside her jeans. There, against the Jeep, with the coyotes singing around them, Lee's fingers glided easily into her wetness. Kate's thighs parted farther, her tongue pushing into Lee's mouth the instant Lee's fingers slid inside her.

Kate's eyes slammed shut as Lee entered her. She threw her head back, her mouth falling open as her hips rocked with Lee. Delirious, nearly overcome with pleasure, she had no coherent thoughts as she held on to Lee. Then Lee's fingers slipped out of her, moving instead to her swollen clit. She stroked her, her fingers moving with lightning quickness. Panting, not caring that she was moaning loudly with each stroke, she felt her orgasm build. As the coyotes howled louder, Kate's mouth opened, her nearly primal scream mixing with the sounds of the coyotes as she came. She clutched Lee, spasms shaking her body, her legs threatening to give way. Never in her life had she screamed out like that. Never in her life had she climaxed so easily.

And never in her life had she felt so incredibly cheap. Standing there against the Jeep, her jeans pushed down to her thighs, the smell of sex ripe in the air.

Oh my God. What have you done?

A lone tear fell down her cheek and she wiped it away, embarrassed. Hurriedly, she pulled up her jeans, turning away from Lee as she righted her clothes.

"Cheap," she whispered. "Just a cheap fuck. Just like all the others."

"Oh, God. No, Kate. No. It's not like that, I swear," Lee said. She grabbed Kate's arm, trying to turn her around but Kate wouldn't look at her.

Kate jerked her arm away, shaking her head. "Please don't. Just take me back. Please."

"Kate, no. This wasn't just my doing and you know it."

"Please, Lee. Just take me back. I can't talk about it now."

Silence smothered the trip down from the upper cliffs. Once at Brenda's, Kate jumped out before Lee had barely stopped. She fled into the house without a word. Lee sat there for a moment longer, then quietly backed up and pulled away. There was nothing else she could do.

CHAPTER TWENTY-THREE

The hot shower did little to wash away her guilt. In fact, her body was still tingling. She washed herself, her hand moving between her legs, everything still sensitive from Lee's touch.

Lee's touch.

She put one hand on the shower wall to steady herself. She couldn't believe what had happened, what she allowed to happen.

"She's right," she whispered. "It wasn't just her doing."

It was mostly your doing.

In fact, Lee had wanted to stop. And for a moment, Kate had been terrified that Lee *would* stop.

And now, she was just one more in a very long line. *Cheap.* She never would have thought she'd stoop so low. Attracted to her, yes. But that didn't mean it had to lead to sex.

But Kate couldn't stop. She just couldn't. Lee gave her an out, she knew. But she didn't take it. She'd practically begged Lee to touch her. And she had. *God, had she.*

Kate turned off the hot water, forcing herself to stand in the cold blast, hoping it would erase what had just happened.

It didn't.

"Kate, darling, are you okay?" Brenda called from outside the door.

Kate turned the water off and stepped out of the shower, looking at the closed door.

"I'm fine."

"I was worried when I got home and you weren't here."

Kate bit her lip. "I . . . I was with Lee," she finally said.

"Oh?"

"She took me up to the cliffs."

"Oh, full moon again." Then Brenda laughed. "Bet it was romantic," she called as she walked away.

Kate grabbed the towel and covered her face, thankful she'd locked the bathroom door. No doubt Brenda would already be inside, asking a hundred questions. Questions Kate was not prepared to answer.

Lee sat in the dark, the hammock nearly motionless. Occasionally she'd shake the ice in her glass, the sangria long gone.

"Incredible," she murmured.

It was a word she'd said over and over since she'd dropped Kate off. Incredible that they'd even kissed. Incredible that she'd touched Kate, been inside Kate. Brought Kate to orgasm. Absolutely incredible.

A mistake. A huge *incredible* mistake.

But it wasn't necessarily *her* mistake. No, Kate could try to blame her, and no doubt she would. But, hell, the fire between them was so strong, Lee knew she had to stop. She tried to pull away. Kate, Kate was the one. Kate took her hand, she put it . . . put it *there*, for God's sake. What was she supposed to do? Tell Kate no? Tell her she didn't want to touch her?

"Incredible."

God, Kate was so amazing. So . . . so responsive, so *ready* for her. It would have been easier to stop breathing than to not go inside her. And no woman had ever screamed out like that from her touch. Never.

Lee sat up quickly, her heart pounding. She stood, paced, glanced up at the moon.

"This is all your fault," she said to the moon. *Another coyote sky. Had to take her up there, didn't you?*

And now what? Was Kate pissed? Was she hurt? Was she blaming herself or Lee?

"And there was nothing cheap about it," Lee whispered. *And God, I wanted her to touch me too.*

Kate lay in bed, staring at the phone as it rang. It was Robin. Kate leaned her head back, her heart heavy with guilt as she answered.

"Hi, honey," she managed.

"I thought it was about to go to voice mail," Robin said. "Am I interrupting your writing?"

"No, no. Actually, I'm . . . I'm reading," she lied.

"You never take the time to read. What's wrong with you?"

"Nothing," she said, her voice sharper than she intended. "Just a book Brenda gave me, about the local history."

"Oh. Sounds terribly exciting," Robin said sarcastically.

"I know you didn't enjoy it here when you visited, Robin. But I do."

"And for the life of me, I don't know why. There's nothing to do there, Kate. I'd go stark raving mad being there as long as you've been."

Kate sighed. "I didn't come up here to be entertained. I came up here to write."

"Oh, I know, honey. That's one reason I'm calling. Do you know when you'll be coming back?"

"I haven't really thought about it. Why?"

"Well, I've been invited to a weekend spa. It's in mid-September. I won't go if you think you'll be back, of course."

Kate frowned. "What kind of spa?"

"Oh, where they pamper you to death for two days. One of the girls from work is going. She invited me."

Kate nodded. "Where is it?"

"Hot Springs."

"Arkansas?"

Robin laughed. "Of course Arkansas. Do you know another Hot Springs?"

Kate rubbed her eyes. Robin had no money. That was one reason she'd moved in with her in the first place. How in the world could she afford a weekend at a spa in Hot Springs? But, it was none of her business, she told herself. After what she'd done tonight, *nothing* was her business.

"Sounds like fun. You go ahead. I doubt I'll be back by then. And if I am, you still go. I won't mind."

"Wonderful! It'll be so much fun. Massages, manicures, pedicures, saunas, the works. Can you imagine how relaxing that'll be?"

"I'm sure it will be."

"Well, I better run. I'm having dinner with some friends."

"Good. I'm glad you're not staying in alone."

"No. It's been fine."

"Good. Well, have fun."

" 'Bye, Kate."

" 'Bye," Kate murmured, but the line had already gone dead. *Strange.* In fact, it was like they were just two friends. And not very good ones.

She was surprised when, a short time later, Brenda knocked on her door. She came inside, carrying two cups of hot tea.

"You're trying to hide from me, darling," Brenda said as she handed Kate a cup. "I don't think I like it."

"I'm not hiding. I'm just . . . well, hiding," she finally said.

Brenda crawled onto the bed with her, crossing her moccasin-clad feet on top of the comforter. She fluffed the pillows behind her back, then took her tea.

"Comfortable?" Kate asked dryly.

"Yes. Now spill it, darling."

"Spill what?"

"Start where you want. End with why you're in bed this early without so much as a word to me."

Kate rested her cup on her stomach, too embarrassed to tell Brenda what had happened. How in the world could she possibly tell *anyone* what had happened?

"Oh, darling, do I have to drag it out of you?"

Kate shook her head. "I can't. It's . . ."

"It's Lee, no doubt," Brenda said. "Did she kiss you again?"

"Oh, Brenda, please don't make me tell you."

"Katie, you're hiding in this bed for a reason. And knowing you, it's because you're overcome with guilt."

Kate groaned, turning her head away.

"So, I'll take that as a yes. Now tell me what happened. Did you make out or something?"

Kate closed her eyes. "Or something," she murmured.

"Oh my God! You *slept* with her?"

Kate shook her head. "I wouldn't really call it that. Not really."

"What does that mean?"

"I can't tell you. Please, I just can't. Like in the book, where you don't want details, like that."

Brenda sipped her tea, her eyes on Kate. "So, you were intimate in some way?"

Kate nodded.

"And now you feel guilty?"

"Extremely."

"And Lee?"

"What about Lee?"

"How does she feel?"

Kate shrugged. "I don't know. We didn't talk. I made her bring me back here."

Brenda patted her hand. "You think Lee is just playing with you, darling? As if you're one of her young pickups?"

"Yes. That's all it is. Because I guarantee you, at the next dinner party, she'll have yet another young *pickup* with her."

"Perhaps."

"Perhaps? *Perhaps?* That's all you've got for me?"

Brenda smiled. "Darling, I didn't come in here to offer you words of advice. I just wanted to know what was going on."

"Well, you're a lot of help."

CHAPTER TWENTY-FOUR

Kate walked quietly up the steps, wondering why she'd allowed Brenda to talk her into coming. She wasn't ready to face Lee, she really wasn't. And if Lee had a date here, Kate wasn't sure she could handle it.

"Will you quit fidgeting," Brenda said again.

"I shouldn't have come."

"You have to face her sooner or later, darling," Brenda said reasonably.

"I'm thinking later."

Brenda grabbed her arm and squeezed. "I think it's been good for you. I saw you writing away like crazy today." She lowered her voice. "Perhaps you now know a thing or two about romance, darling."

"You're evil, Brenda. *Evil*."

Brenda laughed. "Oh, lighten up, will you? So you were naughty? It's not the end of the world."

"I'm involved with someone! I have rules!"

"Oh, pooh."

"Pooh? What is pooh?"

"Pooh is pooh," Brenda said. She knocked once, then opened the door. Tonight, the Mamas and Papas were California dreaming and they both smiled. "I would love to see their music collection. Can you imagine, darling?"

But Kate didn't answer, the smile fading from her face. Her eyes were drawn across the room. Lee was standing next to the sofa, talking quietly with a . . . *God*, a teenager. Kate shook her head, feeling sick to her stomach. No, she shouldn't have come.

"Come, darling. We'll get some wine."

"No, I don't feel like wine."

Brenda pulled her away. "Before you jump to conclusions—"

"She's a teenager!" Kate hissed. "Has she lost her mind?"

"As I was saying," Brenda started, then stopped, motioning with her head. "Why, Lee, so good to see you again."

"Good evening, ladies."

Lee was there before Kate could move away, but she refused to look at her. She stood mutely, her eyes drifting back toward the teen.

"I was about to get us some wine," Brenda said.

"I'll get it," Kate said quickly.

"No, no, darling. I'll get it. I'll be right back."

Kate glared at her as she walked away, then finally looked at Lee.

"I think you need help," Kate finally said. "Seriously."

Lee tilted her head. "Help?"

Kate nodded. "Psychiatric help."

Lee laughed. "Why?"

"You've gone too far," Kate said.

"Are you talking about me and you?"

"No!" Kate hissed. "I'm talking about her," she said, pointing behind Lee. "She can't be a day over fifteen. I can't *believe* you!"

Lee turned. "Gwen?"

"Oh my God, she's got a normal name. That's a first."

"Kate, before you go off, let me explain," Lee said.

"It is really none of my business. God forbid you should go a few days without," she murmured sarcastically as she turned away. But Lee grabbed her arm, pulling her back around.

"Gwen is the daughter of Meredith. They live in the valley. Meredith joins us once a month or so for dinner. Gwen is fourteen. Whenever Meredith travels—she's a home nurse—we all kinda take turns looking after Gwen. I thought she might enjoy a night out. Sunshine has been teaching her to paint, much like Harmony helps Brenda," Lee explained matter-of-factly.

Kate colored slightly, embarrassed for having assumed the young girl was Lee's date.

"Well, I'm shocked then, that you've managed to come without a date." Kate turned to walk away again, and again, Lee grabbed her arm and pulled her back around.

"Aren't we going to talk about it, Kate?"

"What is there to talk about? I'm just another name you can add to your long list of . . . of conquests."

"I know you don't believe that."

"And why not? You're obviously good at seduction, God knows you've had years of practice."

"Seduction?" Lee leaned closer. "If you think for one minute I don't remember you taking my hand and placing it between your thighs, you are sadly mistaken." She moved closer still, her eyes locked with Kate's. "And as much as you wanted me to touch you—and I know you did—I wanted you to touch me more," she whispered. "I was dying for you to touch me."

Lee walked away, leaving Kate standing there, her pulse racing at Lee's words. She looked around, hoping no one heard, no one saw. When Brenda came back, Kate took the wine, nearly downing the glass with one gulp. She felt Lee's eyes on her, but she didn't dare look her way.

"What did I miss? You look all shook up, darling."

"Yes. Lee does that to me."

161

"So, I guess she told you that Gwen wasn't her date. I told you not to jump to conclusions."

"Oh, Brenda, what am I going to do?"

"What are you talking about, darling?"

"Lee. I can't stop thinking about it, about her. I can't get it out of my mind."

"It?"

Kate flicked her eyes at Brenda. "You know what I mean."

"Why don't you just talk to her about it?"

"I can't talk to her. I can't even be around her. I *shouldn't* be around her. I just need to get over it, forget it ever happened. And when I return to Dallas, maybe things will get back to normal."

"Normal? You mean with Robin?"

Kate shook her head. "I don't know what I'm going to do with Robin. I'll have to tell her what happened, of course."

"Why on earth would you have to tell her?"

"Because it was wrong, is wrong. And I know you don't understand, but I feel guilty as hell. I mean, what if she did something like that?"

"How do you know she's not, darling?"

Kate sighed. "I know, and that's not really even the point. The point is Lee. I mean, if this was someone else, someone who didn't date a different woman every week, someone a little safer, then maybe, you know, I could see what happens, where it might go. But Brenda, this is *Lee*."

"First of all, I wish I'd never told you about Lee's dating habits. And secondly, it's not someone safe you're attracted to. It's Lee."

Kate glanced across the room, finding Lee sitting alone on the sofa. She was staring at the floor, looking at nothing. Kate wondered what she was thinking, wondered if, by chance, Lee might also have a hard time forgetting that night.

CHAPTER TWENTY-FIVE

It had been nearly two weeks since the dinner party, two weeks since Kate had laid eyes on Lee. She'd stopped expecting her to come by. And she'd also declined Brenda's invitation to the weekly dinner parties. Apparently, Lee had been skipping them as well.

But Kate was over it, she told herself. The book was cruising. She'd made it past the sex scene—Brenda loved it—and was nearly three-quarters of the way through. Her mind was clear and the words just flowed. She spent the better part of each day perched on the chaise lounge, writing hour after hour. She felt good about this book. Despite her reservations as to how it would be received, she was happy with it. And at this point, that was all she could hope for.

Unfortunately, she hadn't settled on the ending. Do Jennifer and Jordan live happily ever after? Does Jennifer discover that she's gay, but decides that Jordan is not the one for her? Kate was leaning that way. She wouldn't have to continue with this romance nonsense that way, yet she could still let Jennifer out of the closet.

And perhaps later, in another book, provided there was another book, she could allow Jennifer to meet someone else. Someone a little safer than Jordan.

Yes, the book was coming along. It was barely August. Surely she could have a good first draft by her deadline. By October. Just a couple of months away. She looked out at the cliffs, a sight that was so familiar to her now. She would miss it terribly when she left. Occasionally, she missed the things a city could offer, like going out to dinner, or having a pizza delivered, or going to the movies. But she didn't miss the constant noise, the constant *hum* of the city. She'd gotten used to the quiet. And with the quiet came sounds she'd overlooked before. The gentle call of birds as they flitted about the piñon pines. The high-pitched whistle of the broad-tailed hummingbirds that fed at the flowers surrounding the deck. And the occasional scream of a golden eagle as it soared over the canyon. Sounds that had become expected as she worked. Sounds that mingled with smells. The smell of the piñon pines, the fragrance of the flowers when the wind blew, the smell of . . . home. She felt at home here. And she would hate to leave.

But as she sat there now, she smelled something out of place, something foreign. She frowned.

"Smoke?"

She got up, walking to the edge of the deck, looking out over the cliffs, but the sky was clear, only a few, puffy clouds scattered about, as it had been all summer. They'd not had a drop of rain—which Brenda said wasn't unusual. But still, it didn't feel overly dry, overly hot. Not like Dallas felt after a month or more without rain.

But the smoke worried her. Surely no one was burning brush. She had been to town enough to know that there was a burn ban in effect. There had been one all summer.

She stepped off the deck, taking the worn trail she and Brenda used to get to the upper canyon walls. But still, the sky was clear. She shrugged. Maybe she was imagining things.

When she walked back, Brenda was home, still unloading groceries from the car. Kate hurried to help.

"For such a pampered woman, you sure can grocery shop," Kate said.

Brenda laughed. "I tell Sophia what we want to eat, she tells me what to buy. And actually, I find I enjoy grocery shopping, darling. It's just the cooking part I loathe."

"You and me both."

"Yes, I know. If it were left up to you and me, we'd be grilling out every night."

Kate raised her eyebrows. "Speaking of grilling, I thought I smelled smoke earlier. Did you notice anything?"

"Oh, yes, darling. I nearly forgot. I heard about it while I was in town." She handed Kate a bag. "Ice cream. Put that up for me, would you."

"We eat entirely too much ice cream," Kate said.

"Shall we do steaks tonight?"

"Absolutely. But what about the smoke?"

"Oh, yes. There's a forest fire, they say. Started over in the campgrounds in the San Pedro Peaks area. Such a shame, beautiful forests over there, they tell me. I was hoping Lee might take you there."

"Is it close? Should we worry?"

"No, it's on the other side of the river. We should be fine. But the ranchers, I'm sure they're scrambling. Lee left yesterday, they said, so it apparently started then."

"What do you mean Lee left?"

"Well, she's helping out."

"With the fire?" Kate paced. "Doesn't the forest service have firefighters?"

"Of course, darling. But she went to help the Shrikers move their cattle." Brenda shook her head. "They told me at the bakery that a lot of the other ranchers sent men over to help. They go up on horseback, practically to the fire's edge, looking for cattle."

"But why would there be cattle out there? Isn't that national forest?"

"I don't know all the specifics, darling, but I know the local ranchers lease the land for grazing."

"But I don't see why Lee had to go."

Brenda took her hands. "She's the county sheriff, darling. She can't sit idly by during a crisis, now can she?"

"No, of course not." Kate smiled. "And knowing Lee, she probably took along a date."

"Oh, darling, don't be silly."

Kate walked out to the deck, looking at the sky, wondering where Lee was. Wondering if she was safe. And wondering why she even cared.

"Skip, we're getting too close," Lee said. She pulled the bandana higher over her nose, trying to keep out the smoke. She stopped her horse. The only movements they'd seen were elk and deer as they fled the fire. No cattle.

"There's supposed to be close to fifty head up here."

"If you were a cow and there was a fire coming, wouldn't you head down the mountain?"

Their horses danced, nervous from the smoke. Lee didn't blame them.

"Cows aren't real smart."

"Yeah, well we're not being real smart either, man."

They heard a crash as a tree fell, and they both turned in their saddles, just in time to see the fire top the ridge.

"Son of a bitch!" Lee turned her horse. "Come on, Skip. Let's get the hell out of here!"

They rode fast through the forest, escaping the fire and smoke. When they crossed a stream, they both stopped short when they saw a small herd of cattle huddled near the water.

"They yours?" Lee asked.

"Most likely." Skip stood in his saddle, silently counting. "Forty-four. Could be the herd we're looking for."

Lee pulled the bandana off her face and wiped at the sweat on her brow. She took a long swallow of water, then spit, tasting nothing but smoke.

"They're used to horses, Lee. Just take it nice and slow. We'll head them down to the valley. Shouldn't take but an hour or so."

Lee looked over her shoulder. "We may not have time for nice and slow."

The smell of smoke was constant now and Kate could barely concentrate. She glanced at her laptop, seeing only the few sentences she'd managed to churn out. It had been two days, and they still hadn't heard anything from Lee. Brief updates about the fire were broadcast on TV but the local radio station had more information. The fire had apparently jumped a ridge and was heading toward a lush valley. Kate didn't have a clue about the area but Brenda knew of the valley. It was where the Shriker's ranch was. Fortunately, Lee's cabin sat on property across the river, Brenda told her.

"No one's heard a word, darling," Brenda said, waving her phone. "But Sunshine says not to worry, the Fates are watching over her."

Kate rolled her eyes.

"I know, darling, but I told you, Sunshine is a seer." Brenda handed Kate a glass of tea, then pulled her own lounge chair closer. "And she says Lee is fine."

"Lee's got a phone. Why do you think she hasn't called someone?"

"Maybe there's been no time. Maybe there's no service."

Kate hated the fact that she was worried and she tried very hard not to be. Lee was plenty capable of taking care of herself. And it wasn't like she was actually out there fighting the fire. But still, Kate wondered why Lee hadn't bothered to call. Surely she knew they would all be concerned about her. Or maybe she just assumed that they weren't, or at least Kate wasn't. It wasn't like they'd seen much of each other in the last month.

CHAPTER TWENTY-SIX

They all stood on the porch of the Shriker's huge ranch house, staring out at the thick smoke that blanketed the valley. With large tractors, they had plowed up the grass, making a firebreak. Then Lee and the others hauled load after load of water, soaking the ground, hoping to stop the fire's eastward trek. The forest service had the southern end contained. The northern edge was fifty percent contained, which was good. Unfortunately, the southeasterly winds that had been blowing for the last several days were making it difficult to contain the eastern edge of the fire. And the Shriker's ranch house and barns were in its direct path.

They had already moved all the livestock across the river to the normal winter pastures. The trucks were standing by, waiting to be loaded with furniture and clothes, should the fire jump their plowed break. Mrs. Shriker was inside, packing up family treasures, just in case.

"We'll have maybe two hours if it jumps," Skip said. "Not much more."

"It's not going to jump, son," Mr. Shriker said. "We hauled half the lake out there. Even if it does jump, the valley is soaked."

Skip shook his head. "It's a hot fire. Don't be so sure."

The smoke was so thick, they could barely see the flames. Occasionally, they could make out one of the firefighters as he sprayed fire retardant along the break. A crew of nine firefighters was dropped off yesterday morning after the plows had finished. Then helicopters airlifted in basket after basket of water from the lake, hoping to stall the fire. Lee had helped haul the hoses from the local volunteer fire department truck. They had sprayed down both sides of the break, working nearly fifteen hours straight.

She was certain she'd never been more tired in her life. Her energy level was zapped and she was quite amused with herself as she occasionally fingered the small crystal Sunshine had given her several weeks ago. Just for energy, she told herself.

One of the ranch hands came running out of the smoke and they all waited, anxious to hear the news.

"The fire's reached the break," he yelled. "They think it might hold."

Lee sat at the crossroads, her glance going right, toward home . . . then left, toward Kate. She was far too tired to see the irony of it all. And she was far too tired to care. So she did what she did without caring about the consequences. She turned left.

The late afternoon sun was hazy, the smoke-filled sky blocking out the rays. Lee had been too preoccupied the last week to notice, but no doubt the sunsets had been fabulous because of the smoke.

But she wasn't here to watch the sunset. She just wanted to see Kate, if only for a minute.

Brenda's car was gone when she pulled into the driveway and she sat for a moment in her Jeep, wondering if she should just leave. Then she saw lights on inside. Kate must be home. She opened the door, nearly falling out. Taking a deep breath, she walked as steadily as she could to the deck. The side patio door, where she normally entered, stood opened. Through it, she saw Kate standing on the deck, leaning against the railing, staring out to the cliffs. Lee stopped, her eyes locked on Kate, surprised at the instant pounding of her heart.

"Jesus," she murmured.

Kate turned, hearing footsteps. Her eyes widened when she saw Lee.

"Oh my God," she whispered. She walked quickly to her, grasping both her forearms, surprised when Lee stumbled. "You look like hell."

"I feel like hell," Lee said. "I'm sure I smell like hell."

Kate nodded. "That you do." Kate led her into the kitchen and pulled out a barstool. "Sit. I can't believe you didn't call anyone. We were worried." She lifted Lee's arm, her brow creased as she rubbed with her thumb. She thought it was dirt, but it was dried blood. She pushed Lee's sleeve higher, her eyes widened. "What happened?"

Lee shrugged. "I don't remember. I think it was when that tree fell."

"A tree fell? Were you that close to the fire?"

"It's okay. It's just a scratch."

"Have you even cleaned it? It'll be a miracle if it's not infected. It's filthy," Kate fussed. She wet a cloth with warm water, intending to clean the wound.

"I'm pretty sure Sharon cleaned it."

Kate rubbed gently on her arm, shaking her head. "I should have known," she murmured.

"Known what?"

"That a woman was with you."

Lee laughed. "Sharon is Shriker's wife. Skip's mother," she explained.

Their eyes met. "Oh. Sorry. I just assumed."

Lee winced as Kate cleaned her arm. At Kate's raised eyebrows, Lee shrugged. "Hurts."

"Well, I can't believe you don't even have a bandage on it. It's like three inches long. You probably need stitches."

"No, it's not that bad. I just need to doctor it up a bit." Lee studied Kate's face, wondering at the frown there. "So, you were worried about me?"

Their eyes met again. "I was as worried about you as I'd be any friend," she said. "Harmony, for instance."

"Oh, yeah?" Lee stilled Kate's hand, making her look at her. "Now I know that's not true."

"What do you mean?"

"Harmony's not . . . touched you, not been inside you."

Kate tried to pull her hand away, but Lee held her. "Don't Lee." Their eyes held. "Please don't."

"Don't what? Don't touch you? Don't kiss you? Don't *want* you?"

Kate closed her eyes, wishing Lee's words didn't affect her. She shook her head. "No, no, no. We can't do this," she whispered.

"Why not?"

"Why? Because I'm involved with someone. I'm seeing someone," she said. "And you're seeing like . . . like a *hundred* someones."

Lee's fingers slipped from Kate's arm. "Wow. You sure know how to hit below the belt," she said quietly.

"I'm sorry."

"No. You have nothing to be sorry for." Lee shrugged. "It's the truth. I just never thought I'd regret how I've lived my life." She stood up, intending to leave, but Kate stopped her.

"What are you doing?"

"I've got to get out of here. I'm sorry if I bothered you."

"No, you're not going anywhere. You're about to fall down, Lee." Kate took her arm. "When's the last time you've slept?"

Lee shook her head. "I'm not sure. What day is this, anyway?"

Kate smiled. "Come on. You need a shower. Then I'll put something on this cut." She led Lee out. "Then you're going to bed."

"I don't want to be any trouble, Kate. I can just go on home."

"Don't argue with me, Lee." She opened her bathroom door. "Dump your clothes on the floor. I'll throw them in the wash."

Lee laughed. "I don't think they're salvageable."

"I have a pair of sweatpants. Will that be okay?"

"Thanks. You don't have to do this, you know."

Kate smiled. "Strip."

"I thought you'd never ask."

Kate closed the door on Lee's laughter.

"Kate?" Brenda hurried into the house, letting her art bag fall to the floor. "Lee?"

Kate nodded. "She's asleep."

Brenda raised her eyebrows. "Oh? In your bed?"

Kate smiled. "Yes, in my bed. I couldn't let her drive. She was about to fall asleep walking."

"So I take it she's okay?" Brenda asked.

"Cuts and bruises, but, yeah, she's okay."

"Thank goodness, darling." Brenda picked up her art bag again. "Harmony was just saying if we didn't hear from her soon, we'd all trek over to the Shriker's place to check on her."

Kate closed her laptop—she'd not even written a sentence since Lee showed up. In fact, she'd made three trips down the hall to check on her. And Lee hadn't moved. She was curled on her side, her injured arm—which Kate had doctored and wrapped—lay stretched out beside her. She had literally passed out as soon as Kate pulled the covers over her, after mumbling something about Kate sleeping nude.

"The smoke is all but gone," Kate said. "Do you feel like steaks?"

Brenda laughed. "Do we have a choice, darling?"

"Not really, no."

"Maybe we need to have Sophia cook two meals for us each week instead of just the one."

"Maybe we need to learn to cook," Kate said. She stood, stretching. "It can't be that hard."

"And maybe we should just stick to grilling out, darling. For

172

some reason, I can't picture us whipping together a meal in the kitchen."

"You're right. I'd rather open a can of soup."

Brenda laughed. "Which is what you did in Dallas, if I recall."

"No, in Dallas I called in a pizza a couple of nights a week."

Brenda opened the freezer, sorting through the steaks. "Should we do three, darling?"

Kate frowned. "You mean for Lee?"

"Yes."

"Oh, I doubt she'll be up. She's dead to the world."

"Well, you never eat all of yours anyway. Should she wake, I'm sure you can share."

"That's fine. But she hasn't moved a muscle since she lay down," Kate said.

Brenda turned. "And you know this how?"

Kate blushed, then made a production of washing the potatoes. "I may have checked on her," she finally said.

"A time or two?"

"Don't read anything into it."

"Of course not, darling. I mean, this is Lee, after all."

Kate turned around. "What is that supposed to mean?"

"Nothing. It's just Lee. And we know you are immune to Lee because she is so *bad* for you. And then, you know, there's Robin. You should of course ignore this little attraction you have for Lee, because *Robin* is in the wings. We don't want to do anything to upset that."

Kate pointed her finger at Brenda. "This reverse psychology is not going to work. Lee is Lee."

"Yes, darling. Lee is Lee. And why do you suppose she came here first? I mean, obviously she's exhausted. Why not just go home and crash? But no, she came here. To you."

Kate shook her head. "Don't start. It means nothing."

"Oh, darling, of course it does. You're just too stubborn to see it."

CHAPTER TWENTY-SEVEN

Jennifer walked confidently into Paul's office and closed the door, waiting until he finished his call before approaching his desk.

"Good morning, sweetheart," he greeted. "What a surprise. We haven't seen you in the office in three days."

She simply nodded. If she didn't get it out soon, she would lose her courage. So, she lifted her head, meeting Paul's eyes.

"Paul, I'm in love," she blurted out.

His eyes widened. He pointed at his chest. "With me?"

She shook her head. "No." She was surprised to see relief in his eyes. "I've met someone."

He smiled. "Well, that's . . . that's wonderful. Of course now, we'll have to pretend to get divorced!"

"Paul, you don't understand. I met a . . . a woman. I'm in love with a woman."

A look of disbelief crossed his face and he sat down, his fingers nerv-

ously twisting his wedding ring. "A woman? But Jennifer, you're not gay."

"I guess I must be."

"Who? Surely not that detective woman you've been going on about."

She blushed. "Yes. Jordan."

"No, no, no," Kate murmured. "That sucks. Where's the emotion? You're in love! Don't be apologetic about it."

"Talking to yourself again, darling?"

Kate jumped, startled to find Brenda watching her. "I thought you were off painting?"

"That was three hours ago. Have you been working this whole time?"

Kate glanced at her watch, surprised at the lateness of the hour. "Yes. I've been working on this scene with Paul. I just can't get it right. I've written it four times."

"Why does she have to make an announcement to him anyway?"

"Because they're partners, Brenda. They're supposed to be married. She just can't start dating without telling him. Especially a woman."

"What if he suspects she's seeing someone, but he had no clue it's a woman. I mean, he's a private investigator. What would he do?"

"I don't understand."

"He would investigate. He follows her one evening. He sees them together. Perhaps he sees them kiss. Then, the next day, he confronts Jennifer. That way, you don't have to have her confessing as if she's committed a crime."

"Would I rather have her confessing? Or do I want her to have to defend her relationship when he confronts her?" Kate shrugged. "Either way, they're not very positive. She has to be defensive in both."

"I still think it's wrong to have her confess, darling. Maybe she wants to make sure that she's okay with her decision before she tells him. But then he brings it up. She doesn't have to be defensive about it. After all, she's in love with Jordan. That's all that really matters at this point."

"But Paul is one of the main characters. She can't be on the outs with him if I hope to ever write another book about them."

"Paul is one of the characters, but Jennifer has always been the main character. She's the reason middle-aged housewives read it. Not because of Paul, darling."

Kate sighed. "I'm just not good with all this *emotional* crap. Give me some murders to solve and I'm happy."

Brenda smiled. "I think maybe someday you *will* be good at this emotional crap, darling."

"Let's don't go there again, Brenda. It's a waste of time to even discuss it."

"The least you could do is come to dinner tonight. Visit with her. You've skipped the last two weeks. She assumes you hate her."

"If I hated her, I would not have played nurse when she came from the fire. I would not have insisted she sleep for twelve hours to recover. And I certainly would not have made her breakfast." Kate laughed. "Well, attempted to make breakfast."

Brenda laughed too. "Oh, that was priceless. The world's largest pancake, right here in our kitchen!" Brenda leaned closer. "But really, darling. Come with me tonight."

"Honestly, Brenda, it . . . it bothers me to see her with her little playthings. It just reminds me of what I did—what we did—and that I'm just one among many."

"I haven't seen her with a date in two months. In fact, even in early summer when she was bringing dates, I heard she took them straight back to the lodge after dinner." Brenda cleared her throat. "In fact, Sunshine says the dates were just a cover."

"A cover?"

"She didn't want to be there alone. She might seem vulnerable."

Kate laughed. "I think Sunshine's full of crap. I would never use the word vulnerable to describe Lee Foxx."

Brenda took her hand. "Come on, darling. What would it hurt for you to go?"

Kate took a deep breath, then let it out slowly. She would never admit this to Brenda, but she missed Lee. Missed her a lot. So, she nodded. "Okay. I'll go."

"Wonderful, darling."

CHAPTER TWENTY-EIGHT

"Kate, so good to see you again." Sunshine drew them inside, immediately pulling Kate into a dark corner of the living room. "Simone, why don't you get Kate a glass of sangria."

"Of course, darling."

Kate watched Brenda walk away, then nervously looked at Sunshine. Of the three of them, she hated to admit that Harmony had turned out to be the most normal. Sunshine was too mysterious, too *deep* for Kate's liking. And of course, Starlight was just beyond odd. But it was Sunshine who had her hands gripped now, her blue eyes appearing as cold as ice.

"You have a heavy heart," Sunshine said quietly. "So does she."

Kate frowned. "Who?"

There was only a slight smile from Sunshine. "The Fates can be very stubborn. When they have a plan, it is always carried out, no matter how much of a fight we put up."

Kate smiled. "I'm sorry, but I don't have a clue as to what you're talking about."

"Yes, destiny is a frightful thing, isn't it? Especially when we feel like we have no control."

Kate stiffened. "I happen to believe we are all in complete control of our destinies. Decisions and choices we make along our journey shape our destiny, not some silly mythology that the *Fates* are in control."

Sunshine's eyes widened, as if Kate had just spoken blasphemy. She quickly placed a crystal into her palm. "Squeeze tight. You shall need it, I fear. The Fates don't like to be challenged." They both looked up as Brenda approached. Then Sunshine lowered her voice. "The jade Harmony gave you. You need to keep it with you. It will protect you."

Kate stared. "Protect me from what?"

"Here you go, darling." Brenda handed Kate a glass of wine, then looked from Kate to Sunshine as they stared at each other. Then Sunshine turned without another word, leaving them with only a slight nod of her head.

"What in the world, darling?"

Kate slowly shook her head. "I have no clue. They get stranger every time I see them."

"Well, come inside. You can't hide here in the corner all night," Brenda said as she pulled Kate into the living room.

As always, the lights were low, the music just loud enough to be heard. Kate scanned the room, surprised that only four other women were there, two of whom were Sunshine and Harmony.

"Where's Lee," she asked quietly.

Brenda shook her head. "She's not here. Harmony's not seen her all week."

Great. Stuck in the loony bin all alone. She glanced at Brenda. Well, it wasn't really fair to lump Brenda in with them.

"Brenda, it just occurred to me. You're straight."

Brenda laughed. "Yes, darling. Had you forgotten?"

Kate shook her head. "I mean, you're straight. Yet you've been with lesbians all summer. You *hang* with these people." Kate lowered her voice. "Do *they* know you're straight?"

Brenda tilted her head. "Come to think of it, I don't believe anyone's ever asked, darling."

"Doesn't that bother you?"

"Why on earth should that bother me? We're all just people. I find this group positively fascinating, darling." She moved closer. "And if I were a writer, I'd be taking notes. Can you imagine the stories you could tell? I mean, Starlight alone could fill a small book."

"Yes. And I'm not entirely convinced she's real," Kate whispered.

Brenda laughed. "Oh, darling, of course she's real."

They both turned when the door opened. Lee walked in, pausing at the opened door. Kate met her eyes, then slid them to the door, waiting for Lee's date to appear. None did. Lee shut the door behind her, a hesitant smile on her face as she walked over.

"Ladies," she greeted, but her eyes were on Kate. "How are you?"

Kate nodded. "Fine." Then she glanced at Lee's arm. "All healed?"

Lee lifted up her short sleeve, showing off her upper arm. Just a tiny scab remained. "Thank you, doctor. I survived."

"Wine, Lee? I hear they have the best sangria," Brenda teased.

"Thanks. I'll have just a small glass, if you don't mind."

When Brenda moved away, Kate turned to her. "Are you ever going to tell me why you supply these women with sangria?"

"It's my job."

"Your job?" Kate frowned. "Comes with being sheriff?"

Lee laughed. "Not that job. It's a long story. Goes back to my first summer here. I got lost in the backcountry and was rescued by a Pueblo chief. I stayed two weeks with him."

Kate raised her eyebrows, waiting.

"I stayed with him until he died," Lee said quietly.

"I don't understand."

"It's a long story," Lee said again. She moved closer. "Maybe I'll tell you one day."

Kate took a nervous step back. "Well, I'm glad you're all recovered from the fire. I thought you were going to sleep two days straight."

Lee lifted an eyebrow. "By the way, did I properly thank you for your bed?"

"I believe you did," Kate nodded.

"The pillow smelled like you," Lee said quietly. "And I couldn't help but wonder, when you're in that same bed, do you sleep naked?"

Kate caught her breath the instant Lee caught her eyes.

And as their eyes held, Kate felt the familiar tug of this woman. Nervously, she tucked the blond hair behind her ears, wishing she could move, wishing she could pull her eyes away. But Lee held her and as ridiculous as it sounded, time actually did stand still. The sounds from the dinner party muted, the lights dimmed even more, the music faded away. It was just the two of them, just the pounding of their hearts and heat of their eyes.

Kate swallowed. She slowly shook her head.

"Don't you dare," she whispered quietly.

"No." Lee swallowed too. "But I really, really want to kiss you."

Kate closed her eyes. *You can't want this woman like you do. You just can't.* When she opened them again, Lee had taken a step away. The party came back, then Brenda was there, handing Lee a glass of her own wine.

"Lee, why have you been such a stranger?" Brenda asked. "We hardly see you anymore."

Lee looked at Kate and again their eyes collided. "I've just been really busy."

"Well, you need to come over for steaks one night, darling. I know Kate's missed visiting with you."

Kate rolled her eyes as Lee laughed.

"She has, huh? Well, maybe I can come by some night."

"That would be lovely, darling. And of course, if you desire, you may bring a date."

Again, Lee looked at Kate.

"Or not, of course," Brenda said lightly as she witnessed the look between them.

Kate forced a smile to her face. "No little Barbie with you tonight?"

Lee laughed. "Would you believe me if I said I couldn't find a soul who wanted to come with me tonight?"

"No."

"No? You think all I have to do is ask, they automatically say yes?"

"Don't they?"

Lee gave her a lazy smile. "You don't, Kate."

Kate cleared her throat, then glanced at Brenda. "I'm not exactly single," she said.

"Not exactly, no."

Kate bristled. "What does that mean?"

"I think I'll leave you two alone," Brenda said. "I swear, you can't go two minutes without bickering," she murmured as she walked away.

As soon as Brenda was out of earshot, Kate turned back to Lee. "Look, what happened that night, was just a . . . an aberration. I don't do that, Lee. For God's sake, I'm living with someone," she hissed.

"Someone who is completely wrong for you and you know it," Lee shot back.

Kate sighed. "Are we going to start all that again?" Kate shook her head. "And it doesn't matter, anyway. Lee, I'm too old to be one of your groupies. And I so wish that night had never happened," she said quietly.

"But it did happen," Lee whispered. She took a step back. "And you know what? I wish it hadn't happened too. And I wish I wouldn't constantly think of how it felt to touch you."

She walked off, leaving Kate staring after her. Then, with just a brief word to Harmony, Lee closed the door behind her without so much as a look Kate's way.

☙

Lee drove aimlessly along the county road, considering going to the lodge to find Trudy or even Brandy but dismissing the thought quickly. It wasn't Trudy or Brandy she wanted. It wasn't some young, nameless tourist with flawless, tanned skin. And it wasn't a college-age river rat in a skimpy bikini who would take her top off to tease Lee.

It was Kate. A woman who braved a hike down, then up the canyon oasis just so she could frolic in the waterfall. *Naked* in the waterfall, Lee reminded herself. A woman who made Lee laugh without even trying. A woman who chastised her constantly about her choice of dates. A woman who nursed her when she was about to collapse from exhaustion after the fire. A woman whose eyes made Lee quiver, whose innocent touches made Lee's knees weak.

A woman who took her breath away.

"A woman who's in a relationship," Lee murmured.

What an idiot you are!

With the cool night air blowing the hair around Lee's face, she downshifted as she rounded a corner, then turned quickly on the gravel road, heading to the cliffs. She drove without thinking, speeding along the road at breakneck speed, trying to chase Kate from her mind.

But when she ended up at the cliffs, the crescent moon not bright enough to dull the twinkling stars, there was nothing on her mind *but* Kate.

She slammed the door, walking slowly to the table rock. She paused, listening to the faraway call of the coyotes. It wasn't a coyote sky tonight. They were all down near the river, no doubt.

Lee leaned against the rock, crossing her arms and tucking her hands against her side. The air was cool. The daytime temperatures were still warm and pleasant, but she was surprised that September was upon them already. The summer had flown by, and October was fast approaching.

Kate would be leaving in October.

Probably just as well, she thought. Her life had been completely disrupted and Kate was the cause. When she was gone, hopefully,

Lee's life would get back to normal. And normal meant if she saw a pretty girl on the river or in town, she was fair game. And if Lee chose to go out with her, *sleep* with her, then it was nobody's business but her own. There would be no one here to chastise her, no one here to look down on her, to pass her actions off as a childish attempt to regain—and maintain—her college exploits.

Lee tilted her head back and looked to the sky. Is that what she wanted? More young women parading through her life and her bed, whose names she couldn't remember the next day? No.

I want Kate.

The reality of it all hit her like a ton of bricks. Her eyes widened and she sat down heavily on the rock.

"Oh my God," she whispered.

But she shook her head. No. It couldn't be. She didn't *do* things like that. She didn't . . . she didn't fall in love. Not her. Not ever.

She rubbed lightly against her chest, above her breasts.

In love? Are you insane? What idiot goes and falls in love with a woman who doesn't want you? A woman who can't want you because she's involved with someone? Who does something stupid like that?

"Apparently this idiot," she murmured.

CHAPTER TWENTY-NINE

"Are you finished, darling?"

Kate shook her head, but continued to stare out toward the cliffs.

"Can I help?"

"I'm stuck," Kate said.

"Stuck on what? You told Paul about Jordan and he reacted like a typical man. I loved that scene, by the way," she said with a laugh. "And you said you caught the bad guy. What else is there?"

Kate shrugged. "I don't know how to end it. I don't know what's the *right* way."

"Well, darling, only you know what's right." Brenda pulled a chair closer. "What are our choices?"

Kate rested her head on the back of the chaise lounge, staring at the blue sky. "Well, Jenn and Jordan could continue to date, see where that goes. Or Jenn could end things with Jordan, because, you know, Jordan is not exactly a safe catch. Or, Jordan could end things with Jenn because Jordan likes playing the field. Or Jennifer could decide that yeah, she likes Jordan, but she wants to see what else is out there." Kate paused. "Or . . ." she said, her voice trialing off.

"Or what?"

Kate closed her eyes. "Or they live happily ever after."

"What's wrong with that?"

"That's how *all* romance books end. It's a load of crap! That rarely happens in real life."

"Well, darling, first of all, I thought you said this wasn't a romance book. And secondly, I think romance books are here to make us feel good. How depressing would it be if books ended, not when the romance is fresh and new, but years down the road, when things are old and they're breaking up? If that's what you think real life is about, darling, why in the world would people want to read about it too?"

"How do you want it to end, Brenda?"

Brenda laughed. "Well, as a Midwest housewife, I, of course, want Jennifer and Jordan to live happily ever after."

Kate nodded. "Okay, then speaking from the book side of it, you'd like to see Jordan in more books?"

"Well, darling, perhaps Jordan could replace the pansy-assed Paul."

"Do not call him that! He's been jilted. Have some sympathy," Kate said.

"I know you're not serious and I pray that you've not written it that way. Trust me, darling, few are going to be sympathetic toward Paul. They'll want him to move along and get a life."

Kate rubbed her face with both hands. "I think I've just killed this series, Brenda. The Masters. It's about Jennifer and Paul. They're the investigators, they run the show. I can't just ditch Paul now."

"Oh, pooh. The last two books have been all about Jennifer, and you know it. Unfortunately, it was all about Jennifer going nowhere, and Paul was still in the picture. This will be like a breath of fresh air, darling."

"I don't know why I'm listening to you anyway," Kate said with a laugh. "It's not like you're a real Midwest housewife."

They were both quiet, laying in their chaise lounges, enjoying the sunshine. September brought colder nights, but the days were still warm and sunny.

"Does it ever rain here?" Kate finally asked.

Brenda chuckled. "It rained in March and April some, I remember. Harmony says October is the rainiest month."

"And it snows in the winter?"

"Oh, yes. And speaking of that, Starlight showed me her paintings of the snow at nighttime. They are absolutely beautiful, darling. She's going to move them to Harmony's gallery soon for winter showing."

"When did you see them?"

"At the dinner party Tuesday night. She brought them over for Harmony to see."

Kate nodded. "You never said. Was Lee there?"

"Yes. She was there, darling."

Kate looked away. "Was she . . . was she alone?"

"No. She had a young woman with her."

"Figures."

"Now, darling . . ."

"I know, Lee is Lee."

"That's not what I was going to say. You're upset that Lee is dating, yet you have no right to be. It's not a secret that Lee fancies you," Brenda said with a dramatic wave of her hand.

"*Fancies* me?"

"And it's also no secret that you've rebuffed her advances because of Robin."

Kate sat up. "First of all, I'm not sure Lee knows *how* to fancy someone, as you say. And secondly, even if there was no Robin, I'd be crazy to get involved with Lee! She goes through women like most people . . . well, like people go through disposable hand towels!"

Brenda frowned. "What kind of an analogy is that?"

Kate cut her eyes. "You know what I mean."

187

Brenda waved her hand again. "Well, regardless, back to the issue of Lee's dating. As I was saying, you have no right to be jealous."

Kate stood, pointing at Brenda. "Jealous? *Jealous?* Is that what you think I am?" Kate paced along the deck. "Well, that's just silly. I'm certainly not jealous of these *teenagers* she chooses to spend time with. They probably can barely complete a sentence properly." Then she laughed sarcastically. "Oh, I almost forgot, Lee's not interested in that! She's only concerned with what goes on between the sheets!"

Brenda smiled sweetly. "Well, darling, I'm glad to see that you're not jealous. No, not in the least."

Kate stubbornly raised her chin. "Well, I'm not. I want nothing from Lee Foxx. I'm in a . . . a relationship with a . . . a wonderful woman."

Brenda rolled her eyes. "Oh, please, spare me."

CHAPTER THIRTY

"How exciting, darling! Our own gallery showing right here at their house."

"I'd have rather made the trip down to Santa Fe," Kate said, looking nervously at all the cars.

"If it's Lee you're worried about, don't be. I doubt she's going to show. It's a come and go party. And even if you did run into each other, would that be so bad?"

"I could care less if Lee's here."

"Right. That's why you haven't been to the last two Tuesday dinners."

"It had nothing to do with Lee. I was working."

"Of course, darling."

And of course Kate knew it had everything to do with Lee. She just couldn't bear to see her with a date. As much as Kate told herself that Lee was bad news, that Lee used women for playthings, she still could not get her out of her mind. She still could not forget that night up on the cliffs. All she had to do was close her eyes and she could see them together, she could recall exactly how it felt when Lee touched her, when Lee went inside her . . . and when she came.

She closed her eyes now and grabbed the railing for support. Despite everything, she still *wanted* Lee.

"Darling, are you okay?"

Kate nodded. "Yes." She let go of the railing and stood up straight, forcing a smile to her face. "Ready."

Small groups of women were milling about, most of them discussing Starlight's paintings. And most of them were strangers. Kate nudged Brenda.

"Do you see anyone you know?"

"No, darling. These women must have driven up from Santa Fe," she said quietly.

"But aren't these paintings going to be at the gallery next week?"

"Something neither of us knew, but apparently Starlight is quite the big name in the art world. I'm sure these people drove up so they could be the first to see her work." Then Brenda laughed. "Of course, they weren't at the last dinner party. *We* were actually the first to see them."

"Will she be here?"

"Doubtful. She rarely makes an appearance at these things, Harmony tells me. That's one allure to her paintings. Not very many people know what she looks like, who she is. It's all so mysterious."

"Come in, come in," Sunshine called to them. "I had no idea Harmony had invited so many from Santa Fe," she said quietly when she walked over. "I thought it would just be us locals getting a peek."

"How many pieces does she have?" Brenda asked.

"Eleven."

"Oh, my. She's been busy."

"Her energy flows, Simone," she said with arms spread. "I'm

sure it's her meditation. I think it will do wonders for you." Then she looked at Kate. "Have you tried it?"

Kate shook her head, but did manage a smile. "I'm not really into . . . chanting and all that." Before the words had barely left her mouth, Sunshine snatched up both her hands and squeezed them.

"You must be doing something. Your negative energy is nearly gone." Then she leaned closer, her whispered words for Kate's ears only. "It will be gone by morning for sure. Do not turn away the face of love."

As Kate's eyes widened, Sunshine placed a stone in her palm and closed Kate's fingers around it.

"The stone of Aphrodite."

Kate opened her palm, staring at the green stone. Was it another jade? No, it was too bright, too—*oh my God*. "An emerald?"

"The stone of love. Keep it close," Sunshine whispered.

"Sunshine, I can't accept this." She raised her eyebrows. "Unless . . . is it fake?"

Sunshine gasped and touched her chest. "No, it is not *fake*. It has great powers. You cannot fool the mind and body with simple placebos."

Kate shook her head, intending to return it, but Sunshine had closed her fist again.

"It is extremely bad manners to refuse a gift of a healing stone. The emerald has no value to me as jewelry."

Kate looked at Brenda, who just shrugged. Kate sighed and nodded. "Okay. Thank you."

"Do not forget the meaning."

Kate shook her head. "I won't."

Sunshine glided away and Kate held the stone out to Brenda. "It would be funny if they weren't so damn serious about it all."

"Oh, this is lovely, darling." Then Brenda grinned. "You'll know you've hit the jackpot when they place a diamond in your palm."

As soon as Lee opened the door, her eyes collided with Kate's. She saw a multitude of emotions cross her face in only a matter of seconds. Surprise at seeing Lee there, perhaps. Then her eyes softened in a smile and Lee felt her heart catch a bit. Then those eyes slid from Lee and Lee felt Trudy move beside her. When Kate's eyes met hers again, gone was the pleasure that had been there. It was replaced with a look of distaste, of anger, but not before Lee caught a glimpse of hurt—even sadness—in Kate's eyes.

Lee turned to Trudy. "Give me just a second. I'll be right back."

"Take your time. I spied a bottle of champagne. I'll be over there."

Lee walked away without commenting, her eyes focused on Kate.

"Why Lee, darling, we didn't expect you," Brenda said.

"Harmony insisted."

Brenda's glance alternated between the two women, then she politely excused herself.

"I think I'll . . . mingle," she said.

"How are you?" Lee asked quietly.

"Wonderful. You?"

Lee nodded. "Fine."

"Trudy, is it? It must be serious. She's the first woman I've seen you date more than once."

Lee smiled. "You know it's not serious, Kate. In fact, you know me, never serious about a woman." Then she shrugged. "But I needed a date and Trudy was willing."

"Why did you need a date?"

Their eyes met, held. Lee swallowed, her throat suddenly dry. "I needed a date for all the wrong reasons," she admitted.

"I don't understand."

Lee finally pulled her eyes away. "It's all rather silly and childish, if I actually allow myself to think about it." She shrugged. "You don't want me. So I guess I wanted to find someone who did."

"So, it's an ego thing, huh?" Kate took a step away. "I didn't realize you were so shallow, Lee. Of course, I guess I always realized that you couldn't go a single day without the company of a young woman."

Kate turned to go, but Lee grabbed her arm, stopping her.

"That's not true, Kate. You choose to believe something just because of your preconceived notions about me. Which, I admit, in the past were mostly true." She shook her head. "I haven't been with anyone all summer. I haven't been with anyone since . . . since around my birthday." She met Kate's eyes. "Since I met you," she said quietly.

Kate pulled out of Lee's grasp. "First of all, you can't seriously expect me to believe that. I've seen you with *numerous* women over the summer. And secondly, it has absolutely nothing to do with me and I shouldn't even care because—"

"Because you're *involved* with someone," Lee finished for her sarcastically. "But I know that you do care, Kate. You care because there's something between us. You care because you want me too. And you can't stand the thought of me with someone else."

Kate squared her shoulders, her eyes glaring as she looked at Lee. "In your dreams, Sheriff."

Kate turned on her heels, leaving Lee to stare after her.

"Wonderful," Lee murmured quietly. "You sure have a way with her."

"Give me the keys," Kate whispered to Brenda.

"What's wrong?"

Kate shook her head. "I just need to get out of here."

"Are you ill?"

"Of course I'm not ill! I just want . . . *need* to be alone."

"Okay, darling. What's Lee done this time?"

"Why do you always assume it's Lee?" Kate demanded.

Brenda handed her the keys. "Because Lee's the only one who can get you this upset."

Kate lowered her head. "I just need some time. Some alone time," she said quietly.

"I understand. I'll have someone run me home later, darling."

Lee sighed as Sunshine walked over to her. She wasn't in the mood for Sunshine.

"What words of wisdom do you have for me tonight, Sunny? Surely the Fates have told you something?"

Sunshine smiled. "You are angry, hurt, upset. So you use sarcasm. It's a good defense, Ariel, but it won't work."

Lee spread her arms out. "So enlighten me."

Sunshine's eyes turned serious. "Your journey nears its end, Ariel." She took one of Lee's hands and placed a stone there. "It's a jade. Its twin lies with her."

"Her?"

Sunshine shook her head. "Don't pretend you don't know of whom I speak."

"Kate?"

Sunshine nodded. "Go to her tonight. It's time."

Lee shook her head. "I can't go to her. She's involved with someone. She's got a girlfriend and she's made it perfectly clear that she doesn't want me." Lee shrugged. "Besides, I've got a date."

"I have only two things for you Ariel. First, you don't really have a date, do you? You've not been intimate with anyone all summer. In fact, you've not touched another woman all summer, except for that brief moment with Kate up on the cliffs."

Lee's eyes widened. "How . . . how do you know about that night?"

Sunshine smiled. "And two, Kate is involved with someone in name only. And though she won't admit it, Ariel, her heart is not in Dallas. Her heart lies with you." Sunshine squeezed her hand around the jade. "Go to her, Ariel. I shall make sure your friend there gets back to the lodge."

Over the years, Lee had learned not to take Sunshine's words lightly. Although, when the words were directed at her, she did little more than humor Sunshine. But for some reason, her words tonight were different. It was almost like she was *commanding* her to go to Kate. And despite the reservations in her head, she couldn't deny what was in her heart.

Go to Kate.

So she did.

CHAPTER THIRTY-ONE

Kate lay under the covers, her eyes wide open, Lee's words still echoing around in her brain.

"You want me too. And you can't stand the thought of me with someone else."

Surprisingly, it was true. Kate didn't want it to be true, but once Lee had said it out loud, Kate could hardly run from it. Yes, it bothered her that Lee dated. Yes, she was jealous of each and every one of them. Yes, there *was* something between them. And yes, she wanted her.

But still, Lee was Lee. She was a magnet for women and Kate was just one more. Her parade of dates was one thing, but even Harmony and Sunshine weren't immune. Kate had seen the looks, the stares. Hell, even Brenda wasn't immune. So to say there was something between them meant really nothing. The same could be said for countless other women who couldn't deny their attraction to Lee.

And again, Kate was just one more. Because she too could not deny her attraction to Lee. She could hardly stand to be in the same room with her without *wanting* her. That was one reason she hadn't been going to the dinner parties. She didn't want to see Lee with a date and she simply didn't want to *see* Lee.

She heard the car door slam and turned her head toward the opened window, wishing Brenda had given her more time. Not that she expected Brenda to barge into her room. She just wanted to be alone with her thoughts, her feelings.

She heard the side patio door open. That was odd. She leaned up on her elbows, listening. There was movement in the living room, movement in the hall. She saw a shadow in the dim light under her door, where it paused.

Oddly, she wasn't afraid.

The door opened slowly, the light in the hallway making a perfect silhouette. Her breath caught.

Lee pushed the bedroom door open, pausing only for a moment before walking inside. In the shadows, she saw Kate.

Without thinking, she unbuttoned her shirt, ripping the last few buttons in her haste to remove it. She tossed it on the floor, then reached for her jeans, sliding them down her thighs as she stood at Kate's bed.

"*Lee?*"

"There's nothing to talk about, Kate."

Kate stared, still leaning on her elbows. Her heart was pounding so loudly, she couldn't think, couldn't even speak as Lee stood there . . . naked . . . beside her bed. Without thought, she moved the covers aside, welcoming Lee.

"Lee?"

"No. No words, Kate," Lee whispered.

In one quick motion, she pulled the T-shirt off Kate and tossed it on the floor beside her jeans. Then, before Kate could object, her hands slid to Kate's waist, removing the last barrier between them.

Kate knew she should protest, she *knew* she should. But instead, her hands sought Lee, moving up her arms, pulling Lee into her bed. Their kisses were soft and slow—deliciously slow . . . but only for a moment. Then their passion ignited. Kate moaned, her mouth opening, her tongue battling Lee's. Without thought, she spread her legs, her hands on Lee's hips pulling her close.

Lee was too rapturous to think clearly . . . or coherently. All she knew was that Kate's hands were on her body, touching her, guiding her. She settled between Kate's thighs, her hips molding to Kate. She groaned as they touched, but wasn't certain if it was her or Kate she heard. She pulled back, trying to read Kate's eyes in the darkness.

"Kate?"

"I want you," Kate whispered. She didn't care about all the others, she didn't care about Robin, she didn't even care if it would just be this one time that they were together. She wanted her, *needed* her.

Kate could have no idea what those words did to her but Lee's heart nearly melted. She dipped her head, her mouth going to Kate's breasts, her tongue finding a nipple hard, erect. Her lips closed around it and she moaned when Kate's hands moved through her hair, holding her close.

"Oh, Lee," Kate murmured, her hips moving, trying desperately to touch Lee. She spread her legs farther, her hips undulating against Lee. "Please touch me."

The softly spoken words drifted to Lee's ears. She left Kate's breast, her mouth finding Kate's lips again. Her hand slid along Kate's body, pausing slightly at the soft curve of her hip.

"Yes," Kate whispered against Lee's lips.

Amazing what that whispered word did to Lee. Just like that night up on the cliffs, her heart tumbled inside her chest. She lifted up slightly, her hand finishing its journey as it slipped between Kate's thighs.

"Lee," she breathed, her arms pulling Lee closer, her mouth opening, taking Lee's tongue inside as her hips arched to meet Lee's hand. Her eyes slammed shut as Lee's fingers moved inside her.

"Kate, please, I just want to make love to you," Lee murmured. She dipped her head, again finding Kate's breast. But she paused there only briefly, her desire driving her lower. She pulled her fingers from Kate's wetness, her hands gripping Kate's hips as she pulled her close. "Please, Kate," she murmured again. The scent of Kate drifted around her and she was hungry to taste her.

Kate's head burrowed into the pillow, her hands guiding Lee, urging her between her legs. She felt Lee's breath on her damp thighs, felt Lee's hands spread her legs. She moaned, her hips bucking as Lee's mouth, her tongue, settled over her throbbing clit.

Oh God. It had been so long, Lee had almost forgotten the sensation, forgotten how it felt to make love to a woman this way. She had been so careful, so cautious over the years. But tonight, she didn't think about using protection, she didn't think about anything except having her mouth on Kate.

Kate's fists clutched the sheets, her mouth open as she struggled for breath. Lee's hands cupped her hips, holding her close as her tongue moved through her wetness. Kate gasped when Lee's tongue slid inside her, then whimpered as Lee pulled away, only to go back again, this time covering her, her lips sucking gently, then harder, pulling Kate into her mouth. Kate had no time to prepare, no time to try to stifle her scream. Her hips arched once as her orgasm claimed her and she held on, pressing Lee's mouth hard against her until her spasms subsided.

Oh God, oh God, oh God.

Her hands fell limply from Lee's head, her eyes still squeezed shut, her chest still heaving as she tried to catch her breath.

Lee too, lay with her eyes closed, her face resting on Kate's wet thighs. She finally released her grip on Kate's hips, but then felt Kate's fingers entwine with her own.

"Lee?"

Lee was too afraid to look up, too afraid of what she might find in Kate's eyes. She rolled her head, still nestled at Kate's thighs.

"Lee, please," Kate whispered, her hand moving to brush at Lee's hair.

Lee shook her head. "I'm sorry. I shouldn't have come here like this. I shouldn't have . . . ambushed you like I did."

"Shhh." Kate tugged on her hand. "Come here."

Lee looked up, letting herself be pulled to Kate. She met her eyes, but the shadows hid them. "Kate, I don't know what to say," Lee whispered so quietly, Kate barely heard the words. "I just *needed* you so much. I . . . I . . ." Lee buried her head against Kate, surprised—shocked—at the tears that were threatening. She shook her head, not knowing how to explain.

"Shhh," Kate murmured. She gathered Lee to her, gently kissing her forehead. "It's okay, sweetheart," she whispered. "I wanted you, Lee. I needed you too." She couldn't understand Lee's tears, couldn't even begin to until she felt Lee's hand caress her breast, felt Lee's lips brush her neck gently. She squeezed her eyes shut, her heart nearly exploding as Sunshine's words came back to haunt her.

Do not turn away the face of love.

And then she understood. Lee was crying because she'd just made love to Kate. It wasn't sex with a stranger. Lee made love to her. And Kate trembled as she realized she wanted . . . *needed* to do the same.

"Lee," she whispered. She forced Lee's head up, her fingers gently wiping at her damp cheeks. She leaned closer, her lips moving across her face, finding her mouth, softly kissing her. "I'm going to make love to you, Lee," she murmured against her lips. "I'm going to make love to you."

Tremors physically shook Lee's body. She felt them, she knew Kate could feel them too. But she couldn't stop her trembling as Kate pushed her down, as Kate's body covered hers, as Kate's mouth found her small breast.

Kate moaned as her tongue swirled around Lee's nipple, feeling it harden even more before her lips closed around it. Her hand found Lee's other breast, and she caressed it gently before moving her mouth there.

Oh, Kate. Lee's eyes closed as she savored the feel of Kate's hot mouth on her. She couldn't remember the last time someone had made love to her. College, maybe? No. Even then, it was just sex. Just an act. But God, Kate's hands were soft upon her skin, her mouth gentle at her breasts. Her breath caught as Kate spread her legs, her knees urging Lee's thighs apart.

"You're so soft, Lee," Kate whispered against her skin. "So strong, but so soft."

Lee moaned, waiting, as Kate ran both her hands along Lee's inner thighs, dangerously close, but not close enough. Lee's hips arched, silently begging Kate to touch her.

Kate bit her lip as her fingers moved to the edge of Lee's wetness. Then she straddled her, lowering herself again until her body pressed flush against Lee. Lee grabbed her hips, grinding against her, seeking release.

"Let me," Kate whispered. She slipped her hand between them, Lee's wetness enveloping her fingers. She moved inside her without another thought, her fingers sliding easily through her wetness. She bent her head, finding Lee's breast with her mouth, her fingers delving deep inside Lee.

But it wasn't enough, she wasn't close enough. She moved to Lee's mouth, kissing her hard, her tongue raking against Lee's before she pulled away. She used her knees again to spread Lee's thighs and she pulled her fingers from Lee as she grasped her hips.

"Kate, please," Lee whispered. "Don't stop."

"No. I've only just begun."

Kate knelt between Lee's legs, her hands opening Lee to her mouth. She moaned as she covered her, her tongue snaking out, finding Lee's swollen clit.

"*Kate,*" Lee hissed, her hips moving against Kate's mouth. *Oh Kate.* It was an act that only Lee performed. Lee hadn't had another woman's mouth on her in more years than she could count. Maybe that was why she came so suddenly, so hard, that she lifted them both off the bed as her hips arched, and she did something she never, ever did. She screamed out her pleasure.

With her eyes still closed, she pulled Kate up her body, gathering her into her arms, holding her close.

"God, Kate, you have no idea," she murmured, her lips moving softly against Kate's face. "So beautiful, so incredible. You have no idea."

Kate smiled against Lee's skin, inhaling her scent, snuggling closer to her warmth. "Yes, I do," she murmured just as quietly.

Lee rolled them over, settling her weight on top of Kate. She touched Kate's face softly, gently tucking her hair behind her ears. She kissed her lightly, moving her mouth to Kate's ear.

"Please, Kate, let me stay with you tonight." Her hand cupped Kate's breast, not understanding the need she had to be close to Kate. "I want to sleep with you, Kate. I want to wake up with you."

Kate pulled Lee's mouth back to her own. Yes, she wanted to wake up with Lee too. Only she wasn't quite ready to sleep.

CHAPTER THIRTY-TWO

Brenda stared at the phone, her eyes widening as she saw the name displayed. She glanced nervously down the hall to Kate's closed bedroom door, then looked back at the phone. Well, she couldn't very well let it ring.

"Good morning," she said cheerfully.

"Brenda? It's me. Robin."

"Why, Robin, what a surprise," she said, glancing again toward Kate's bedroom.

"I know it's early, but I took a chance Kate would still be in bed."

Brenda smiled wickedly. "Oh, yes, she's still in bed."

"Well, I wanted to surprise her, but I'm afraid I'm lost."

Brenda sat up, her eyes widening. "Lost? Where are you?"

"Well, I'm here. Somewhere."

Brenda stood quickly, pacing. "Here? As here, in Coyote?"

"It's Kate's birthday."

Brenda rubbed her eyes, nodding. Yes, she'd forgotten. "Well what a surprise that will be," she managed. She glanced again at Kate's door. "But where exactly are you?"

"Well, I must have missed your turn because I'm heading into town, it looks like." A pause, then, "Oh, yeah, now I recognize it. There's the bakery."

"Okay. Well, I can direct you back this way. But you know, Kate would probably love it if you picked up lunch, since you're right there at the bakery. Tell them it's for me. They'll know what to send."

"Sure. I'm starving, anyway. I could only get a late flight. I'd intended on driving up last night, but I knew I'd get lost for sure."

"Well, darling, it's a good thing you waited, then. And all you have to do is head back out of town the way you came. You'll come to a fork in the road. You'll want to go left. Stay on that road about five miles. Our road is to the right. There's a huge yucca behind the mailbox."

"Oh, I remember now. Kate pointed it out to me."

"Well, call me back if you get lost."

"I will. But don't tell Kate. I want it to be a surprise."

Brenda smiled. "Of course. I won't mention a word to her."

As soon as she disconnected, she hurried down the hall, pausing at Kate's door, listening. She knocked, rapping her knuckles on the door several times.

"Kate, darling. Are you awake?"

She knocked again, this time opening the door and peeking inside. The sight before her warmed her heart and she smiled broadly. "Oh, my sweet darlings," she whispered. Kate and Lee lay tangled together, the covers a twisted mess around them. Brenda hated to wake them, but she knew she must.

"Kate. Lee."

She walked closer, gently shaking Kate's shoulder. "Katie."

Kate stirred, her eyes opening slowly. "Hmmm?"

"Kate, darling, wake up."

"Brenda?" Kate rubbed her eyes, then sat up. "What time is it?"

"Oh, my," Brenda murmured. She pointed to Lee. The sheet had slipped to her waist.

Kate jerked the sheet up, covering them again. Her movements woke Lee, who rolled toward Kate, her contented sigh making Kate want to close her eyes again.

"You need to get up," Brenda said. "You both need to get up. Now."

"What is it?"

"Robin."

Kate sat up again. "*What?*"

"She's on her way."

"Here? *Now?*"

Brenda nodded. "Surprise. It's your birthday."

"Oh, good God, no. No, no, no."

"I'm afraid yes, yes, yes," Brenda said.

"It's your birthday?" Lee asked.

Kate shook her head. "It's the fifth."

"Saturday," Brenda said. "Tomorrow."

Kate buried her head in her hands, then felt Lee touch her, rubbing lightly on her bare back. She turned, meeting her eyes.

"I'm sorry."

Lee shrugged. "I understand."

"I'll, er, I'll be in the kitchen," Brenda said quickly, leaving them.

"This isn't how I envisioned us waking up," Kate admitted. She wasn't able to stop her hands from moving to Lee, from caressing her breasts. She wasn't at all shy, with the sun shining in around them. Her thumb raked across Lee's nipple, watching in fascination as it hardened.

"Kate, don't do this to me," Lee whispered.

Kate smiled sadly. "You're right. I'm sorry." She pulled her hands away. "It's just—"

Lee nodded. "I know." Lee cupped her cheek, meeting her eyes. "Not enough time. We should have talked last night."

Kate laughed. "Talking was the last thing on both our minds."

"Kate, last night, I know I nearly forced you. I barged into your room, I—"

"You made love to me," Kate whispered.

Lee nodded again. "And now your girlfriend is coming." She took a deep breath, then tossed the covers off, walking naked around the bed to her clothes. She jerked on her jeans, then looked around for her shirt.

"Lee." Kate pulled her own T-shirt back on, then stood before Lee, taking her hands. "I'm sorry. I don't know what to say. I wasn't expecting her."

"I know. It's just . . . I don't think I've ever been in this position before."

"The other woman?"

"No." Their eyes held. "Jealous. I don't think I've ever been jealous before."

"I'm sorry," Kate said again.

Lee shrugged. "She's your girlfriend." Lee turned to go, then stopped. She walked back to Kate, then quickly pulled her into her arms.

Kate didn't resist. As usual with Lee, she couldn't. Her mouth met Lee's, their kisses hurried . . . and not nearly enough. She watched Lee leave, watched her move quietly down the hall, heard her muted greeting to Brenda. Then the Jeep drove off, the sound fading, and still she stood there.

"Kate, darling, are you okay?"

She looked at Brenda, and again, a sad smile. "Just lovely."

"Well, as much as I want to hear all about it, don't you think we should change the sheets?"

Kate looked at the tangled mess of the bed and laughed. "I'd say." Then she ran both hands though her hair. "What am I going to do, Brenda?"

"Well, first, just so we don't have a major scene here in about ten minutes, you're going to shower. I'll change the sheets and make your room presentable."

"Presentable? I've just spent the entire night and most of the morning making love with another woman. How am *I* going to be presentable?"

"You're going to muddle through it like you always do, darling. Then you'll send Robin back to Dallas so that you can sort out this thing with Lee."

"Sort it out? What is there to sort out? So Lee and I slept together? That's hardly news around here where she's concerned."

Brenda took her hands, making Kate look at her. "I know you feel something for Lee, darling. You can try to lie to yourself, if you wish, but don't lie to me."

Kate shook her head. "No."

Brenda smiled. "Yes. All I have to do is look at you and know."

"I don't want to *feel* something for her. Lee is Lee."

"Yes. Lee is Lee. But I don't think you have a choice anymore, darling. Just as Lee has no choice. You've both been running from this for most of the summer. It's about time it finally caught up with you."

Kate just stared. She had nothing for a rebuttal. It was true, after all.

"But please, I do not wish for a scene, darling." She shoved her toward the bathroom. "Shower, please."

Lee drove without thinking, her hands clutched on the wheel. Twice she stopped, wanting to turn around, wanting to go back to Kate, to tell her . . . *to tell her what?* So they had a night together? They had been dancing around it all summer. It was bound to happen sooner or later. Sexual attraction. That's all. And now she could just move on to the next, just like always.

But no. Not this time. Lee hated to admit it, but it wasn't just like always. God, when Kate touched her, when Kate made love to her, when . . . when her mouth had claimed her, God, Lee thought she was going to pass out.

"I'm in love with her."

And, Jesus Christ, her girlfriend is coming.

CHAPTER THIRTY-THREE

"What a surprise!" Kate said with forced cheerfulness. She moved into Robin's hug but it was awkward and she felt herself stiffen. "You should have called first."

"Oh, it was spur of the moment, anyway," Robin said. "I thought perhaps you'd come back by now, and we could have a party in Dallas, but you hadn't mentioned a word of it." She spread her arms. "So, I thought I'd surprise you up here."

Kate and Brenda exchanged glances.

"Well, darling, we'll just have to have that party right here, then," Brenda said. "And honestly, if you hadn't shown up, I'd have forgotten completely about Kate's birthday. It's not like she's reminded me."

"I hadn't actually thought about it," Kate admitted. She watched with dismay as Robin carried her bag into Kate's bedroom. She glanced again at Brenda.

"I wish I could help you, darling," Brenda whispered.

Kate sighed. Here they were, hadn't seen each other in months, and they get by with a short hug and barely a kiss on the cheek. What did that say about their relationship? Was that why her writing was so stilted, so reserved? Was it simply a mirror of her own life? No passion. No *desire*.

But that hadn't applied last night. No, last night, with Lee, she had turned into the kind of woman she always thought she was. Passionate. Desirable. No, with Lee, she'd become nearly insatiable. Lee's touch upon her skin was like fire. And when her own hands had moved across Lee's body, she felt a power she'd never known before. No woman had ever trembled from her touch. No woman had ever begged for her kisses.

She closed her eyes and turned away, wishing things were different, wishing it was Lee instead of Robin.

"So, you haven't said, how's the book coming?"

Kate turned back around, forcing a smile to her face. "Actually, it's just about finished. I just haven't had the right feel for the ending. I have about four possibilities that I'm toying with."

"You always said the endings were the easiest part."

"Yes. I usually know the ending before I'm even half done." Kate glanced at Brenda. "This one's different."

"Why don't you let her read it, darling?"

"Oh, Brenda, that would be a first. Kate never lets anyone read them before they're published," Robin reminded them.

Kate laughed. "Well, this one has been difficult for me. And actually, Brenda's read it."

"But it was pure torture," Brenda said with a laugh to Robin. "I had to pretend to be a housewife from the Midwest."

"Well, if Brenda's already read it, I think it's only fair that I get to too." She linked arms with Kate. "Besides, how else am I going to occupy my time around here?"

Then why did you come? But Kate bit back her retort. She should be flattered that Robin had made the effort to surprise her on her birthday.

"Why don't you two go out to the deck?" Brenda suggested. "I'll bring out a pitcher of herbal tea."

"Wonderful," Kate said. "We'll enjoy the sunshine. It's warmed up nicely."

"Was it cold here this morning?" Robin asked. "It was very pleasant down in Santa Fe."

Kate pulled two chairs out into the sunshine, offering one to Robin. "It's been in the forties the last week or so but we're still hitting the seventies during the day. There's not a lot of color change here but higher up, the oaks have turned red. Up in the ski areas is where most of the color is," Kate explained. "Aspen trees."

Robin laughed. "You've certainly changed, Kate. I hardly recognize you anymore."

Kate bristled. "What do you mean?"

"Talking about the weather and the trees." Robin pointed at her. "And look at you. You're all tan, relaxed. In Dallas, you always seemed so stressed. You were always in a hurry. I never would have thought you could stand being out of the city as long as you have."

Kate nodded. "I was stressed. And *everybody* is always in a hurry. Maybe things are slower up here because there's no place to go," she said with a laugh.

"Well, here it is October and you've not mentioned coming back. I sometimes think you may not ever come back."

Kate looked toward the cliffs and the blue, blue sky behind them. "I've never thought of *not* going back, Robin. But honestly, I really haven't given much thought *to* going back, either."

"Here you go, girls," Brenda said, handing them each a glass of tea. "I've put the burritos in the oven to warm. We'll have an early lunch since we all missed breakfast."

"Oh? You skipped breakfast too?"

Kate and Brenda exchanged glances.

"Kate slept in. I think it's the cool mornings now that keep her in bed longer."

Kate hid her smile but gave Brenda a slight nod.

They were all quiet for a moment, then Kate noticed Robin impatiently tapping the arm of her chair. She'd barely been there an hour. Was she already bored to tears?

"So, what do you do with your time?" Robin asked. "I mean, what do you *do* all day?"

"Read. Take walks," Brenda said. "I paint. Kate writes. We talk. We sit out here and soak up the sun." She looked at Kate. "Sounds awfully boring, doesn't it, darling," she said with a laugh.

"Yes. But I'm sure it's done wonders for my blood pressure."

"Why don't you get your laptop out, darling, and let Robin read. Then you and I can begin planning this big birthday party we're going to have tomorrow."

"Oh, Brenda, we don't have to have a party. It's just another birthday."

"Nonsense. It's your day. And instead of bothering Sophia, I think we'll do something we've not done all summer. Grill burgers outside. How does that sound?"

Kate smiled. "It actually sounds fun. Thanks." She turned to Robin. "What do you think?"

"Burgers on the deck? Well, I had thought we could drive down to Santa Fe, maybe have a nice dinner somewhere, take in a movie. You know, normal stuff."

Kate shook her head. "You know, I don't know what it is, but I just have no desire to go into Santa Fe. Brenda and I went one weekend and we had a good time, went to a couple of galleries, had dinner." She shrugged. "But I'm just not in the mood."

"I can't believe you've turned into such a homebody," Robin said. "You used to love to go out to dinner."

"Yes, I did." She looked out at the vastness of the land surrounding them, not understanding the pull she felt, the connection. And certainly not understanding the peace that settled over her just by walking outside and breathing the fresh air, feasting on the sight of the cliffs. She knew of no words to explain it to Robin, but she didn't want to leave it.

"Well, like I said earlier, I hardly recognize you anymore."

Brenda laughed. "I think you may be right, Robin. I haven't noticed it, I suppose, since I've been around her, but Kate has mellowed quite a bit, hasn't she."

"Mellowed? Is that what you call it?"

"And what would you call it?" Kate asked.

Robin smiled. "I didn't mean anything by that, Kate. I'm just saying you've changed. It's not necessarily a bad thing."

"Well, Robin, maybe if you sit out here, enjoy our scenery, read a good book, you'll understand what we mean," Brenda suggested. "I'll go check on lunch."

Kate looked at Robin. "Well?"

"Sure, Kate. I'll sit out here and read, and try to contain my excitement."

"Look, if you dislike it here so much, why did you come?"

"Because it's your birthday. I thought that's what I was supposed to do."

"Well, maybe if you'd called first, we could have discussed it and you would have learned that it wasn't something you *had* to do. Honestly, I hadn't given a thought to my birthday. And as scary as it may sound, one does lose track of time up here."

"Oh, I'm sure a few days of this won't kill me. My flight back is at noon on Sunday." She held out her hands. "Now, where's that book you want me to read?"

"You know, darling, it would be so much simpler if you just told her."

"Her flight is not until noon on Sunday. Do you really want to be around her for two days after that?"

"Not that we've had a chance to talk, darling, but you are going to have to share a bed with her."

"I know."

"Surely you're not going to sleep with her."

Kate sighed. "We haven't seen each other in four months. Don't you think she's going to expect sex."

"And you would do it? Even after Lee?"

"After Lee what? Who's to say that she's not rounding up her next date as we speak?"

"You are so blind. Blind and stubborn. I never thought I would say those things about you, darling."

"That's just it. I'm not blind. I know exactly how Lee is and she wouldn't give it a second thought to sleep with someone else."

"So that means you are going to sleep with Robin?"

Kate shook her head. "No. I can't. I'm not."

"Because you have feelings for Lee and because you're falling in love with Lee. Why won't you just admit it?"

Kate gasped. "Falling in love with *Lee*? I'd have to be insane."

"Call it what you want, darling." She pointed to their lunch platter. "Six enough?"

"Six is plenty. I doubt Robin will eat two." She looked out to the deck where Robin was reading. "And I'm not going to sleep with her because of me, not because of Lee."

"Because of you what?"

"Because you know my rules. It would just be sex and I don't do just sex. Whatever Robin and I had is gone. I look into her eyes and there is nothing there. It's almost like we're strangers. I can't see being intimate with her. It nearly disgusts me to think about it and how sad is that?"

"Again my point. Why don't you tell her? Get it over with." Then she leaned closer. "So, if it wasn't just sex with Lee, what was it?"

"I swear! Can't I say anything without you always twisting it around to Lee?"

"Okay, darling. But I love teasing you." Brenda picked up the platter of burritos. "Bring the tea and napkins." Then she stopped. "How do you plan to get out of sex?"

"She can't handle alcohol. She'll pass right out." Kate raised her eyebrows mischievously.

"Sangria," they said in unison.

"Oh my God, Kate! A woman? Jennifer is a *lesbian*?" Robin shrieked.

Kate paced on the deck. "You think it's too much?"

"No! I love it. It's just so unexpected."

"You think so? The last few books, you didn't get the impression that Jennifer might be gay? That she and Paul weren't really in love?"

Robin blushed. "Well, I didn't actually read the last two, Kate." She shrugged. "I mean, I started them—"

"But you couldn't make it through," Kate finished for her. "It's okay. You're not the only one." Kate looked at Robin's empty glass. "More wine?"

"Sure. This stuff is great. Who makes it again?"

Kate cleared her throat, hesitating only slightly. "Lee. Sheriff Foxx. You probably remember her."

"Who could forget? She's a knockout."

"Yes. A knockout," Kate murmured as she went in search of more wine. Brenda already had another glass ready to go.

"This is number three," Brenda whispered. "Is she going to be able to stay up for steaks?"

"I'm thinking we should start them now. Wine and a heavy dinner will put her right out."

Brenda shook her head. "It would be so much easier to just tell her."

"Yeah. And if she's really, really pissed, she goes back to Dallas, to *my* apartment," Kate said. "Where my things are. Who knows what she might do?"

"She doesn't seem to be the angry type. Or the excitable type. No passion, darling."

"Maybe it's me. Maybe I just wasn't able to bring it out in her. Just like she doesn't bring it out in me."

"Then why on earth have you spent two years together?"

Kate took the wine. "Nobody's ever brought it out in me before." She met Brenda's eyes. "Until now."

Brenda smiled gently. "I know, darling."

CHAPTER THIRTY-FOUR

"What about that one?"

Lee followed where he pointed, a cute redhead, maybe twenty-three or so. She shook her head. "I told you, Skip, I'm not in the mood."

"So we're just going to sit here and drink? We haven't done this in years."

"Then let's pretend we're staking out the place." She nudged him, then motioned to the pool table.

"Oh, man. That's the little bastard that broke in here. I told Opal he should've pressed charges."

Lee laughed. "And he's got some balls coming back here. Why don't you go give him the what-for, big guy."

"He almost peed in his pants when I caught him. I can't believe he's here." Skip stood up. "I'll just go say hello."

Lee glanced again at her watch. After ten. Were they in bed already? Were they touching, kissing? She closed her eyes, trying not to imagine another woman touching Kate, making love to Kate. She told herself she shouldn't care, that it really wasn't any of her business what Kate did. Just because they slept together didn't mean they had any kind of rules now. It didn't mean anything. Kate's girlfriend was here. Of course they were going to have sex. And if Lee had any sense at all, she'd take Skip's advice and go talk to the redhead.

She looked down the bar again. No, she had no interest in the redhead. She cupped her cheek in one hand, hoping—praying—that she could get over this silly attraction she had for Kate.

She shook her head and closed her eyes. *Hell, you're in love with her. It's past a silly attraction.*

"You okay, Lee?"

Lee looked up, smiling at Skip. "Of course. I'm fine. Did you put the fear of God in him?"

"Cocky bastard," Skip muttered. "I told Opal he should've pressed charges."

"I take it he wasn't scared of you?"

"Oh, he and his buddies had a good laugh."

"He's just fucking with you."

"Yeah, well I'm going to be Opal's private security for awhile. I told him I want to bunk over here."

"Skip, the kid's not going to hit this place again."

Skip raised two fingers to Opal, pointing at Lee. "But just in case, I want to be ready."

Lee laughed. "Okay, Barney Fife, you can do a stakeout."

Skip bumped her shoulder. "I hate it when you call me that." Then he bumped her shoulder again. "So, what about the redhead?"

Lee shook her head. "Not interested."

"Look, are you sick or something? It's Friday night."

"Thanks, Opal," Lee said when he placed two bottles on the bar. "And I'm not sick," she said to Skip.

"Are you like, pining for someone?"

"*Pining*? No, I'm not pining. Geez."

"So you have someone at the lodge for later then?"

"No! Jesus, Skip, can't I just be alone? What's the big deal?"

"Man, testy too."

Lee sighed. "I'm sorry." She tapped the bar with her fingertips as she stared at her beer. "Okay, maybe there is someone," she said quietly.

"Are you serious? Who?"

"You think I'm going to tell you? You gossip like a woman. It'd be all over town."

"Well, of course! This is big news. Lee Foxx in love," he laughed.

She grabbed his arm. "I never said in love," she hissed. "Don't be spreading rumors."

"Okay, I'm sorry." He leaned closer. "So, who's the lucky gal?"

"Maybe not so lucky."

"Oh, Lee, you know what's sad? I'm the only son of the richest man in the county, and you still get more dates than I do. So, who is she?"

Lee cleared her throat. "Kate Winters. She's the woman staying with—"

"The writer. The one you took hiking," Skip said.

"Yeah. That one."

"I've not met her."

"No."

"So what's the problem?"

Lee shook her head. "Too much to go into." She tipped her beer at him. "But she'll be leaving soon. Hopefully things can get back to normal."

"She was just here for the summer?"

"Yeah. I think she's leaving this month."

"Does she know how you feel?"

"Of course not. You think I'm crazy?"

CHAPTER THIRTY-FIVE

"Oh, honey, that sex scene was absolutely delicious!"

Kate stared blankly at Robin. "You think so?"

"Really. It was so . . . so passionate. I didn't know you could get all worked up like that," Robin said with a laugh.

Kate blushed. "Well, it's certainly something new for me."

"I love it." Then Robin winked at her. "And if I can stay awake tonight, maybe we can try to duplicate it."

Kate gave a nervous laugh. "Well, it'll be a long night. Brenda's got that little dinner party planned, you know."

"Yes. And maybe burgers on the deck will be more fun than the sit-down affair she had the last time."

"Maybe. Although it will probably be the same group."

"That's okay. They were a little strange, but I enjoyed chatting with the sheriff. That one has got some kind of charisma, doesn't she?"

"She's just loaded with it," Kate murmured quietly as she tried to suppress the twinge of guilt that showed it ugly head.

"What? You don't like her?"

"Oh, I like her fine. It's always interesting to see who she'll bring to these little get-togethers. Her age limits are somewhere between eighteen and twenty-two, I believe." Guilt mixed with jealously was a terrible combination, Kate decided.

"Well, as cute as she is, I'm surprised someone hasn't snatched her up."

Kate tried to smile, but she wasn't sure it reached her eyes. "I don't believe Lee wants to be caught." She stood suddenly, pointing to the laptop Robin held. "I'll let you finish. I'm sure Brenda needs help in the kitchen." She didn't wait for a reply as she walked quickly inside.

"What's wrong, darling?"

Kate shook her head. "I'm not sure I can do this."

"I told you to just tell her."

"I'm not talking about Robin."

"Lee?"

"I swear, Brenda, if she shows up here tonight with a date . . ."

"What will you do, darling? *You'll* have a date. Why isn't Lee afforded the same consideration?"

"Because I can't *help* but have a date," she snapped. "If Lee brings someone, it's a conscious act on her part."

"You're being ridiculous and you know it."

"Why must you always take Lee's side?" Kate demanded.

"Because I'm a romantic, darling. And when I walked into your room and found the two of you in bed together, my heart nearly melted right there on the floor." Brenda waved her hand dramatically. "I saw love, darling," she said quietly. "I'm sorry you don't see it."

Kate shook her head. "I . . . I care about her. But I'm certainly not in love with her. I'm not *that* crazy."

CHAPTER THIRTY-SIX

Lee stood nervously beside her Jeep, wondering why she was putting herself through this. She should have told Brenda she couldn't come. Brenda would have understood. Hell, Kate would have understood.

But in the end, she couldn't stay away. She had to see Kate. She had to see Kate with Robin. It seemed like days . . . weeks, since they had been together. Hard to believe it was just yesterday morning she'd walked out of Kate's bed.

And Robin walked in.

She was nearly eaten up with jealously. In her mind, she saw Robin touching Kate, saw Robin kissing Kate, making love to Kate. And she had made herself nearly physically sick thinking about it. She never thought she'd be one of those women who could become so consumed with jealously, but she was.

Another glance at the house, another deep breath and she finally took the first steps toward the patio. She heard voices on the deck and she paused, listening. She felt somewhat comforted by the peaceful sound of Sunshine's voice. Perhaps she could find some time alone to speak with Sunny. Just to see what the Fates had planned for her this evening. Maybe give her a heads up.

Funny, Lee.

She smiled, glad she could still find the humor in it all.

"You can't grill the veggie burgers, Brenda." Kate took the box from her hand and read the directions. "Pan fry lightly in olive oil," she read.

"Do we have olive oil?"

"I swear, vegetarians are a lot of trouble."

"I'm sure cows think they are no trouble at all, darling."

Kate laughed. "Well, we'll do these last. They only take a few minutes."

"I'm not going to start the grill just yet, darling. I'll wait for Lee. And she better get here soon. I don't think we have enough wine to get us through this evening."

"Did you ask her to bring some?"

"No. But she always does," Brenda said as she carried the tray of hors d'oeuvres out to the deck.

Kate shook her head. "I have got to find out about this Pueblo chief and this recipe," she murmured.

"Who are you talking to?"

She spun around, finding Lee staring at her. Their eyes met.

"Hey."

"Hey." Kate gripped the countertop, wondering at the sudden impulse to fling herself into Lee's arms. "I . . . I didn't hear you come in."

"Used the side door," Lee said. She took a step closer. "Everything okay?"

Kate considered lying. But instead, she managed a sad smile. "Just peachy."

Lee looked across the bar to the others on the deck, including Robin. She slid her glance back to Kate. "Can we talk?"

Kate hesitated. She shouldn't, she knew. She shouldn't be alone with Lee. She seemed to lose all her self-control around Lee.

"Just for a second, Kate."

Kate nodded. She slowly reached out to take Lee's hand. Their fingers entwined immediately and Kate felt the quickening of her pulse at even this simple touch. She led her back the way Lee had come, through the side patio door. Once outside, Kate walked into the shadows, leaving the muted voices and soft patio lights behind. Unconsciously, she looked to the sky. The moon—three-quarters full—not quite a coyote sky, hung lazily over the cliff walls.

"I . . . I missed you. Last night," Lee said quietly.

Kate turned slowly, finding Lee's eyes in the shadows. No matter how often she told herself that Lee was dangerous, that Lee was just out looking for her next bed partner, that Lee couldn't possibly be trusted with her heart, she simply could not fight her attraction. Lee's eyes held her, pulled her closer.

"Skip took me out to Opal's last night," Lee said, her fingers still holding Kate's hand tight. "He was trying to set me up with . . . with this redhead," Lee said quietly.

Kate tried to ignore the pain in her heart. She didn't know why the words caused her pain. It was what she'd suspected Lee had done last night.

"And you know, I knew you were here with Robin. I knew she was in your bed." Lee cleared her throat. "I knew she was touching you. Making love to you," she whispered as her eyes closed. "And I . . . I just couldn't stand the thought of you together." Lee touched her chest, rubbing lightly against the ache in her heart.

"So . . . so I guess the redhead made it all better?"

Lee shook her head. "No. I wasn't in the mood for anyone's company."

Their eyes held and Kate was surprised at the pain she saw in Lee's. She took a step closer.

"You know what? I wasn't in the mood for anyone's company last night either." Not that Robin hadn't tried. Apparently, they hadn't fed her enough sangria. But Kate had complained of a *terrible* headache and Robin had finally fallen asleep.

"What does that mean?" Lee whispered.

"It means she wasn't touching me, wasn't making love to me."

Lee closed her eyes, letting her breath out slowly. "Oh, Kate," she whispered.

Kate moved without thinking, her hands sliding up Lee's arms, pulling her closer. "I missed you too," she whispered against her mouth.

Lee pulled her closer, nearly crushing Kate to her. This *need* she had for Kate was overwhelming. She couldn't seem to get close enough. Their mouths fought for control, neither winning. Lee moaned loudly when Kate boldly cupped her breasts, both hands covering her.

"Oh, God, Lee," Kate murmured, her lips moving from Lee's mouth, traveling down her throat, seeking the throbbing pulse in her neck.

Lee closed her eyes, her heart pounding from Kate's gentle exploration, her hands and mouth moving lightly across her body. God, she wanted to take her to the ground and make love to her right here. She wanted to touch her so badly, she trembled. She knew they should stop, knew the others would miss them. But with Kate's mouth moving across her skin, with Kate's hands moving to her hips, sliding down to her thighs—teasing her. *God . . .* no, she couldn't stop.

"I want you so much."

"Oh, Lee . . . you have no idea," Kate whispered. She forgot about the others. She forgot about the party. There was only Lee. There was only Lee and the moon.

But Lee didn't forget. When Kate pulled Lee's shirt from her jeans, when her warm hands would have slid up to Lee's breasts, Lee stilled them.

"Kate, we can't," she whispered. "Not here." She glanced nervously toward the deck, seeing the others as they mingled. How long had they been gone? Ten minutes? Twenty?

Kate groaned, leaning her head heavily against Lee's chest. No, they couldn't. Jesus, all she wanted was to touch Lee. But no, they had a goddamned party to deal with. And she had Robin to deal with.

"I'm sorry," she murmured. She pulled out of Lee's arms, taking deep breaths, trying to still her racing heart. "Jesus, I'm so sorry."

Lee didn't know what to say. She was afraid to touch Kate, afraid she couldn't stop. "You should go back," she finally said.

Kate nodded. "I know." She looked up, meeting Lee's eyes. "I know."

Lee watched her walk away, her heart breaking with every step Kate took. She was going back. Back to the party, back to Robin . . . back to her life. She turned away, her eyes moving to the sky, finding the moon. She took a deep breath, then closed her eyes, aware that she was wishing—praying—that Kate would not go back to Robin. But it was out of her hands. There was nothing she could do. It was all up to Kate.

"Ariel?"

Lee turned slowly, not really surprised to see Sunshine standing behind her on the trail.

"Your journey is over, Ariel."

"Yeah? Well, it kinda sucks."

Sunshine moved closer. "How does it feel to be in love?"

Lee shoved her hands in her pockets. "Well, it ain't all it's cracked up to be," she said lightly. "In fact, I didn't think it was supposed to hurt this much."

Sunshine smiled. "To quote an old song . . . love hurts, Ariel."

"I have a really bad feeling, Sunny." Lee looked away. "I'm not sure Kate feels the same, you know."

"Why do you doubt?"

"Well, you know, Robin is here, for one. And two, she's got issues with me." Lee shrugged. "Issues with my past dating habits."

Sunshine laughed. "You can't blame her for that, Ariel."

"No. I know."

"And as for Robin, no, there is no energy there, Ariel. There is nothing between them. I don't think there was ever anything between them."

"There *is* something between them. They've been together for a couple of years, they live together. So, yeah, there's still something between them."

"Ariel, you must trust. You must trust the fire between you. Kate knows, just as you know."

Lee stared. "Knows what?"

Sunshine smiled. "The fire between you . . . it's *true*, Ariel."

Lee slowly shook her head. She didn't know what to say.

"Didn't I tell you the Fates always win?"

CHAPTER THIRTY-SEVEN

"I didn't think they'd ever leave," Robin said as she helped Kate and Brenda with the dishes.

Kate and Brenda exchanged glances.

"It's barely after ten, darling," Brenda said.

"And that's two hours longer than normal people can stand talking to Harmony." Robin reached into her pocket. "My God. Look at this shit."

Kate and Brenda smiled, then laughed outright as Robin held out a palm full of crystals.

"What the hell am I going to do with this? She said I needed to work on my negative energy. Can you believe that?"

Kate and Brenda again exchanged glances.

"Harmony and Sunshine are very *attuned* to energy levels," Brenda explained.

"Well, they're weird. And I'm sorry. I know they're your friends and all but they kinda freak me out."

"They are absolutely harmless," Brenda said.

Kate put the last of the dishes in the dishwasher, wondering at her urge to defend Harmony and Sunshine. Yeah, she thought they were kinda weird too. But as Brenda told her months ago—they grow on you.

"I don't know how you two stand it up here. Even Lee was acting weird tonight. I swear, she didn't say five words all night."

Kate flicked her glance to Brenda, then looked away. No, Lee hadn't said much. She sat in a corner of the deck, brooding, watching as Robin doted on Kate all night. In fact, Kate couldn't seem to get away from her. She and Lee didn't have another moment alone and without warning—without even a good-bye—Lee had gotten up and left.

"Lee is having some personal issues," Brenda said. "It has nothing to do with the group." She smiled. "And Kate and I stand it up here just fine, darling. Perhaps it is you who should reconsider the next time you have the urge to visit."

Brenda left without another word, the door to her bedroom closing rather forcefully.

"What is it with everyone tonight? I can't believe she just spoke to me that way."

"Well, Robin, it's the truth. Each time you've been here, you've done nothing but complain."

Robin stood in front of her, her eyes questioning. "Why are you still here Kate?"

"What do you mean?"

"Your book's all but done. You've been here since May. Five months, Kate." She shrugged. "I guess I want to know if you're coming back to Dallas or not."

"Well, of course I'm coming back. I have an apartment there, I have my things there."

"What about me, Kate? What about us?"

Kate swallowed, then cleared her throat. "What about us?"

"Oh, come on, Kate. I hardly know you anymore."

Kate nodded. She pulled out a barstool and sat down. It was

time. Past time, really. She leaned her elbows on the bar, resting her chin on her hands.

"I know I've changed, Robin. But I'd like to think it's in a good way." She cleared her throat again nervously. "You may not agree, though." She took a deep breath. "I've . . . I've met someone, Robin. And it's made me realize that what you and I have isn't . . . well, it isn't *love*."

They stared at each other, Kate waiting for the angry explosion she expected. It never came.

"You met someone, huh? Well that's good, Kate. I mean, it wasn't like we were exclusive or anything. It wasn't like we'd declared our undying love."

"*What?*" Kate hissed.

Robin took a step back. "We never once talked about that, Kate. I still dated occasionally. I thought you did too."

"*What?* When?"

"Well, I don't know, whenever you and I weren't doing something."

Kate closed her eyes. "Let me get this straight. We've been *dating*? We've not been in a monogamous relationship?"

"Well, no. What gave you that idea?"

"Oh, I don't know," Kate said sarcastically. "Maybe because you've been living in my *bedroom* for one thing!"

"You offered me a place to stay," Robin reminded her.

"Yes. And when you moved into my bedroom, I assumed that meant you weren't out *dating*. Jesus, I cannot believe this."

"I'm sorry. It wasn't like I went out all the time or anything."

Kate stared. "And while I've been gone?"

"Well, I've been going out, yes. In fact, I met someone too."

Kate rubbed her eyes. She had a sudden urge to laugh hysterically. The guilt she'd carried with her most of the summer vanished with Robin's words. Even the anger she'd initially felt was gone as quick as it had come. She and Robin's relationship was just a farce, a sham.

"You've met someone too? The Hot Springs massage person?" Kate guessed.

Robin blushed. "Yes. How did you know?"

"So, just a few weeks ago, you were sharing a romantic weekend with her. Yet last night, you wanted to have sex with me?"

"Well, we're not really exclusive, either. I mean, she's been staying at the apartment with me, but—"

"Are you kidding me?" Kate stood, her voice rising. "You've had another woman staying at *my* apartment while I've been gone?"

"I didn't think it'd be a problem, Kate."

Kate stared. She didn't know what to say. To say she was *floored* by Robin's words would be a gross understatement. Months ago, when she'd first told Lee about Robin, Lee had questioned the exclusiveness of their relationship. Kate remembered being shocked that someone would assume she and Robin were not monogamous. Apparently the thought had never crossed Robin's mind. *Monogamous.* Most likely, that word had never crossed Lee's mind either.

"You know what? It is a problem, Robin. I should have never let our relationship develop as it did. I knew I wasn't really in love with you. I shouldn't have asked you to move in. I shouldn't have accepted that what we had was good enough. Obviously, *you* didn't. But despite all of that, it's still wrong what I've done. In my mind, we were a couple. And this summer, I met someone, someone who made me feel all the things you didn't. But I should never have let it go as far as it did with her, because you and I were still officially a couple. And I have been eaten up with guilt, Robin. And yes, I was going to end things with you." She walked toward the deck, staring through the glass doors. "I don't know what's going to happen or what I want to do now." She turned back around. "But when we say good-bye tomorrow, I don't ever want to see you again."

CHAPTER THIRTY-EIGHT

Kate pulled the blanket around her, trying to chase away the chill. The moon had traveled across the sky, yet still high enough to light up the cliffs. In the distance, she heard the lonely call of a coyote.

She had been out here for hours, it seemed. Robin was in bed. Kate had claimed the sofa, although she couldn't sleep. She didn't doubt Brenda had heard them, but she'd not come out of her room. Perhaps she sensed Kate's need to be alone.

"What a fool you are," she murmured to herself. Two and a half years she'd been dating Robin. Counting all the months she'd been up here, they'd shared an apartment for nearly a year. And it was all nothing. How *stupid* could she be?

And Lee. God, what was she going to do about Lee? She could no longer use the excuse that she was involved with someone. She rolled her eyes. As if that excuse had worked lately anyway. Officially, she was single now. If she stayed here for awhile longer, what would she and Lee do? Would they *date*?

I don't want to date her.

No. Tonight she realized she was past that stage. The brief time they were together tonight, the few kisses they'd shared—the stolen moments when they couldn't stop touching—Kate accepted what it felt like, what it meant.

She was in love with Lee. It was as plain as day to her now. And it was most likely a *huge* mistake. After all, Lee was Lee.

Tonight, after Lee left so abruptly, where did she go? Kate doubted she went home. At least not alone. No, she'd watched Robin, had seen Robin touching her, hugging her. Robin had kissed her unexpectedly. When Kate looked up, Lee was there, watching, staring at them. She saw the pain in Lee's eyes. But there was nothing she could do. And shortly thereafter, Lee simply got up and left.

No, she doubted Lee was alone tonight. The ache in her heart worsened and she rubbed lightly against her chest.

Lee stood still, not noticing the cold, her eyes staring out at the moon-kissed cliffs across from her. The occasional call of the coyotes only made her sullen mood worse. It had been hours, but she still couldn't get the picture of them kissing out of her mind. She knew that it was Robin who had kissed Kate. She knew that. But still, the image was there. And it was so obvious that they were a couple, the way they touched, the way they looked at each other.

It wasn't really Kate, she reminded herself. But that hardly mattered. Here she was, alone, standing at their spot, standing at the spot she'd never brought another human being to—except Kate. And Kate was in bed with another woman. She didn't want to think beyond that. Kate had said they hadn't slept together. But their actions on the deck indicated otherwise.

"Sunshine was wrong," she murmured.

Trust the fire.

"I guess the Fates really don't like me after all."

CHAPTER THIRTY-NINE

Brenda watched them drive away, curious as to the tight hug Kate had given her. She could see the uncertainty in Kate's eyes and as much as Brenda loved her, there was nothing she could do for her now. She let her leave, knowing she had to work this out on her own.

She went back inside, intending to have the last of the coffee out on the deck now that the air had warmed up. The phone interrupted her and she put the coffeepot back, thinking Kate must have forgotten something.

"It's me. Please, I've got to talk to her, Brenda."

"Oh, darling, I'm sorry. You just missed her."

"What do you mean?"

"They're on their way to the airport, Lee. I'm sure—"

Brenda stared at the phone before putting it down, wondering why Lee had hung up on her. "Women, I swear," she murmured, again grabbing the coffeepot.

Lee downshifted as she took a corner too fast, dangerously sliding the Jeep on the rocks then speeding up again. Once she hit the county road and pavement, Lee shifted into fifth, speeding along as she attempted to catch Kate. She didn't pause to think about what she was doing, she only knew she couldn't let Kate leave.

Finally, up ahead, she spotted the rental car. Without thinking, she flipped on the police lights and siren, not caring in the least that it wasn't protocol.

"What the hell?"

Kate slowed, her eyes fixed on the rearview mirror.

"What is it?" Robin asked.

"It appears to be Sheriff Foxx."

"Were you speeding?"

Kate rolled her eyes. "No, Robin, I wasn't speeding." She pulled over to the side and stopped. She was out of the car before Lee even opened the door to her Jeep.

"What the hell are you doing?" Kate demanded.

Lee stared. "I . . . I, er . . . you were speeding."

Kate put her hands on her hips. "Like hell."

"You were. Really."

"Fine. You going to give me a ticket or what?"

Lee shifted nervously. "Kate, please . . . don't go."

"What?"

"Please don't leave."

"Lee—"

"Hey! We've got a flight to catch," Robin yelled.

Kate glanced at her watch. "I'm sorry, Lee."

"Please don't do this, Kate. Don't leave."

Kate frowned. She wished they had time to talk, but now was not the place. Not with Robin right there. "I've got to go, Lee."

Lee stood in the middle of the road, watching in disbelief as

Kate drove out of her life. She was sure her heart stopped beating as the car faded from sight.

I love you, Kate.

"What did she want?"

Kate shrugged. "I'm not really sure."

Robin turned in her seat, watching Kate. "You said last night that you'd met someone, but you didn't say who. Is it Lee?"

Kate paused, then nodded. "Yes. It's Lee."

"No wonder she was acting so strange last night. She was jealous. I'm sorry, Kate. I had no idea."

"I know. It's my fault. I should have told you."

"So, what's going to happen with you two?"

"I don't know." Then she smiled. "I feel kinda funny talking to you about this."

"Yeah. I guess."

"And I did some thinking last night. There's really no reason for you to have to move right now. I mean, I don't know when I'm coming back."

"Really? That'd be great. Because I really like it there and it's close to work."

Kate nodded. "But I'm not going to continue paying all the rent. I'll pay half, since I have all my furniture there but that's it."

"Fair enough."

God, they were being so civilized with each other, it was almost nauseating. No doubt Robin was as relieved as Kate was to formally end their relationship. She let her thoughts drift back to Lee, puzzled by her odd behavior. Lights and siren? What was up with that?

234

CHAPTER FORTY

Lee drove in a daze, going to the only place she knew she would find solace. She found her on the deck, out in the sun. They looked at each other, then Brenda motioned to a chair.

"Sit, darling."

Lee nearly fell into the chair, her head hanging.

"What's wrong, Lee?"

Lee shook her head. "I just can't believe she left. I can't believe she left without even talking to me."

"Kate?"

"Of course Kate." Lee stood, pacing along the deck. "There's something between us, Brenda, I know there is. She knows it too." Lee clutched at her chest. "She *knows* it, Brenda. But she thinks she can't trust me." Lee shrugged. "I can't blame her. Hell, I've been with more women than I can count. But it's different now. It's different with her. I mean, I can't even *think* about being with someone other than her." Lee stopped pacing, standing in front of

Brenda. "How could she just leave me? Without a word? I mean, not one goddamned word. Did it mean *nothing* to her?"

"Lee, what are you talking about?"

Lee spread her arms. "I'm talking about Kate! I'm talking about me!" she nearly yelled. "How could she just go back to Dallas without a word?"

"Darling, she didn't go back to Dallas. Whatever gave you that idea?"

Lee bent down, grasping Brenda's chair. "She didn't go to Dallas?"

"No, darling."

"Then where the hell did she go?"

CHAPTER FORTY-ONE

Kate let the drapes fall back into place, thinking that maybe this wasn't such a good idea after all. Sunset had become her most favorite part of the day and she missed the view of the cliffs. The parking lot outside her window, with the windshields of the cars reflecting the waning sun, could hardly compare to the cliffs.

But, as she'd told Brenda, she needed some time to think, time to sort out her feelings, time to reconcile what had just transpired in her life.

Time alone.

She fluffed the pillows on the bed, then lay back, absently tossing the remote between her hands. The hotel was nice, as Brenda had said it would be, but she felt confined by the four walls. She hadn't realized how comfortable she'd become with the openness of their home. She smiled. Yes, home. Home in a rented summer house, shared with a somewhat eccentric old friend, in a place she'd never been before. Who would have thought she'd fall in love with the place?

And who would have thought she'd fall in love with Lee?

Oh, Lee. She shook her head. What was she going to do? No doubt Lee would totally freak out if she told her she was in love with her. Lee, with her love 'em and leave 'em style, would probably run for the hills to escape her.

Or would she?

Kate was still puzzled about Lee's earlier behavior. What had caused her to stop them on the pretense of speeding, using lights and siren, no less?

Don't go.

Kate drew her brows together, remembering Lee's words.

Please don't do this, Kate. Don't leave.

It hit her suddenly. Lee thought she was going back to Dallas with Robin. Lee thought she was leaving. And Lee was begging her not to go.

She closed her eyes. Yes, Lee had the look of panic when she was asking Kate to stay. The big idiot. Why would she assume Kate was leaving?

Well, she did see you kissing. And what other reason would you have for driving a rental car to the airport?

"Oh, Lee," she whispered.

She jumped, startled by knocking on the door. She had not yet called for her dinner.

"Who is it?"

"Room service."

She got up, her heart pounding as she stood at the door. Brenda promised she would not tell Lee where she was. Kate paused, looking up at the ceiling, wondering why she was surprised. Surprised, but not angry. Her assertion to Brenda that she needed some time alone to sort through everything was true enough. At least at the time it had been.

"Kate?"

Kate stood there, finally letting a smile touch her face before opening the door to Lee.

"You have impeccable timing."

"I, er, I thought maybe you needed to talk."

"Is that what you thought?"

Lee shrugged, their eyes colliding. "I thought you might need me."

Kate nodded. "Yes, you're right." Kate wet her suddenly dry lips. "I do need you, Lee." Slowly, she reached over, taking Lee's hand, letting their fingers move together. She gave a slight tug, leading Lee into the room. "Tell me about this morning."

Lee frowned.

"Lights and siren. *Speeding*?"

"I thought . . . I thought you were leaving."

"Going back to Dallas?"

Lee nodded.

"With Robin?"

Lee nodded again.

"And . . . so?"

Lee ducked her head nervously, rubbing her damp palms on her jeans. She looked up again, meeting Kate's eyes. "I . . . well, I . . . *Christ, Kate* . . . I . . . I thought you were leaving me," she finished in a rush. "And I didn't know what to do," she whispered.

Kate shook her head, moving closer. "Not leaving, Lee. I just needed some time to think, to sort out what I was feeling."

"About Robin?" Lee asked hesitantly.

Kate smiled. "No, not about Robin. I ended things with Robin." She shrugged. "There wasn't a whole lot left to end, as it turns out."

"So then, I guess that means you needed time to think about . . . about me?"

Kate met her eyes. "Yes. You see, I don't quite know what to do about these feelings I have." Kate walked away, her back to Lee. "You told me once how boring it would be to sleep with the same woman, night after night after night," she said quietly. "So I'm wondering how in the world I could have let this happen," she whispered.

Lee closed her eyes, hearing the words Brenda had spoken to

her only hours ago. *She's in love with you, Lee. But darling, I doubt she'll ever tell you. She's afraid of getting hurt.*

"You didn't let it happen, Kate," Lee finally said. "It was out of our control all along."

Kate turned around. "What was?"

Lee moved, taking the few steps that separated them. She reached out, her fingers softly touching Kate's face. She leaned closer, her lips gentle as they moved across Kate's, lightly tasting.

"Oh, Lee," Kate murmured. Her arms slid around Lee's shoulders, pulling her closer. "I don't know what I'm supposed to do."

"It doesn't matter, Kate." Lee's hand had found Kate's breast, and she swallowed Kate's moan, her tongue teasing along Kate's lips. "I'm going to make love to you tonight." She moved her lips to Kate's ear, gently kissing. "I'm going to make love to you for the rest of my life."

Kate tried to pull away, but Lee held her. "No. It's true. I swear to you, Kate," she whispered into Kate's ear.

Kate clutched her tight. "Swear what?"

"I swear that I will be true to you. I swear that you can trust me with your heart."

Kate squeezed her eyes shut. "Tell me why."

"Because I'm in love with you, and I want to be with you. I love you, Kate."

Kate relaxed, moving away from Lee just enough to see her eyes. And she saw all she needed right there. She smiled gently.

Lee grinned.

"I guess it's pretty obvious that I've fallen in love with you too."

Lee laughed. "Not so obvious, no."

Kate's eyes turned serious. "I think I fell in love with you the night we danced by the cliffs," she admitted. "And after that, it just killed me to see you out with others."

Lee shook her head. "There were no others. There's been no one, Kate. They were just . . . fake dates," she said. "I didn't want to be alone around you, so it was safer to bring a date."

Kate met her eyes. "You swear you won't hurt me?"

"Cross my heart."

Kate's fingers were already unbuttoning Lee's shirt as she pulled her toward the bed. But she stopped.

"I have . . . I mean, you may not know this, but I was having a really hard time coming up with an ending for my book."

Lee's hands rested lightly at Kate's waist, her thumbs slowly stroking warm flesh. She tilted her head. "You mean with Jenn?"

Kate nodded. "Jennifer fell in love with someone very much like you." Kate pulled her eyes away, her gaze dropping to Lee's lips. "I didn't know what to do with her . . . with them."

Lee nodded. "I see."

"Jennifer is a little afraid, I think."

Lee shook her head. "She shouldn't be afraid." Lee's hand traveled slowly, cupping Kate's cheek. She smiled as Kate leaned into her touch. "You know the ending, Kate. They live happily ever after."

"Is that truly possible?" she whispered.

Lee's eyes turned serious. "My heart says it's possible. What does your heart say?"

Kate closed her eyes for a moment. "I love you. It says I love you."

Lee pulled her closer. "Does it also say you might stay in Coyote with me?"

Kate touched Lee's lips with her own, whispering against her mouth, "And live happily ever after."